THE HIDDEN TREASURE OF GLASTON

ALSO BY
ELEANORE M. JEWETT

Told on the King's Highway
Big John's Secret

the hidden treasure of glaston

by Eleanore M. Jewett

Illustrated by Frederick T. Chapman

BETHLEHEM BOOKS • IGNATIUS PRESS

BATHGATE, ND   SAN FRANCISCO

Cover illustration © 2000 Gino d'Achille
Cover design by Davin Carlson

Interior artwork by Frederick T. Chapman

First printing, June 2000

ISBN 1–883937–48–5
Library of Congress Control Number: 00–101259

Bethlehem Books • Ignatius Press
10194 Garfield Street South
Bathgate ND, 58216
www.bethlehembooks.com

Printed in the United States on acid free paper

DEDICATED

TO

Anne Lloyd

FRIEND OF OLD GLASTON

AND

BELOVED FRIEND OF MINE

table of contents

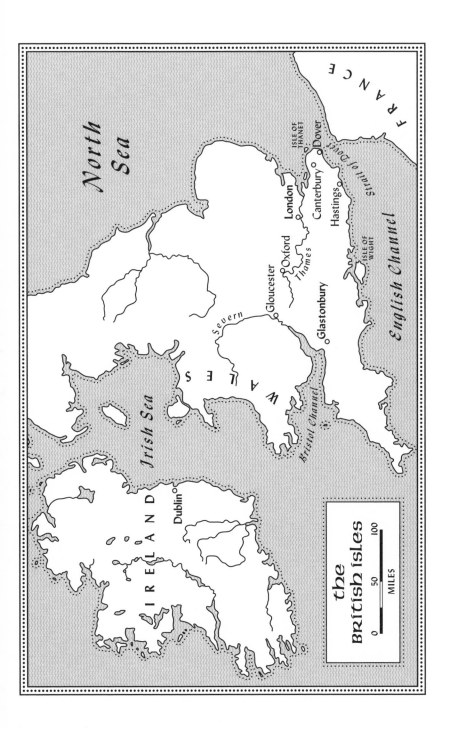

the hidden treasure
of glaston

i. the coming of hugh

IT WAS A NIGHT of sweeping storm, a spring night when the rivers were brown and full, the freshets boiling and the marshes around the abbey more boggy and treacherous than usual. Cold it was, too, bitter cold for March, and the wind-driven rain slashed against doors and walls and beat the muddy roads into a running ooze. God pity all poor souls abroad on such a night! Those who had shelter, be it ever so poor, clung to it, and within the great draughty halls of the monastery the good brothers rubbed their chilly hands together or muffled them in their black sleeves as they hurried through the cloisters to the church. The bell for Compline, the last service of the day, had just rung and after that there would be a chance to toast themselves a few

14

moments, silently, in front of the huge smoky hearth in the common room before going to bed in the cold dormitories.

The master of the guest house, however, the brother whose duty it was to greet any stranger of importance who came to the abbey, did not attend Compline that evening. Before the bell had ceased ringing there came a thunderous knock on the outer gate. A porter hastened to draw the bolts, opened the heavy doors and admitted, with a furious blast of wind and rain, a knight swathed in a heavy cloak and followed by a stout servant half supporting what might be a child, perhaps, or some slight or ailing person. Outside the porter could just discern by the flickering light of his lantern two horses standing, heads down, tails close to their reeking shanks.

He bowed the two men into the guest house hall, then ran quickly to fetch Brother Arnolf, the guest

master, catching him just as he was about to enter
the church.

"There be strangers come to the gate, Brother
Arnolf," said he, "a knight, one nobly born I would
think from the manner of him, and a squire or servant with what might be a child or young lad."

The guest master turned back toward the buildings beyond the cloisters, bidding the porter see to
the horses. This he did with willing speed for it
were ill to keep even a beast standing uncared for in
such cold and wet.

When Brother Arnolf reached the hall he found
the strange knight, his wet cloak thrown aside, walking impatiently up and down the rush-strewn floor.
Near the glowing brazier which was kept alight on
bitter nights like these, stood a boy, delicately built,
with large dark eyes in a thin, pale face. The servant
had gone out again to the horses and, as the boy
moved closer to the fire, Brother Arnolf understood
why he had not entered unsupported and sturdily on
his own two feet. One thin leg dragged pitifully; indeed it seemed as if he could scarce bear his weight
at all upon it without falling.

Brother Arnolf bowed dutifully to the knight and
raised his eyes and hand for a moment, in the customary prayer and blessing. He had scarcely finished
before the stranger spoke, quickly, nervously, yet as
one accustomed to authority, asking to see the abbot.

"Most surely," said Brother Arnolf, "my Lord Abbot shall be summoned immediately after Compline
which is even now being said, and while you are

awaiting him, will you not seat yourselves before the brazier and grow warm in comfort? The lad seems chilled and as soon as the service is done, I myself will fetch wine from the cellarer and see to your beds."

"I cannot stay the night," said the man, "but I would welcome wine, for it is raw indeed without. And make ready one bed, for the boy rests with you. However, I will keep my plans for the abbot's ears. Do you call him as presently as may be."

Brother Arnolf bowed again and departed. He was puzzled and curious. Guests were frequent enough, none knew better than he whose task it was to make all the arrangements for housing and feeding them. Often the guest house dormitory was nigh full, to say nothing of the occasional princely visitors who were lodged in my Lord Abbot's own quarters, and the always plentiful supply of beggars and vagabonds who found food and shelter in the almonry, a building near the gate, set apart for that purpose. For in those days (it was the year 1171) the monasteries scattered over the countryside, often on lonely roads and in desolate places, offered almost the only hospitality available for travelers. And welcome indeed must those great piles of buildings have appeared to the eyes of weary souls when they came upon them, perhaps after a long journey beset with manifold dangers and difficulties. All men, whether princes or beggars, merchants or pilgrims, wandering holy men or strolling mountebanks and peddlers, knew that they would be received graciously and without question at any monastery. They would be housed and fed for two days and two nights, and then they would be sped upon their journey with God's blessing and not so much as a penny to pay—unless they were minded to give a gift to Our Lady or to the patron saint of the place or, perchance, leave somewhat for the abbot to use at his discretion.

The coming of this knight and boy to the abbey, however, had about it something out of the ordinary. For one thing, none traveled after sundown except upon necessity. Thieves and cutthroats were too frequent upon the dark lonely roads, pitfalls and mudholes and the danger of losing one's way too constant in the best of weathers, and on such a night as this—! Moreover this man was evidently one of noble birth, accustomed to authority, and his clothing betokened wealth and comfort. What was he doing abroad in all this storm, unaccompanied except for that sickly boy and one servant, and apparently upon business too pressing to admit of even a night's delay? Lords and nobles did not lightly thus inconvenience themselves. Ah well, the duty of Brother Arnolf was to obey orders, fulfill his tasks as guest master and not ask questions. Compline was over now, he would hasten to fetch the abbot and bid the cellarer bring food and wine to the guest house hall.

Abbot Robert was a tall man, thin, erect, with iron-gray hair and dark somber eyes, and he moved with the gracious dignity of one accustomed to honor and obedience. He glanced keenly at the knight and the lad as he entered the room, then greeted the former in quiet courtesy and bade him come with the boy to the church, as the custom was, that they might be sprinkled with holy water and ask the blessing of Our Lady Mary upon their stay within the abbey walls.

But the knight interrupted him somewhat brusquely. "My Lord Abbot," said he, "I pray you have done with all these courteous entreaties and customary formalities. I know well the hospitality and good will for which Glastonbury is famed, and I would linger the night with joy save for a grievous necessity which speeds my journey, be time and weather ever so foul. And so, good Father, let me but speak that which I am come for without delay and be off upon my way."

The abbot glanced keenly at the knight wondering if perchance some unlawful business might be the reason for his haste. He inclined his head, indicating his acquiescence, and the knight continued, "The lad yonder is my son, my only son. He is called Hugh."

He paused and looked at the boy who still stood shivering in spite of the blaze of the brazier and turned toward them large unhappy eyes that had in them fire as well as tragedy. In his father's expression was a mingling of sorrow, pity, and perhaps scorn, and under his gaze the lad's white cheeks reddened, but his eyes did not drop.

"You may see for yourself how it is." The knight addressed the abbot again, his voice sounding strained and hard in his effort to keep emotion from it. "A cripple, sickly, with nothing in him on which to build a fighter, and the business of a baron's son is war and naught else, as all the world knows."

"Nay," said the abbot quickly, interrupting him, "there are other ways of living save in fleshly combat and other foes to fight save those in mortal armor. I, too, was born the son of a noble line." He stood tall and proud in his black monk's robe, and his long thin hands clasped each other firmly, suggesting need for self-control.

"Aye, the Church," continued the knight still bitterly, "religion and the cowl for weaklings and cripples. Forgive me, Father—"

The abbot had raised his hand again in a gesture of reproach.

"Nay, in truth I meant not any harm or rudeness. My heart is torn and broken this night and I scarce know what harsh saying may leap from my lips. And, in sooth, it is but natural a father should desire a stalwart son to carry on the honor of his house in valiant knighthood."

The abbot's hand had dropt and his eyes were now full of compassion. "Have patience, my son, it is but a young lad; time and the mercy of God may still give him a strong and vigorous body, and by the look of him he is now no weakling in soul."

"The lad has mettle in him," admitted the knight. Then for a long moment he said nothing but gazed unseeingly into the heart of the bright brazier. "His mother is dead," he added abruptly.

"God rest her spirit," said the abbot, crossing himself. The other went on:

"She was a gentle soul, yet brave withal; the kind of courage women have that endures much and says little. Our chaplain taught her to read and she loved parchment and vellum better than jewels. The boy Hugh is not unlike her. But come, I have delayed long enough; let us to business. I have brought the child here to be reared and schooled by you."

"As an oblate," questioned the abbot, "vowed to the monk's life? Perhaps you do not know that it hath recently been decreed from Rome that no child shall be vowed by his parents any more except upon the understanding that he himself shall choose between the world and the Church when he has come of age."

"That is as it should be," agreed the knight, "I would not force the boy against his will, but for the present—I do not wish to take him with me. My life is hedged about with grievous dangers—I—"

He hesitated, seemingly at a loss for words.

The abbot regarded him questioningly. "You need not fear to speak openly to me, my son. You are, perhaps, fleeing the country, and would see the lad safe before you go?"

The man shrugged his shoulders impatiently. "As you will," said he. "I need not burden you with details; I desire only that the boy remain with you. Somewhat I have to pay for the boon which I ask."

The knight turned and strode toward the door of the great hall. He flung it open and motioned to his servant, who was standing without, to enter. The man advanced bearing a bulky leather satchel which, at a nod from his master, he placed at the abbot's feet.

"Open," ordered the nobleman curtly.

The servant knelt upon the rushes and, with

clumsy, unaccustomed hands, struggled with refractory buckles. When the cover was at last loosed and
the contents of the satchel pulled out and laid carefully upon the floor, the abbot bent forward, exclaiming with surprise and delight.

"Books! Five, eight, more than a dozen! Why, good
sir, there is nigh a nobleman's ransom in the contents of that leather bag!"

The knight smiled. "Aye, it is a goodly treasure,
or so they say that value the scrivener's art. I know
naught of such things." There was a suspicion of
scorn in his voice and the wrinkled cheeks of the
abbot flushed with displeasure but he kept his eyes
on the manuscripts which lay tumbled on the rushes
at his feet.

"A princely gift truly," he continued, picking up a
large volume, the binding of which was studded with
semi-precious stones and inset with a plaque of blue
enamel. "There is no need to pay for the lad with
such bounteousness. Indeed, he would be welcome
among us for himself, without payment at all. If I
seemed to hesitate it was but out of honesty, for our
teaching is not what it once was, our discipline is
relaxed, and scarce any others are here now to bear
him company."

"Such conditions please me the better," said the
other. "Let him do what those in authority bid him;
do, and keep silent. That is the rule, is it not? The
fewer friends he has, the less he will talk and the
better for him, as for me. I have spoken too freely as
it is. The books and the boy are thine, Father. Do
with them as thou wilt."

His voice softened as he dropt into the more familiar second person form. For a moment he glanced past the abbot toward his son as if he would speak to him. Then he turned and, with a sudden motion as if he had not intended to do so, knelt before the abbot, his head bowed.

"Give me thy blessing, Father," said he in a voice scarce audible; then, barely waiting for the blessing to be spoken, he rose and, looking neither to the abbot nor the boy, without a word more, went hastily to the door. The servant quietly followed him, their quick footsteps echoed down the hall, grew fainter, and were gone.

The abbot remained standing in silence, his gaze turned again upon the books at his feet. A slight sound caught him out of his reverie. The boy Hugh was lying on his face on the floor, trying vainly to stifle with his sleeve his heartbroken sobbing.

Father Robert knelt beside him, felt his thin body shaken by the violence of his weeping and drew him into his kindly arms.

After awhile the sobbing grew less and Hugh lay back exhausted upon the rushes. The abbot rose stiffly from his knees and smiled down at him in gentle, friendly manner but said nothing. He knew well that no soothing words would comfort that tragic young figure, scorned by his father, caught up into the midst of circumstances painful, bitter, filled perhaps with terror, and now dropt down among strangers into a strange new life. He drew up a bench before the manuscripts, sat down and began picking up first one, then another.

"Hey-day, but your coming will be matter for great rejoicing in our abbey, young Hugh!" said he, more to himself than as if expecting the boy to answer. "Our aumbries—the presses or cupboards where books are kept, child,—or perhaps you know such monkish furniture?" He glanced at the lad who had arisen and was limping wearily toward his bench.

"Aye, Father," said he, "we have an aumbry at home for our own books, bought from a monastery—or we had," he corrected himself, looking down in pained confusion.

"Our presses, as I was saying," continued the abbot, his eyes again upon the handsome volume in his hands, "are all too scantily filled with books. Father Henry, God rest his soul, he who was abbot before me, loved our Glaston passing well and would build and build. Nigh half the fair new structures on our grounds were of his dream and planning, and that left in the treasury but little for the purchase of new books. True, our scribes are busy daily copying and illuminating, yet the shelves fill slowly, very slowly. Aye, these are the welcomest gifts your father could have brought us. We shall dedicate them at the High Altar on the morrow. You yourself shall take part in the ceremony, if you wish. Do you know aught of letters, lad?"

Hugh had by now drawn up beside the abbot and was looking wistfully over his shoulder at the volume in his lap.

"Yes, Lord Abbot, I can read the script a little. My lady mother's clerk that she brought out of France taught me and my sisters when my father was away. He liked not the thought of learning in a knightly son—but—I could not run and ride at the quintain like other boys and—Oh, Father Abbot, the stories in that book are goodly! I know almost all of them!" He stooped and picked up a large, square, leather-covered manuscript from the floor. "And this one," he continued, a note of eagerness in his voice, as he handed another to the abbot, "hath the softest vellum pages! The feel of them is gentle and I like well the smell of them."

The boy's listlessness had left him and there was animation in his tone and face. The abbot watched him with a little smile of understanding and satisfaction, noting how lovingly his thin hands caressed the beautiful cream colored sheets of vellum.

"I would I knew the ending of the longish tale at the beginning of this book," Hugh ran on, "the one with the great gold initial on the red ground. I would have finished it a few days since—but I could not." The boy broke off with a little sigh and the abbot replaced the volume gently on the floor with the others.

"We must have Brother John summoned," said he. "Step to the doorway, boy, and bid one of the brothers come hither."

He watched curiously as Hugh dragged his halting limb across the floor, but the errand was accomplished without hesitation, the message dispatched, and the boy's face and bearing were less sad and downhearted as he took his stand again beside the abbot's bench.

"Bibles, missals, Psalters, stories of saints," enumerated the abbot, his eyes again on the books at his feet. "I fear me Brother John will not sleep this night for joy of our new treasure! And why couldst thou not read thy story a few days since?" he continued gently, dropping into the more familiar pronoun.

"It was then that—that our troubles came upon us. But I pray, Lord Abbot, ask me not about myself further, for my father hath forbidden me to say aught save—" he paused, his voice shaking and again the look of haunting tragedy in his face.

"Save what, lad? I will not ask thee more than thy father would have thee tell."

"Save that my name is Hugh; I am twelve years of age; my mother is dead, and my father gone—I know not where. That I have no longer home or family or anything out of the past." He had spoken as if repeating a lesson learned, but ended with a bitterness that was his own.

At that moment Brother John, the librarian of the monastery, or armarian as he was called, appeared at the door. When his eyes fell upon the books, his thin face flushed, his hands flew up to his chest and he could scarce mumble his dutiful greeting to his superior before falling on his knees in front of them.

The abbot laid a hand upon Hugh's sleeve and gently pushed him forward. "Brother John," said he, "we must thank the lad here, and his father, for this princely gift; it is because of the coming of Hugh that our aumbry shelves shall receive such goodly store."

Brother John cast a keen glance at Hugh, rose up and, to the boy's great confusion, kissed him on one cheek, then on the other, then without a word, returned to his knees and an eager examination of the books.

"Oh, my Lord Abbot, praise be to all the saints, here are the *Dialogues of St. Gregory!* And two Bibles and a goodly gloss! And homilies and—and—by my faith! the Roman pagans! Virgil, Horace, Ovid—one, two, four of them! Father, you will not deny us the reading of these? Some are noble, truly, and the Abbey of Croyland has, so they say, a fair collection of them, and the brothers read them in recreation hours."

His tongue rattled on, he paused not either for answers to the questions he threw out, nor for comments to match his own. His fingers trembled with eagerness, his cheeks were pink and his eyes shone with delight as he lifted them from some fair parchment to the smiling face of the abbot seated above him. At last he sat back on his heels sighing with satisfaction.

"Boy," said he, "these books will find some fair and worthy companions upon the shelves of our aumbries. You shall see for yourself on the morrow." He turned toward the abbot again. "Father," said he, "is the lad to sleep in the guest house or in the common dorter? There is an empty bed beside mine among the brothers—"

"Mine?" corrected the abbot. "How often, Brother John, must you do penance for that little word forbidden upon the tongue of any Benedictine?"

The monk stammered in confusion. "Father, I—in sooth, the richness of the books has muddled my poor brain! I had but thought to say that the little brother —I have already forgot the name—mine aumbry, my own living aumbry, who has brought this precious gift—the lad here—"

"My? Mine?" the abbot was laughing in spite of himself. " 'Tis late, Brother, and thy wits are most certainly addled! Take the boy and between the two of you, take the books. Place them in the cloister niche which is nearest the church, ready for dedication on the morrow. Then betake you both to the common dormitory and sleep on the beds Holy Church has most graciously provided for you!"

He arose; Brother John and Hugh gathered up the books carefully, and the three moved toward the door. As Hugh paused to pick up his cloak and a small bundle of clothing which the servant had left on a bench near the brazier, he heard the abbot speak again to Brother John.

"Were you not asking for a novice," said he, "to help in your work for the scriptorium? The novices can ill be spared from their studies, and there are all too few of them. This lad is over young, yet he has had the beginnings of a clerkly training. Under your teaching he can at least mix colors and pound gold for the illuminating of parchments and in time he may be taught to copy. We will make a scribe of him."

Brother John's reply was spoken too low for Hugh to hear, but evidently he had agreed. The boy stifled a sigh as he approached the two men again. So his life would be given to books, to reed pens and crackly parchments, to lead rules and colors and long hours over a desk. The life of a monkish scribe; he knew what it was, and one part of him warmed at the thought, but another part of him suffered in disappointment and humiliation. He wanted to be a knight, gay, proud, brave, successful, whom all the world would look up to with shouts and admiration as he rode abroad on a matchless steed! And his father! How his father would despise him even more than he did now, if he grew stooped and thin-chested bending over a desk, with all his interests centered on written pages. No, *that* must not happen. . . . But his father was gone, gone clean out of his life, no doubt, for in all probability he would never see him again. And here was he, a boy with a limping foot, cast out of the active world into a monastery. He sighed deeply, then lifted his chin and threw back his head. Well, what of it? There was no room in life for despair. His mother had taught him that. Sometimes he had thought his mother more truly brave than his warrior father; that time when there was plague in the village, for instance; she had gone about among the poor, helping and nursing with her own hands. And other times, horrible times of siege. Hugh was glad for her sake that she had died before this last bitter experience had come upon the family. Yes, glad, though he missed her cruelly. His mother loved books and here in the monastery at least one might love them openly and without fear of ridicule.

The abbot and Brother John had passed through the hall of the guest house and out through a side door to a path that led into the midst of the conventual buildings. Hugh quickened his step as best he could to catch up with them. It was dark and still cold without, though the wind and rain had abated somewhat. Soon they came to the cloisters built around an open square or garth, with the walls of the abbey church towering up on the north side and the great dorter nearer them on the east side. In the cloisters they paused to place the precious books in the aumbry nearest the church. A flare was burning in a stone bowl which cast a dim, uncertain light over the press, the little alcove in which it stood and, more dimly yet, over the walks and pillars of the cloister which lost themselves in blackness not far beyond. They climbed a flight of outside stairs so dark that Hugh must feel his way with his hands before each step, yet seemingly so familiar to the two men that they never hesitated.

At the door of the great sleeping room the abbot left them. Evidently his quarters were apart from the others. Brother John reached for Hugh's arm and guided him between rows of beds wherein he could faintly discern the monks sleeping. A pale ray of moonlight suddenly streamed in from the glass-less window high up at the end of the room.

"Ah!" whispered Brother John, "the moon has come out of her clouds to welcome thee! Here are pallet and blanket; thanks be to the moonlight, thou canst see them and look about a little. Lie down now, lad, and sleep, for I doubt not that thou art very weary."

Weary! he had not thought of it, but as he laid aside his outer garments and sank down upon the straw-filled mattress and drew the rough blanket over him, it seemed to him that never in his life before had he been so utterly exhausted. His muscles twitched, his head swam with colored images; he tossed about, wide-eyed and restless and wondered if sleep would ever come to him. And then, heavily, dreamlessly, he fell into the depths of slumber.

II. BROTHER JOHN
AND DICKON THE OBLATE

HUGH WAS AROUSED from his exhausted
sleep by a din of bells. He opened heavy eyes to
find the big dormitory room full of dim, flickering
light and moving figures. Brother John, in a whisper,
bade him lie still. It was the midnight service, he said;
Matins were for the monks and novices, not for weary
half-grown lads, and the halls and walks were bitter
cold. He finished with a great sneeze and hurried into
his soft, furred boots, shivering the while but making
no complaint.

The boy leaned on his elbow and watched. Stone
bowls stood at the ends of the long room with burning wicks in them which cast a wavering, uncertain
light over the brothers as they hastily donned their
cowls and habits. Novices appeared, with dripping
flares making the room seem quite bright, and when

the bell at last ceased its importunate clanging, each monk stood with bowed head and folded hands at the foot of his bed. Then, in companies of six, led by a novice, they marched out, padding softly in their furred winter shoes. Hugh, left alone in the dim light from the bowls, strained his ears to listen and soon heard the rhythmic intoning of the service from the abbey church beyond the cloisters.

He lay back, closing his eyes, but sleep did not come again immediately. He could not seem to shut out the mental pictures he so wished to forget; the cold angry faces of a mob, flames licking along the floor of the room in which he slept, his father's bitter, tragic face as he looked back at the ruins of his home, the long weary ride on the stormy roads to Glaston; and then his father, kneeling before the abbot in the guest house hall, asking for the blessing that he must feel in his heart he had no right to claim. His father—Hugh loved his father, yet always with the memory of him, even from his babyhood days, came pictures of broils and combat, sudden anger that often as not resulted in bloodshed, fear, hatred, intrigues. The boy sighed heavily. His father was a hot, impulsive man of action, but he had his quiet, lovable side too. If only the king had let him alone! If only the people had not been so swift to rise against him! Again the memory of that frenzied, ill-smelling mob and his own stark terror in the face of it. He shivered and drew the rough woolen blanket closer about him. Below, the chanting of the psalms rose clearer. He listened, marking the antiphonal rhythmic beat of them. Gradually his tense body relaxed and he breathed evenly and quietly again. A sense of security and peace stole over him. Here no bloodthirsting brutal mob could break in, here no desperate deeds could be done and then as desperately and futilely repented. Here one might love music and books and quiet, and not be ashamed. He turned on his side with a sigh, not of unhappiness and fear this time, but of relief.

How long the service lasted he did not know for he soon fell asleep, with the soft Gregorian chant still in his ears, and did not wake when the brothers filed back to the dorter and into their beds again. Indeed, before long he learned to sleep through the night office and only stir and dream when the midnight bell broke the dark quiet.

The next day the books which his father had brought with him were duly dedicated at the High Altar, Hugh himself taking a small part in the ceremony as Abbot Robert requested, knowing that it would ease the lad somewhat of his hurt and sorrow. Then they were taken to a little alcove off the north cloister walk where stood the Painted Aumbry. A large press or wardrobe this was, adorned on the panels, inside as well as out, with pictures of saints and angels in vivid reds, blues, greens, and yellows. The drawings were uncouth but the coloring strong and bright and, in Hugh's eyes at least, delightfully cheerful. It pleased him that the treasury of books from the home that was lost to him should here be housed so nobly, and he watched with pride as Brother John laid each volume carefully upon a shelf where it would not be crowded or injured.

There were two or three other cupboards for manuscripts in recesses off the cloister walk, but these were unadorned and in them were kept mostly the novices' lesson books, the monastic records, and some few service books in constant use. The Painted Aumbry contained the real library of the community and it was the pride and joy of Brother John's life. Every morning after chapter meeting he would confer importantly with the abbot, then go at once to the Painted Aumbry, take out such books and writing materials as were needed for the day's task of copying and illuminating, and also deal out books for those who did no copying, for all the monks were expected to read a little, daily, in the cloisters at certain hours.

Hugh accompanied Brother John every day and helped him, being familiar enough with books and script to know at least how to find what was called for.

But one day, shortly after his arrival, Brother John beckoned to him and, leaving the cloisters, set forth across the abbey lawns, slowing his quick, nervous step that Hugh's limping foot might keep up with him.

"Where are we going?" the boy asked.

"To the kitchen," answered Brother John. "I would

boil up my ink and show thee how the Byzantine gold must be powdered and the root juices treated."

The big kitchen stood apart from the other monastic buildings and none save those who had business there was permitted to enter. It was clean and spacious, with shining copper pots, kettles, and big caldrons ranged round the sides, and several huge fireplaces; a warm, good smelling, delightful place, truly. Brother John had a bench and table to himself in one corner and there he could mix his gallic acid, sulphate of iron, and gum for the good durable ink, boil down his roots for stains, stretch and dry or scrape his parchments, and melt the precious gold leaf which the rubricators used for their most choicely illuminated pages. The place was quite deserted when Brother John and Hugh entered, letting themselves in with a huge key.

"I like well to work here at this hour," said the brother bustling about, laying out copper and iron pots and taking small packages of various materials from a cupboard near his table. "The lay brothers and the cellarer are all out in the garden, field, market, or elsewhere, and I need not fear sullying dust or grease for my fair, clear colors. Here, boy, mix this gum with a little water; there is a bucket yonder, fresh from the well. When it is soft, add the soot—I will give it thee—and mix until thou hast a good black, and the right consistency. The novices are so wasteful of their practice ink, I seem to be ever in need of more."

Hugh set to work and did as he was told, pounding and mixing in a large, mortar-like bowl, while Brother John began boiling down roots for dyes. He talked incessantly. So many hours during a monk's day must be spent in silence that it was a relief, no doubt, to let his tongue run on, even if his listener were nothing more than a young lad. And Hugh, as the days went on and he became more accustomed to the busy brother, began to talk more freely also.

"The fairest book we had," said he one time, "was one fetched from Iona where St. Colum once lived. It was very old, and the pages were all stained and the script faded and strange and hard to read. We kept it wrapt in fine linen in the bottom of the aumbry, but Alleyn, our clerk, let me look at it now and then, and once he read to me out of it a little."

"What became of it?" asked Brother John, full of interest.

"It was burned," said Hugh in a hard, bitter voice. "When they came, the enemies of my father, they made a great fire and flung into it much, much that we loved. Those that my father brought here were all the books we could save, and that was through the quick wit of Alleyn. How I hate those men! And the king! I hate him! I hate him!"

"Tut, tut, boy," said Brother John, pausing and looking up from the parchment he was stretching. "You must not hate the king—that savors of treason. Indeed, 'tis not well to hate at all. Doubtless you have reason, but there is no comfort in hating, be the reason ever so good. Give over hating, child, while you are young and loving is easy."

"I loved Alleyn," said the boy in a low tone from which the bitterness had not gone. "And I loved my lady mother who is dead and gone, and my sisters —aye, and my father too, though I'm thinking he cared not at all for me. They are all gone—because of the king—and I shall never see them again. How can I help but hate him?"

"Never is a long word," Brother John continued with his work, talking the while. "Maybe they are not all gone forever; and what is sure at any rate, is that you will learn to love others. The world is not so bad a place—if you let not hate poison it. Look up, lad, and forget thy troubled past, whatever it may be. Books will help thee and I see right well thy liking for those!"

"Books *are* goodly," agreed Hugh, "but I would be a knight and ride abroad adventuring. 'Tis not enough to sit in the cloister walk and read about great deeds; I want to be doing them!"

Brother John's glance at the boy was full of understanding but for the moment he said naught. His attention seemed entirely absorbed in a pile of old and broken parchment sheets.

"Go stir that vermilion powder in the kettle," said he at length. "Small wonder if it be not burned with all our tongue wagging. Nay? Well, then, set it on the table to cool and now fetch me two knives and the pumice and we will scrape parchment. It is so costly these days, the good white parchment, and old sheets of accounts can be scraped clean and used over again. Adventuring did you say, lad? Nay, adventure ofttimes may spring up like the grass under our feet—'tis not always needful to ride after it."

Hugh brought the knives and pumice and settled himself again beside the monk, to work on an old cracked sheet covered with figures and ancient reckonings. Nothing could be duller, less adventurous, he thought, than this scraping, soaking, rubbing of worn yellow parchments to make them usable again. Yet there under his very finger tips, little though he knew it at the time, lay the makings of an adventure that was to color the pattern of his whole life.

But before he had got into it came an important happening without which the adventure could not have been, or if it had, would have proved dull and lonely. Though at first he had thought he might not see a lad his own age again as long as he stayed in Glaston, quite unexpectedly, Hugh found a friend.

Perhaps Brother John was aware of a lonely restlessness in the boy for, as the spring weather came on and deepened into summer, he frequently pushed him good-naturedly away from his parchments, saying:

"Lad, thou hast done enough for the nonce. Go out into the fields and to the grange. Bring me back some new sheepskins if the lay brothers have got any cured. And, Hugh, there be eels in the stream back yonder, and a dish of fried eels for Friday, should you happen to catch any—!"

His sentence would trail off as he hurried back to his ink and parchments. Good old Brother John, thought Hugh, he wouldn't know, himself, whether he were eating eels or angleworms! He is only thinking that fishing would be rare sport for me—and 'twould indeed be, if I could find another fellow to fish with me!

He would start forth then by himself and wander hither and yon over the vast abbey grounds. At first his dragging foot made him tire easily but as the days passed, almost without his realizing it, he began to limp less, hold himself straighter and, as Brother

John noticed with gratification, seemed in all ways to have grown ruddier and sturdier.

One day Hugh followed the River Brue along its winding path, deep into the marsh lands, going farther afield than he realized. At length he sat down on the reedy bank of a backwater pool, to rest before retracing his steps. The air was very quiet, too late in the day for much bird song, and not a breath of wind stirred the tall lank rushes. Hugh could see his own reflection clearly in the still water and watched idly as the minnows darted about beneath the placid surface. Suddenly he was startled by a whizzing sound and an arrow bedded itself in a willow tree trunk directly across the pool from him. Through the tall rank grass some little distance from him, a boy came running. He stopt short directly in front of Hugh and began crossing himself, his eyes fairly bulging out of their sockets. He had on a rough, rather soiled woolen tunic such as peasants wear and over it what looked like the ragged remains of a monk's habit. A round borel cap atop of his round, open-mouthed, astonished face, made such a comical picture that Hugh burst out laughing.

"By my faith!" cried the boy. "By all the saints! I thought you were a duck—a wild duck! You *were* a water fowl! I swear you were! Enchanted maybe, under a devil's spell!" He crossed himself again. "And sure I know not whether it be the greater miracle that you be changed this moment from a fowl into a boy, or that I did not pierce you dead with my arrow!"

Hugh ended his laugh with a friendly grin. "As to that," he said, "I am no water bird nor ever was one, enchanted or otherwise! But it is truly a near miracle that yon arrow did not lodge in my head. And glad I am that your aim was not altogether true!"

The boy seated himself on the bank, pulled off his cap and made a lunge with it at a streak of sunlight that shone through the shade of the willows near him.

It was Hugh's turn to look astonished. "Whatever are you doing?" he asked.

The boy laughed rather sheepishly. "Trying to hang my cap on a sunbeam. It's been done, you know; Saint Vincent hung his hat and his pilgrim's cloak on a sunbeam whenever he had a mind to—and they always held. A miracle, of course, but just an everyday kind of one. Some day it is going to happen to *me*, or a miracle of some kind—I know it is!"

"But you aren't a saint, are you?" queried Hugh, laughing again.

"That I am not! But it isn't always saints that get the wonders. Almost anything could happen in a place like this—to just anybody. So I'm on the lookout! Who are you, anyway? And if you were not that fat wild duck I thought I saw, where did you come from?"

"I'm Hugh; I belong in the monastery."

"Oh, an oblate?"

"No, not exactly." Hugh spoke hesitantly as he always did when questioned about himself. "My father did not vow me to the life of a religious; he—he—just—left me here while he—while he went off to the wars. I might stay here always and again I might not."

"So you are free! I wish I was! I'm an oblate and

no question about it. My father gave me to the monastery as a thank offering when he got well of the
plague. I was but a young infant, but I guess I squalled
even then. I don't want to be a monk, or a lay brother,
ever! I want to be a yeoman and fight and travel
about and seek adventure!"

"I'd like that too," agreed Hugh heartily. "I'd like
to be a knight but—"

The boy followed Hugh's involuntary glance down
at his lame foot.

"I see," said he, "but, by Our Lady, there be miracles a-plenty these days! And here, most especially;
why, I wouldn't wonder to see you healed of *that*
most any time!"

"Why here in particular?" queried Hugh.

"Don't you know about old Glaston? Sure, it's as
full of saints' bones and hallows as the Brue is full
of eels! I'll warrant there's scarce a saint worth men-
tioning in the whole of Britain, or the land of Eire
either, that has not stopt the night at least at our
Glaston. And seems like they all left things behind
them. There was Patrick and his bell—I've seen that
many a time—and St. Bride. She left her loom and
wallet and weaving stick, they say, over at Beckery
where she lived in a hermitage. And, of course, St.
Dunstan; did you know he had a forge here and
worked in metals? And one time the devil came and
Dunstan got him by the nose with his pinchers. They
are hereabouts somewhere, too, his pinchers. It's the
most wonderful place in the world, our Glaston."

"You love it, don't you?" said Hugh. "It's just a

place to me; but maybe I'll get to love it, too, some day. Have you been here long?"

"Since a small child; I am near thirteen now."

"I am near thirteen, too."

There was a moment's silence between them but the two seemed to draw nearer to one another in spirit. An instant liking deepened, and each felt instinctively that he had found a friend. The silence threatened to become awkward.

"Do you—do you ever fish for eels?" said Hugh, more to say something than because he particularly wanted to know.

"Sure," said the other. "And I go hunting with my short bow. I made it myself, see?" He handed the bow he had been holding to Hugh who felt its smooth surface appraisingly and tested the gut string.

"Nice piece of work," said he.

"Of course I am not *allowed* to fish and hunt," continued the boy, "and every so often Guthlac, the lay brother at the grange, gives me a drubbing, but he is glad enough to eat what I bring him. You see things aren't as they used to be, or so he tells me; they used to keep their oblates very strictly, with their noses to their books and a switch held over their heads while they conned their service music. But me—I couldn't read notes to save me, and the letters in the Psalter books are beyond my cunning, so they have turned me out on the farm to help with the creatures. I like that well enough and, if they must make a monk of me, I'll serve that way. 'Tis not so bad, really, and there are the long afternoons when the lay brothers are dozing. That's when I go where I please and—and—" He stopped suddenly in the middle of his sentence and edged closer to Hugh with a questioning look.

"I guess you're the right sort," he continued, after a moment. "I'll tell you a secret if you vow to keep it close."

"That I will!" agreed Hugh eagerly.

"I hunt—other things beside birds and eels," said the boy in a solemn tone.

Hugh waited questioningly.

"I hunt treasure. I've a private hoard hidden away. Things I have found buried in caves or in underground passages, and some even in the marshes around the Brue."

"What kind of treasure?"

"Saints' relics; bones and jewels and coffers—and—but I'll show them to you some day. Want to see them?"

"Do I!" exclaimed Hugh, his heart beating high with interest and amazement.

"But first I think we should swear brotherhood and eternal secrecy. My name is Dickon—I guess I didn't mention it. Now who are you, really? And how do you come to be here? You just said you were Hugh, and nothing further. What's the rest of it?"

All the happiness suddenly died out of Hugh's face. "I can't—I can't tell you—much more. My father—we had enemies who burned our home—my father brought me here—and is gone—out of England—and—I guess I'll have to be just Hugh to everybody."

"But not to me if we are going to be sworn

brothers!" Dickon's tone sounded hurt. "You could tell me anything—I'd never breathe it. I'd vow on the bones of a saint, or anything. Even if your family had been traitor to the king, I wouldn't mind; I'd keep it hidden, though I should die for it."

Hugh shook his head sadly. "I can't; I just can't tell anybody. My father—"

But he got no further. The boy gave him a look in which disappointment and anger were blended, lept lightly across the stream and retrieved his arrow, then, clapping his cap on the back of his head, he remarked with an air of finality:

"It was a fit beginning for true friendship, my arrow finding you in this marsh and near slaying you, but there can be no secrets hid between sworn brothers. If ever you be minded to tell me your story, the whole of it and the truth of it, seek out Dickon the oblate at the grange over yonder."

He moved off a few paces, then turned back saying, "There is nothing of me or mine, either past or present, that I would keep from thee, Hugh, wert thou minded to be my true friend." Then, as Hugh made no reply he walked on without a word or look more.

In spite of his clumsy mixture of clothes, his figure held a certain dignity, and Hugh watched him with a very heavy heart. He liked the boy immensely, and nothing would have made him happier just now than a friend his own age to whom he could talk freely. For a moment he felt he must run after him and say to him, "My father made me vow I would tell naught! I cannot break my solemn vow!" But even while he was thinking he would do so, the boy's quick stride had taken him out of sight.

iii. ꜧue anꝺ cry

DISCONSOLATELY Hugh turned his steps back toward the conventual buildings. He thought he would take a short cut, so left the windings of the Brue and struck through a bit of woodland. Before long he realized he must have missed his way for no familiar landmarks appeared. The trees grew sparse, the land more open; he passed through an apple orchard and brought up before an ancient stone wall, evidently marking the end of the monastic property. Beyond the wall ran a rutty country road, and when he had got onto it Hugh could see in the distance the bell tower of the new chapel, the one which Abbot Henry had begun and which had not yet been finished. It seemed a long way off but the boy sighed with relief to see it. He was growing tired

and hungry, too, for it was approaching sundown and the noonday meal had not been overfilling. He trudged along, his lame leg dragging more than usual.

The road ran through a straggling village, with squalid peasant huts on either side of it. Pigs rooted and chickens scratched about in the mire before the blackened doors; gaunt, mangy looking dogs snarled at him as he passed but, except for a few half-naked, dirty children who stared at him curiously, there seemed to be no human beings about. Doubtless they were all still busy on the long strips of culti-vated fields that lay beyond the village. One hut, a little larger and more prosperous looking than the rest, had a byre beside it, outside of which stood a heavy farm horse hitched to a springless cart. Hugh wished he might borrow the cart and drive himself back to the abbey. No one seemed to be about to ask and he was passing on when something caught his attention, a figure moving cautiously out from behind a high pile of stable refuse toward the cart. He looked furtively in each direction and, catching sight of Hugh, started and seemed about to retrace his steps, then seeing it was but a boy alone, came on. He was ragged and unkempt, his cloak, which must have once been gay with gold and scarlet, hung soddenly about him as if many times soaked in rain and mud. It was drab and torn, as was the cap with the bedraggled plume pulled down low over his forehead; not so low, however, as to cover completely an ugly cut with dried blood about it near the left eye. Hugh stared at the man for a moment, then a little cry escaped him and his hands flew to his mouth as if to crush back any further sound.

The stranger stared back, scarcely less astonished, then, looking around him fearfully lest anyone be within sight or sound, he beckoned the boy closer, exclaiming in a hoarse voice:

"Hugh! Young Master Hugh! Faith, I had thought you safe in France ere now! How comes it you are thus free and well-cared for and alone and unmolested in this filthy village?"

"I am with the monastery folk—Glaston. But, oh, Jacques, how come you in such sorry case?"

" 'Tis harried and hunted I am, young master, as are all your father's house that have not already fled the country. Even the king's protection would scarce serve us now; the people—the fierce hatred of the mob—" He shivered as he spoke and moved nervously nearer the cart. "I had thought to steal a ride, so low am I fallen. Nights in the bare fields, days without food, hiding and slipping from village to village, afeared of my own shadow. Nay, I am even now near done for!"

Hugh groaned. "The mob! I know well what that means! Jacques, we cannot face a mob gone wild again."

At that moment a peasant appeared far down the road, running. He was shouting and, as he drew nearer, others joined him. "Hue and cry!" he bellowed in a great voice that soon brought the village folk pouring in from the fields, down lanes, and out of byres and huts which but a moment before had seemed so still and lifeless. "Hue and cry! Hue and cry! 'Tis a criminal fleeing from justice!"

The man at Hugh's side looked desperately at the oncoming crowd and seemed for the moment frozen into inactivity.

"Quick!" cried Hugh scrambling clumsily onto the high-wheeled cart. "Quick! Climb in! We'll make Glaston before they can catch us! Sanctuary! You'll find sanctuary at the abbey!"

Jacques needed no second bidding. Up by the hub of the wheel and into the empty cart he tumbled.

"Lie low!" shouted the boy over his shoulder. He had already caught up the thick reins and cowhide whip and was beating the horse into action.

The jouncing of the springless wagon over the ruts of the road as the big lumbering horse plunged forward would have thrown Hugh out if he had not crouched into a sitting posture and clung desperately to the front board with one hand while holding both reins in the other. The whip he dropt almost at once, being unable to hold that also, but he would have had no further use for it anyway. The horse, startled by the quickness and the unfamiliarity of the hand and voice behind him, and still more by the shouts and running feet of the growing crowd coming down the road, made all the speed possible to get away from them. The cart swayed and tipped, first on one wheel, then on the other. Jacques bounced about like a pea in a hopper and Hugh hung on with all his might.

A few of the swifter-footed boys among the pursuers gained on them for a few moments and ran along beside the cart, but they soon fell back, unable to keep the pace. The calls and shouts of the crowd grew angrier and more savage as they saw the prospect of their prey escaping them. A stone flew past Hugh's head, barely missing him; then a clump of mud struck him between the shoulders. More stones and mud followed; a terrific jolt of the plunging wagon tore his grip loose and he would surely have fallen out had not Jacques' arms caught and held him. Somehow they managed to steady each other. The abbey church seemed nearer now—but still so far! Could they make it? At least they were outstripping the crowd, but the horse had got the bit in his teeth now and was almost out of control of the reins.

Suddenly they took a right-angled turn on one wheel; the cart tipped perilously, then lurched to the other side. It was too much. Hugh lost his hold and he and the fugitive were both flung out onto the road. The horse shied in added fright, wrenched the reins from the boy, who was still clinging to them, and ran madly on, the empty cart clattering behind him.

"Are you badly hurt, lad?" asked Jacques, picking himself up and leaning over the boy anxiously. The cut in his face had broken open again and was streaming fresh blood.

"No," gasped Hugh, "I guess—I'm not hurt much if any. Don't bother about me; you must run on; the crowd will be caught up with us again in a few moments. Run, Jacques, run! Get to the Galilee Porch of the abbey. 'Tis sanctuary there and none can touch you!"

They could hear the shouting and running of the villagers drawing nearer. Jacques laid his hand on Hugh's shoulder in a swift gesture of gratitude and, without a word, ran on.

Slowly the boy gathered himself together and stood up. He was shaken, bruised, exhausted, but except for torn clothing, an ugly cut below the knee, and a bleeding hand where the reins had torn it, he seemed none the worse for his tumble. He limped back from the road and leaned against a tree trunk. Would the crowd mob him? he thought in near panic. But he crushed the fear down. Would Jacques make it? That was what mattered. If the man could only reach the north door of the abbey—the Galilee Porch—then, according to the law of the land, he could claim sanctuary, for a time at least; just how long the boy was not sure.

The running feet drew nearer. The first of the pursuers were upon him. "Hue and cry! Hue and cry!" They rushed on down the road, too intent on the fleeing figure far ahead of them to do more than glance at the boy leaning wearily against the tree by the roadside. Men and boys, the swifter runners, passed him first, then women, many with brooms and sticks in their hands, and old men hobbling awkwardly along on rheumaticky feet, and even quite young children. Their faces were hard and intent with a wild sort of savagery, the cruel thrill of the hunt. Hugh fell in with the last stragglers and hurried along beside them. He found himself keeping pace with an old gaffer who was wheezing and helping himself with a stout staff, but making surprisingly good headway.

"What is it? What hath the man done?" asked the fellow, breathing heavily. "Know you who 'tis and what he be a-fleeing for? Be it murder or thievery?"

"Neither!" said Hugh passionately. "He hath done naught at all!"

"Hey day! Is it friend of yours that you know whereon you speak?"

Hugh bit his lip. He must be careful how his tongue tripped him.

The man halted abruptly, seized Hugh's arm and swung him around, then looked him critically up and down.

"By my faith, 'tis the boy that was driving the cart with the murderer in it! And 'twas Jehan's cart! Hey, neighbors, stop a bit! Here be one that is a felon too!"

But most of the villagers were already far ahead and paid little heed to his shout. He shrugged his shoulders and hurried along after them, glancing suspiciously at Hugh every few moments, as if he did not intend to let the boy escape him.

"What do you know of the fellow yourself?" asked Hugh, anger and resentment still hot in him.

"Naught whatever," replied the old gaffer, "save that he be a man running. When folk raise the hue and cry I would be after whatsoever they hunt and harry. 'Tis wonderful pleasant to give chase, and I would cast my stones with as good an aim and a better will than any, saving only that age hinders the speed in me."

"And does no thought come to you as to whether there be justice in the case, or that the poor hunted creature might be innocent?"

"Justice and innocence be questions beyond simple peasant folk like me." Then he grinned. "Except where it toucheth our own skin! But what is it to you, and who are you anyway?"

"I am of the monastery folk," said Hugh.

"Oh, so you be of Glaston?" The man looked at him with a new expression. "They be good folk—yonder."

By this time they had reached the main gate of the abbey grounds and pushed in with the others. They passed the almonry and the guest house and ran on to the church; in the northwest corner was an entrance with a paved court in front of it, the Galilee Porch. It was there that the crowd had gathered and halted. Their prey had escaped; the man had reached the great north door and was clinging to the bronze knocker. Sanctuary! Hugh, peering over the shoulders and under the arms of the pursuers milling around the grounds, breathed a great sigh of relief as he caught sight of him. They were still muttering angrily but dared not approach closer. Sanctuary! Thank God for sanctuary! Jacques was safe for the present, at least. The bell in the tower began to ring, clamorously, insistently. That would tell the abbot and the brothers that a hunted creature claimed the protection of the Church. Just what they would do with him or what would happen next, Hugh was not certain.

He squirmed and elbowed his way through the press of folk until he had got to the front and could see better. Jacques stood close to the door, his tall, slight figure drooping with weariness, his clothes freshly torn and stained with blood, sweat, and mire. He had lost his cap and his heavy shock of brown curling hair, matted and clotted with blood from his cut, fell straggling over his forehead and cheeks. After a few moments he braced himself, controlled his laboring breath with an effort, turned and faced his pursuers with squared shoulders and head held high.

"What hath the fellow done?" asked someone near Hugh. The question was passed back and forth among the crowd. None seemed to know any more about the matter than the peasant with whom Hugh had talked, though several held ugly rocks in their hands, which they had been about to throw, doubtless following after many another which had been thrown already.

A sudden squirming and displacement among those

beside Hugh resulted in the eruption of a round borel cap and a familiar face under it. The boy Dickon emerged, apparently from beneath the feet of the men towering above him, and took his place shoulder to shoulder with Hugh, where he could see without hindrance everything that went on. He gave Hugh an odd look which held in it something of admiration, and the lad smiled back, eager to be friendly. But Dickon merely nodded, making no remark.

"Who started the hue and cry?" asked a voice in the crowd.

"The manor beadle," answered someone.

"And said he what 'twas all about?"

"Aye," cried a new voice from the outskirts of the group. " 'Tis said the creature is of the household of one of them that slew the good Archbishop— Thomas à Becket."

There was a murmur of horror, then an awed silence. Hugh's eyes never left the figure standing so tragically at bay before the door of the Galilee Porch. His lips were shut in a thin, tight line, as if words might leap out in spite of himself, and his eyes burned defiantly in his white face. Dickon turned from staring at the fugitive and watched Hugh curiously.

By now the bell had ceased ringing and the abbot and some of the monks had come forth upon the church porch. Hugh saw Brother John among them and the sacristan, and Brother Symon, the almoner, an old man with a quiet, pitying face, and many others whom he had already come to know, or at least recognize.

Abbot Robert addressed the fugitive who still stood close to the protecting door of the church, but had turned from the menacing villagers to face him.

"Young sir," he said gravely, "are you here to claim sanctuary of Holy Church?"

The man nodded, the expression on his face a mixture of hunted fear, entreaty, and the defiance of despair.

"Of what are you accused?" continued Father Robert. "Or are they present who would bear witness against you?"

Before Jacques could answer, a voice from the edge of the crowd called out, "There should no sanctuary be granted him, Father Abbot; he is of the devil's own brew, he is one of the party who slew our Archbishop, Thomas à Becket!"

Exclamations of astonishment broke from the group of monks behind the abbot and some of them involuntarily drew back, gazing at the fugitive with a new expression in which hostility took the place of friendly or indifferent curiosity.

"Aye," cried another voice and the beadle of a neighboring manor village stood out from among the crowd. "Aye, 'tis known to us that the Archbishop, God rest his soul, was hacked to pieces before the High Altar itself, over Canterbury way. And this fellow saw the deed done and stayed it not— nay, took part in it himself, no doubt. Give him no sanctuary!"

A stone flung from somewhere in the crowd struck against the doorjamb and fell clattering to the floor, barely missing the head of the fugitive. Snarls of

hatred, curses, and yells from the crowd were mingled with the more subdued mutterings of the monks.

The abbot stept directly in front of the young
man so that if another stone were thrown it would
find its target in him, and raised his hand with an
imperious gesture.

"Silence!" he commanded. "Know you not that
every man must be accounted innocent until he be
proved guilty? And you know the law of sanctuary,
all of you—and some of you have used it to your
own profit ere this!" A short laugh interrupted him
and the humor of the crowd grew lighter. The abbot
continued, "No matter what his deed or crime this
young man can claim sanctuary in the name of the
Church and of English Law here in Glastonbury
Abbey for the space of forty days. And after that,"
the abbot turned from the crowd and addressed himself more directly to Jacques, "after that time, if you
be indeed fleeing from justice you must adjure the
realm, betake yourself to the nearest port, and go
into exile in some foreign land."

The fugitive bowed his head and the abbot went
on. "And now, my son, speak up, declare boldly for
yourself in the presence of these people, what you
have in truth done that you should be thus harried
and hunted; what you are accused of, both justly and
unjustly."

The man tried to still the trembling of his hands
by clenching them. "Father Abbot," said he, "I will
tell all, nor hide anything. Only let me not fall into
the hands of yon frenzied mob! I am—or was—of
the household of my Lord Hugh de Morville, he

who with three others sought to prove their loyalty to our liege, King Henry, by siding with him in his quarrel against the Archbishop Thomas à Becket. Thou knowest, Lord Abbot, far better than I, who was but a dutiful follower of those above me, what were the causes of their bickerings. I only know that on an evil day we stood, the four lords and their attendants, in the presence of the king and he thundered forth those ill begotten words: 'Becket! that accursed Becket! Is there no friend of mine loyal enough to rid me of the fellow?' And then—"

"Ah, yes, I know!" interrupted the abbot quietly. "And then the hot-blooded young fools, your masters, rode away to Canterbury and slew the Archbishop before the very altar."

Again an ominous snarl broke from the crowd, but the abbot held up his hand imperiously.

"But you," said he, still addressing the fugitive, "what part did you play in this dastardly deed?"

"Good Father Abbot, by my soul I swear no hand or weapon of mine nor of my master's touched the Archbishop! True, we held back the crowd and suffered the deed to be accomplished and, in the riot that followed, I fought and slew innocent folk—God forgive me—to protect my master. Our souls are thus much stained with blood in this dread matter, but we are like to suffer all the punishment falling upon the other three, who themselves did the actual deed. And yet, good Father, none of it was of our intention and I, for my part, am most truly penitent."

There was a moment of intense silence in the

crowd. Hands still clutching stones were lowered, faces lined with hatred relaxed.

"God forgive us all, for we be sinners, too, every one of us," muttered someone.

Heads nodded in agreement and again attention centered on the abbot who was speaking in a voice gentler and less stern:

"What did you then, young sir, after the murder and the riot?"

"We fled away, all of us, and harbored ourselves in Hugh de Morville's castle fortress of Knaresborough. The king would have protected us, but he could do nothing to stem the anger of the people and the greed and ill will of our enemies at court, who took this opportunity to ruin and despoil us utterly. We were attacked, besieged by a frenzied mob, driven out, and the lands and castle of Sir Hugh ravaged, burnt, and destroyed before our eyes."

Dickon who had been alternately watching the scene on the Galilee Porch and noting the expression on Hugh's white face, slipped an arm through his; a friendly gesture, but Hugh seemed too absorbed in the conversation that had been going on, and in his own bitter thoughts, to be conscious of it.

"We scattered," the man Jacques continued. "Since then we have lived like hunted beasts in forest or lonely field or byway. My few companions have been killed or separated from me, so that I know naught of them, and I have wandered alone these many weeks, subsisting as I could, hoping the storm against us would die down at last and that I might find

some peaceful harborage, or else take ship to France.
Surely, Father Abbot, you will not deny me sanctuary? I be all but spent and fore-done!"

He knelt upon the stone pavement of the porch,
his hands upraised in supplication.

"Nay, indeed nay," said Abbot Robert laying a
kindly hand on the bent shoulder. "There is nothing
to fear in the House of God. Thou shalt rest in
peace within these walls. And now, thy name, my
son?"

"Jacques de Raoul." The man rose, an expression
of immense relief on his face.

"Of Norman birth?"

"Not I but my father's father. We come of a Norman line and followed William of Normandy."

"Then exile means home in France?"

"Nay," said the young man sturdily. "No land but
England can be home to me." He sighed as he spoke
and looked out over the monastic grounds, the green
velvety lawns between the ancient wooden buildings,
the gray stone of the newer ones and, farther away,
the conical shaped hill of Glastonbury Tor.

"So," said the abbot watching him sympathetically, "another son of England will be driven from
our land because of the quarrels of kings and barons.
Alas, how many they are! And we can ill spare sons
who love their England, be their blood Norman or
Saxon. But come, we must see to your present needs.

"Our almoner will give you the fugitive's cloak,
our monks will furnish you food and tend your injuries, and I myself, my son, will hear your personal
confession and absolve you in good time. Then get

you to the high road and, in the protecting garb of the sanctuary seeker, hasten to some port and escape to France."

As they were talking Brother Symon had fetched a black robe with a yellow cross on the left shoulder of it. This he handed to Jacques, thereby signifying to the world that he was a fugitive from justice, but under the direct protection of the Church.

The abbot bade the crowd of people disperse, which they did quietly enough. The monks, too, followed by the abbot, turned away and went back to the cloisters, all save Brother Symon, the almoner, and Brother Cuthbert, the infirmarian, who busied themselves tending the cuts on the young man's face and head, and bringing him food and wine. He must stay near the Galilee Porch both night and day, they told him, lest some fanatic attack him; or else go forth soon to the nearest port while folk remembered that the sanctuary law protected him.

Only Hugh and Dickon heard these words of warning. When the rest of the crowd had departed they had still lingered on, watching; Hugh eager to have another word alone with Jacques, Dickon unable to keep his eyes from Hugh's face.

At last the two monks finished their kindly ministry and left Jacques to himself. He drew the black robe around his shoulders, never raising his head from its dejected drooping and, without a word or sign of recognition to Hugh, stept inside the door of the church.

"So that is it," said Dickon quietly, nodding his head.

Hugh had been staring at the closed door and now brought himself to with a start. "*What* is it?" he questioned, giving Dickon his full attention for the first time. "What do you mean?"

"So thou art of *his* household, the great lord, Hugh de Morville—one of those four—"

Hugh nodded silently, his face tense and tragic.

"But why didst thou not tell? It is not anything against *thee* who had naught to do with that murder?"

"Thou seest how it is!" cried the other bitterly. "The whole world will hate my father and all his house because of that deed—forever and ever!"

"But not our Glaston!" interrupted Dickon. "We would have welcomed thee hadst thou been the wickedest man alive. We hate nobody here in Glaston; we couldn't! Brother Symon says our Glaston is so sacred a spot that Christ Himself may come here some day. He is always expecting one of the beggars in the almonry to turn out to be Christ in disguise. And you should see him tend them himself, all sorts of filthy beggars. And many be thieves and cutthroats, no doubt. But it makes no difference to Brother Symon whether they be good or bad, clean or leprous, they be all, *all* come as the children of God and brothers of our Saviour. I cannot tell thee as he does—but surely there could be no hatred at all toward anyone here in our Glaston."

The boy spoke with a warmth and assurance that touched Hugh to the heart and for a moment he could scarce keep the tears back. At length he said, "I—I would like to have told everything to Brother

John—and the abbot—he is kind and friendly—
and you, too, Dickon. But my father made me vow I
would say naught to anyone and would start new as
if I had never had even the name of De Morville.
But I can't do that—I just can't be as if I hadn't any
name or past or anything!"

"Of course you can't, and of course you could not
break your vow either, but now I have guessed about
it. Your vow is all whole and unbroken, yet we know
about each other through and through, and we can
be sworn brothers after all. You would like to be,
wouldn't you?"

"I would—more than anything! And I am glad
you have guessed my secret! It was a heavy burden
to carry alone."

The two boys looked at each other in silent understanding for a moment and then, both feeling
suddenly awkward after such an unusual display of
sentiment, Dickon seized his cap and made a thrust
at a streak of sunlight slanting in a long line between the trees of the grounds.

"Not yet!" said Hugh laughing. "You're no saint
yet! The sunbeam won't hold, and that is the last
sunlight of the day. 'Twill soon be time for Vespers.
By my faith, I had forgot the horse and cart we took
in the village! I wonder—"

"The owner has no doubt got them home by now,"
Dickon assured him. "I saw the horse and the overturned cart by the side of the road before I joined
you here. Jehan was in a great to-do about them; he
is the peasant who owns them, you know. I told him
you were one of us, one of the abbey folk, and must

needs help any sanctuary seeker in any way you could. That soon pacified him. They all love our Glaston, the peasant folk—and they'd better, with all the brothers do for them!"

Hugh looked relieved. "I feared they would want to be after me in a mob when they had finished with Jacques," said he. "All I thought of at the time was to get him here safe, and the horse and cart were handy—"

"You were fine!" said Dickon approvingly. "Finer than I would have been—with two whole legs to me." He turned red and embarrassed, thinking Hugh might be hurt at the allusion to his infirmity, but the boy was only pleased with the praise.

" 'Twas nothing," said he modestly; "the least I could do for a friend of my father's, for anyone of my father's house."

"That is the way I feel about Glaston folk, all of them. I would risk my life for Glaston any day— may the saints so help me! But come, we must seal our pact of undying friendship! We must draw blood on it and swear that hereafter there shall be naught hid between us, either good or bad!" Dickon thrust his hand under his tunic and drew forth a knife knotted clumsily with a hempen cord tied around his waist.

"But no!" A new thought occurred to him and he returned the knife to its somewhat dangerous place of concealment. "I've a better idea! We'll make a ceremony of it in my secret cave. We'll swear brotherhood over my treasure of hidden hallows. What time art like to be free on the morrow, Hugh?"

"Maybe Brother John will let me have the afternoon off; we have a good supply of scriptorium materials on hand. Otherwise I would only have the hour after the noon meal when the brothers are resting."

"We'd need more time than that," said Dickon. "I have something very special to show you. I'd be free anytime. I just go off when I've a mind to; Brother Guthlac sometimes thrashes me when I get back, but usually he's too lazy."

Hugh did not quite like the thought of running out on Brother John; he had been so friendly. "Let's leave it that I will be here on the Galilee Porch tomorrow at two," he said. "If I am not here you will know I just couldn't get away."

"Agreed," said Dickon. "Two by the sundial. I'll be there—my brother!"

iv. hidden hallows

THE NEXT DAY, having got leave easily enough from Brother John, Hugh stood on the Galilee Porch at two o'clock. Jacques de Raoul was nowhere to be seen. Hugh had hoped to speak to him again; he had gone back early that morning when the brothers left the building after the service of Prime to look for him, but had found the place empty. Evidently he had thought it wise to set forth at once instead of waiting the allotted days of sanctuary. Times were troublous and even the protecting black cloak with the yellow cross of the fugitive might not insure his safety on the high road. Better get himself clear out of the country as soon as he could.

Hugh was sad at his going, wise though he knew it to be. His meeting with Jacques was the last link,

he told himself, that connected him with his family and his old life. Now only the unknown and the new existence lay ahead of him.

Dickon was late and, after waiting an hour, Hugh became restless. Perhaps the boy already regretted his promised friendship, but no, he was not that sort; and before long he spied him coming across the abbey lawn on a run. He grinned his greeting as he came up, rather breathlessly.

"I went along with *him*," he said, pointing to the porch where Jacques had been. "Thought maybe he would be off early so that he could make a port before folk could be yapping at his heels again. I got here before dawn and he was just setting out. I went with him five miles or so, for I had a notion it might be well for him to have somebody from Glaston right beside him. Everybody seems to get into such a dither at the mere mention of the murder of Thomas à Becket."

Hugh winced and his cheeks flushed. For a few

moments he walked along beside Dickon with troubled eyes fastened on the ground.

Dickon glanced at him uneasily, wishing he had not referred to the tragedy of the Archbishop. "Of course I know *he* didn't really have anything to do with it—Jacques, I mean—any more than you did—"

"I know how it is," said Hugh. "It sort of spreads a blackness over everybody, a terrible deed like that, even over folk whose hands are clean of all guilt in it. I feel it all the time over me, as if everybody must hate me and all my family."

"But it isn't a matter of hate at all," said Dickon, standing still in his earnestness. "Not in Glaston, it isn't! And you belong to Glaston now."

Hugh smiled a little. "I guess you're right about Glaston; maybe I'll feel about it the way you do, sometime. Now it seems as if I hadn't quite the right to belong."

"Well, come along now, let's walk faster," continued Dickon, still uncomfortable for the turn the conversation had taken. "We've quite a way to go to my secret cavern. Oh, I forgot!" He slowed his quickened pace immediately, glancing at Hugh's limping foot.

"That's all right!" Hugh flushed uncomfortably again, then threw back his shoulders and grinned, making Dickon feel less embarrassed. "I can get along as well as most."

"I should say you could!" said the other heartily. "Jacques said he never would have got to Glaston whole if you hadn't climbed into that cart quicker than a rabbit and used your wits even quicker than your feet!"

Hugh's depression of spirits warmed at the praise. "That was good of Jacques," said he, adding modestly, "I did naught. And Dickon, it was good of you to go with him."

"Oh, I was glad to, but it made me late meeting you, because when I got back, I had all my morning tasks to do, and Brother Guthlac was standing with the sleeve of his gown rolled up and a stout switch in his hand!" Dickon made a rueful face.

"So you got a drubbing for your pains?"

"No, he barely touched me! He's too fat to catch me or hold me if he does! And I got everything done before I came here, but it took time; he'll be over being cross with me when I get back this evening."

All this while the two boys had been walking north and away from the monastic buildings. Just before they reached the old north gate, Dickon turned aside into the fields, striking off toward the west where the moorland was wildest. After a little they came to a depression in the ground almost like a deep hole, and near the bottom, partly concealed by a rock, was a cleft just wide enough to wriggle through. Dickon wormed his way in and Hugh followed, scraping his legs and tearing his clothes a bit, for it was a tight squeeze; but once they were inside the boys were able to stand upright without difficulty. They found themselves in a cave dimly lit by the cleft through which they had entered. Beyond them was a dark opening apparently leading further underground.

Dickon struck flint and lighted a tallow candle, both of which articles he unearthed from a hiding place in a corner of the cave. Then he led the way into the dark passage, Hugh following closely. It was high and wide enough for them to walk upright, single file, and gave the impression of a man-made tunnel leading deeper and deeper into the earth at a very slight downward grade. At one place it dropt abruptly into a small open cavern but it climbed out again directly, on the opposite side, and continued, narrowing somewhat and turning, then proceeding with astonishing straightness for what seemed like a long distance. Hugh was filled with astonishment.

"What is this place?" he asked, his voice loud and reverberating in the close, walled space.

"I am not sure," answered Dickon, speaking low to avoid the re-echoing. "It might be part of an old drain abandoned long ago, maybe when the Romans left Britain. I've heard Brother Sacristan tell about the Romans and the roads and water works they built. Or maybe—and this is what I really think—it is a part of a secret passageway between Glaston and the sea, a way of escape for the brothers in the old days when the Danish pirates harried the land."

"Does it lead all the way back to the monastery buildings?" asked Hugh.

"That is the only trouble with my theory," said Dickon; "it stops in just a bit. You'll see."

A sudden turn and they reached an arched doorway which led into a low stone-lined room perhaps sixteen feet square. Along two sides of it were ranged heavy black oak chests, and against the wall directly opposite the entrance stood a large wardrobe or press, also of wood, blackened with age, tall, extending up to the rough stone ceiling. In a corner, not far from this aumbry, the wall had been broken through, leaving an irregular round hole and much rubble and loose stone on the floor beneath it. Through this hole came a damp draught which flickered the candle in Dickon's hand.

The boys looked around for a moment in silence. Then Dickon moved toward one of the chests. The top was covered with dust and he blew on it and flapped his gown, removing the worst of it, and apologized like a housewife for the condition of his premises.

"I've not been here for many a long day and dirt collects, though I can't imagine where from."

But Hugh's eyes were fastened on the jagged hole in the wall. "Dickon," said he, "however did that hole get there and what is beyond it?"

"That puzzles me more than anything else, though there are plenty of queer things about this place."

"What do you think it is, really? What is it all about?"

"This must be a secret storeroom; you can guess that when I show you what's in here." Dickon lifted the lid of the chest which creaked and groaned on rusty hinges. Then he handed his candle to Hugh and devoted both hands to bringing the contents of it carefully out. Hugh forgot for the moment his questions, in astonishment over what was brought to light.

First a narrow box of metal inlaid with enamel and having crystal and amber and dull red and purple stones set in it. The inside was lined with gold and it contained a single white bone.

"A reliquary," explained Dickon, "and that might be the finger bone of some saint."

Hugh crossed himself and looked with added awe upon it. Dickon put the box carefully on the floor and reached into the chest again, bringing forth a curious object, quite large, of blackened metal wrought in the semblance of a castle. It opened in the middle showing a place to burn incense.

"That's a censer, evidently," said Hugh, "and what a beautiful one! Look at all those delicate little turrets hammered out of—is it bronze or iron? It's hard to tell, it's so black—but if it were polished—"

"And here's a book satchel with gold clasps," Dickon continued, taking things out and, after showing them to Hugh, placing them beside the others on the floor. "And look at this bell, dull metal with square corners and a bone clapper." He rang it softly and a full sweet tone came from it. "St. Patrick's bell is like that; they keep it in a special reliquary at the abbey. This might have belonged to somebody about his time. And look at this." He handed out a round, flat object with ivory carving on one side, covered with grime but exquisite in workmanship, and on the other a mirror.

"Well, by my faith!" exclaimed Hugh, "how did that get in here with all these churchly things?"

"It doesn't belong in here," said Dickon, "I found this outside, over by the Tor in the marshes, but it seemed so wonderful I brought it in to be with the other treasures!"

Mirrors had not played any part in Dickon's young life before and he turned and twisted this ancient one, looking at himself and grimacing, placing his round cap at a rakish angle over one eye, and blowing out his cheeks comically, delighted to see the expressions on his own face given back in the uncertain light from the candle. But to Hugh a mirror was no curiosity. "What else is in there?" said he, bending over the chest himself.

"This key," continued Dickon, putting the mirror down and diving into the depths of the chest again. It was fully ten inches long, heavy and dull, but had curious grill work at the end of it. "I found that outside, too; not so precious as the other things, but it may come in useful some time. And here's a bishop's staff with jewels on the handle; and now—this is the greatest treasure of all."

With both hands he lifted something out that was large and heavy, carried it to one of the other chests and set it carefully upon the top of it. "Doesn't seem as if this ought to touch the ground alongside those other things; it is so special and—and holy."

Hugh gasped and stared, for a moment unable to say anything. It was an oblong boxlike article about two feet long and eighteen inches wide with a stone top, in the center of which had been set a huge and magnificent sapphire. The intense blue of it and the lights caught from the shine of the candle seemed to fill the dark underground chamber with a soft radiance. The sides and front were of gold, with other precious and semiprecious stones set in it, but the great sapphire dominated the whole.

"Dickon!" exclaimed Hugh at last. "I never saw anything so beautiful! What *is* it?"

"I think it's a portable altar," said the other, awe and reverence mingling in his voice, "the kind the saints used to carry with them when they went to convert the pagans. Nobody knows what holy man may have consecrated it and taken it about with him."

"Or what adventures it may have had!" Hugh's imagination was on fire with the thought. "It may have been present at a martyrdom, even!"

Dickon nodded and they continued to gaze at it. "It's so beautiful," repeated Hugh. "Don't the brothers know about it—or this place?" he continued in a moment, coming back to his wonder about the whole discovery.

"I'm sure they don't," said Dickon. "I've questioned carefully Brother Sacristan and several of the others. I've an idea this is a secret storage place, as I said and that there once was a passage underground all the way from the monastic buildings to the sea, so the brothers could get away and carry their treasures with them when they were besieged or raided. But it must have been walled up or blocked by a cave-in or something, because there is no way out of here except the way we came in, and nobody bigger than us could get through that cleft in the moor into the cave. And what's more nobody *has* been in here for ages and ages. You should have seen the blankets of untouched dust that lay over everything when I first happened on that cleft and followed the passageway in here!"

"And you found all those things except the key and the mirror right in here?"

Dickon nodded. "In these chests—or two of them, rather: the other has old books and parchments in it, torn mostly."

"Books!" Hugh's interest blazed afresh. "Let's look at them!"

They went over to the chest Dickon indicated, threw open the lid, and this time Hugh handed over the candle and bent over the contents himself to investigate. Loose pages mostly, worn, cracked, discolored, but many of them with the script still legible upon them, and down at the bottom were several bound books with heavy gold and silver clasps, their leather bindings old, but the boards beneath the leather still whole.

Hugh looked intently at the writing on some of the loose pages. "That's not at all the way the scribes write now," said he, "and it's not very plain though the letters are so round and big. It's Latin, evidently. Dickon, could I take a few of these pages out? It's hard to see clearly in here, and they might be interesting."

"Of course!" answered Dickon readily. "This place is yours as well as mine, or will be as soon as we've sworn brotherhood. Let's do that now and make a real ceremony of it, shall we?"

Hugh put down the parchment sheets and watched

as Dickon found an irregular place in the wall where he could set the candle so it would hold. Then he put the reliquary with the white bone in it on top of the chest whereon the sapphire altar rested, and said:

"It is really binding, this vow we're going to take, and that altar and the reliquary with the bone in it make it *sacred*. You stand beside me now and say everything I say. Are you ready?" Hugh nodded.

Dickon then dug under his tunic for the knife he apparently always wore tied around his waist, and took it from its clumsy leather sheath. Hesitating just a moment, he scratched the point sharply across the underside of his arm and drew a little blood, then he handed the knife to Hugh and bade him do likewise. He took a drop from the arm of each on the tip of his knife and then laid it on the chest before the jeweled altar.

"I do solemnly swear," Dickon began, "before this sacred and hidden treasure and before this bone in the reliquary, the bone of an unknown somebody, most probably a saint, that he whose blood is mingled with mine, will be my brother forever and ever."

Prickles of excitement were running up and down Hugh's spine. The mysteriousness of the place, the intense quiet except for the sound of their own voices and movements, the sense of being hidden completely from the knowledge of all men, alone, the two of them, in a forgotten underground chamber, got hold of his imagination and thrilled him. And more, still, the beauty of that shining blue sapphire, the rich gold, the soft mellow color of the marble into which it was set, and the sense of what that jeweled rectangular object was, filled him with awe and a sort of exaltation which was more than excitement and made of the ceremony something very deep and vital. He repeated Dickon's words without faltering over one of them; they seemed to be burned into his memory so that he would never forget them.

"I will keep nothing hid from my brother," Dickon continued in the same solemn voice; "all that I have shall be his also and for him I will die, if need be, willingly. Go on, Hugh."

And Hugh repeated these words also, slowly, meaningfully.

They stood a moment in silence and then the spell seemed to break. Dickon gathered up the treasures he had left on the floor, and replaced them in the chest. When he picked up the bell he rang it once or twice, savoring the beauty of the tone and listening to the echoes dying away in the mysterious underground darkness. The reliquary was also put away and Hugh lifted the jeweled altar with breathless care and they placed that too in the chest and closed the lid.

"The candle is burning low," said Dickon. "We'd better go out now. I wouldn't like to get caught here in the dark."

"What is in that cupboard?" said Hugh. "You haven't said anything about that. It looks as if it might be for vestments like the one in the abbey." He approached the tall black piece of furniture opposite the arched doorway.

"Oh, that," said Dickon, "that's locked. I've tried

to pick the panel open but couldn't without hurting the wood. Sounds empty; listen." He rapped his knuckles sharply against the paneling. A hollow reverberation came back to them.

"It could still sound hollow if it was not completely filled." Hugh ran his fingers around the edges of what surely were intended to be doors.

"Well, it's stuck or fastened in some way. Come on, it must be getting late."

Hugh could not bear to tear himself away. "Can we get some more candles from some place, and come again as soon as I can have another day off? I want to see what's beyond that hole and look at everything again. Dickon, I think this is a wonderful place!"

The other nodded appreciatively, then looked at the stump of his candle with a calculating eye, and moved toward the passageway. Picking up the loose parchment sheets he had left on the top of the chest, Hugh followed him quickly, realizing that they would indeed have to hurry if they were to get through the long passage to the cleft in the moor before their light gave out entirely.

And indeed, they had not gone very far before the candlewick began to sputter and in another moment Dickon dropt it with an exclamation as he put his burnt fingers to his mouth.

"Couldn't hold it any longer," said he, speaking out of the appalling blackness which had immediately enveloped them. "By all the saints, but it's dark! Feel along the wall and follow me close."

It seemed to Hugh as if he had gone suddenly

blind; he could not see his own hand when he raised it to touch his face. But with the inability to see, his sense of hearing became more acute. The boys moved slowly and in silence, feeling their way along the rough cold stones of the passage wall and pausing every now and then to listen, though why they did this they could not have told. Faint and far off they heard a trickle of water, then some pebbles or loosened earth fell with a soft swish, like grating sand. The sound of their own breathing and their shuffling steps as they felt their way, stumbling over the unevenness of the flooring, seemed unnaturally loud. Hugh suddenly crouched down with a little cry of fear. Something had flown by him; he felt the motion of wings, though of course he could see nothing.

"Only a bat," said Dickon reassuringly. "Hear him scolding us?"

The high piping gibberish reassured Hugh that it was indeed a bat, but that sound, too, was eerie and strange as it grew fainter and died in the distance.

"The way seems longer than when we came in," whispered Hugh.

"It would," agreed Dickon stoutly. "Light makes a great difference. But we can't go wrong; there's no other passage. What's *that?*" It was his turn to pause, breathless.

"I didn't hear anything," breathed Hugh.

They both listened intently. Utter, complete, intense silence and then it came again. Hugh heard it this time, though very faint and distant—the ringing of a metal bell.

"Come on! We've got to get out!" gasped Dickon, plunging ahead in the darkness, only to stop again in a moment with a groan, having cracked his head against a projecting boulder in the roofing.

Neither said a word but, breathing hard, made the best speed they could along the passageway till they spied at length a narrow shaft of light and knew that they were close to the cleft that would let them out above ground and into the safe upper world of daylight. When they had finally squeezed through the opening, they lay on the soft moor grass, still shaken and trembling.

"What *was* it? What could it have been?" said Hugh.

"A bell ringing. It couldn't have been anything else; but *what* bell and who was ringing it? I tell you there's *no way* into that hidden chamber but this—and nobody passed us going in. They *couldn't* have! Nobody larger than us could get through that cleft in the moor and nothing but a mouse or a bat could get by us in the passage without our knowing!"

The two looked at each other speechlessly.

"Could it be something—somebody—not human?" suggested Hugh questioningly after a pause.

Dickon nodded and then crossed himself. "That's what I was thinking."

"But a ghost or spirit would not make a real sound or ring a real bell, would it?" Hugh continued.

"*Anything* could happen in Glaston," declared Dickon.

"But it would be a *good* happening—a sort of *holy* happening in a place where so many saints have been, wouldn't it? So we needn't have got so scared." Hugh spoke more confidently.

They were quiet for a moment, thinking things over.

"You—you won't be afraid to go back another time as we planned? I guess—I'm not—too scared, either." In the light of day on the solid, familiar earth, Dickon's courage was returning. Hugh's also. He nodded his assurance.

"I'll tell you what it might have been!" said he. "Your bell, the treasure one you said was like St. Patrick's, it might have tipped over in the chest. Sounds would seem loud and carry far in that dark, narrow passage."

Dickon looked doubtful. "Maybe," said he, "but it wasn't the same tone. Well, we've just got to find out!"

"And we'll dig out that hole in the corner and explore further!" Hugh added.

The boys stood up and turned toward the abbey. They said little, each being busy with his own thoughts.

Hugh found himself still holding the sheets of parchment he had taken from the chest in the treasure chamber. He was glad he had not dropt them in his excitement, and rolling them into as small a bundle as he could, he concealed them in his sleeve, wondering where he could hide them from the keen eyes of Brother John, yet have them handy for closer inspection and study.

Before reaching the cloisters they passed the Old

Church as it was called; the queer rectangular building of wood and lead that enclosed the flooring of
the oldest place of worship in the Island of Britain—the Chapel of St. Joseph. Neither Hugh nor
Dickon knew as yet the history of it, but it was an
object of daily, almost hourly, view, for it stood just
to the west of the Church of St. Mary where all the
services and offices of the monastic community took
place.

With a sudden impulse Hugh moved toward the
door of the Old Church, Dickon following him. Just
inside he found a conveniently loose board in the
wall to the left of the entrance. A wooden casing
had evidently at some time long past been built over
the original structure of the church and Hugh, feeling inside the broken boarding, could reach down to
the floor, a deep, ample, and wonderful storage room
in which to hide the parchments.

"There!" said he with satisfaction. "That is a perfect place! I can keep all the pages I want to in
there, and slip away at odd times and study them
without anybody's knowing. I guess nobody comes
in here much, do they?"

Dickon shook his head. "No, they have all their
services and church doings in St. Mary's now. I've
never seen even Brother Sacristan going in here."

"I somehow think those books and loose pages in
the underground chest will make interesting reading." Hugh spoke with animation.

"Maybe," said Dickon dubiously.

"We might even find something that would tell

us about the treasure chamber—what it was built for and when it was used—"

"That's so!" Dickon showed more interest. "But what I want to know *now*, more than anything on earth, is who rang that bell—or what—and everything." He ended lamely enough.

v. missing pages

IN SPITE OF their eagerness, several days passed
before Hugh and Dickon were able to pursue their
underground adventures further. Brother Symon, the
almoner, found work grown suddenly heavier because
of a fresh inroad of destitute and ailing men from
the village, and Dickon was transferred from the
grange to the almonry to help him. That meant
long busy hours for the boy and much tramping
through the roads and near-by villages, while accom-
panying the good brother on his missions of charity,
as well as aiding him in his work with the poor who
gathered daily about the gates and within the grounds
of the abbey.

As for Hugh, it seemed to him that Brother John
was minded to keep him at scriptorium work longer
and more steadily than even the traditional choir-

schoolboys in the old days. Ordinarily he would have worked contentedly enough, for the smell of parchment was ever pleasing to his nostrils and he had already grown proficient in mixing colors, grinding gold, and cutting new quills as well as in making the ink for the novices, which seemed always to be in fresh demand. He liked to sit in the shady cloister copying the script and was getting astonishingly good at it. But now, with his mind full of Dickon's hallows and the mysterious room and passage underground, he fidgeted restlessly, whatever his task, and drew down more than one reproof on his head from the usually gentle brother, until finally something happened which pointed to a possible connection between his daily routine work and that day of adventure with Dickon.

The bell for Sext, the noontide church service, usually caught both Hugh and Brother John in the midst of work in the kitchen, often at a stage most difficult to leave. While the ink was still gummy or the minium, the scarlet dye, was too pale, or a piece of parchment just ready to come out of its soaking and be stretched, the bell would summon them clamorously and Brother John would dry his hands, swing a kettle on a crane back from the hotter part of the fire, and obediently prepare to leave his work where it was. Sometimes, however, on very busy days, he would abruptly bid Hugh stay on until he should return, or until the task in hand should be finished.

One morning he sent the boy early to the kitchen, not even waiting for the customary hour or more of study and copying in the novices' cloister, and he himself followed soon after, coming in with his arms full of dusty, old, board-covered manuscripts and loose sheets. Hugh sighed when he saw him, well knowing what that meant; soaking in milk, scraping carefully with pumice stone, erasing, as best he could, records and accounts which had no present-day value. Parchment and vellum were growing more costly every day, so Brother John said, and it would be a wicked waste to use new sheets for kitchen accounts, or for the novices to blot and scratch when they first graduated from wax tablets to writing real script.

As far as possible skins from their own Glastonbury sheep, calves, and goats were used for scriptorium work and the final preparation of these fell to Brother John and any assistant he could get hold of. That was tiresome enough, Hugh thought, for each skin must be washed thoroughly, unhaired, scraped, and washed again, then stretched evenly on a frame to dry. But then you had something worth showing for your pains. Hugh soon came to feel toward a new sheet of soft, fine texture some of the satisfaction that showed in Brother John's face when he inspected a finished skin minutely, putting his eyes close up to the frame, noting the color and grain of it, and nodding his head in silent approval. But making an old parchment fit to use again was a dull and thankless task, Hugh thought, no matter how one might look upon it. And now Brother John was depositing on a table a load of old stuff that would mean endless labor for both of them.

"I have been in the vault under the big church," said he, "and I found a press that had been quite forgotten. There seemed to be nothing in it of any value, only accounts and paltry records and some very ill-written scripts. But the parchment is still firm and good."

Drawing up a stool, he sat down and began rummaging among the heap of old pages and broken bindings, picking out sheets here and there that were less cracked and torn than others.

Hugh had pricked up his ears at the mention of a vault beneath the great church and listened eagerly for more, but Brother John's mind was on parchment.

"Now these pages are excellent," he said, "strong and heavy. They will stand much erasure and will come out as good as new. Get the tubs ready, boy; some of these can doubtless be washed clean with clear water, or milk of course, if the ink proves refractory."

He handed Hugh a bundle of loose sheets and

then bent his nearsighted gaze on a book in large, square, board binding.

"And this," he continued, "hath the look of very old parchment, but the script is scarce more than a century. An account of monies, of no value to us, not even dated. But if I mistake not, the ink is durable. Milk and meal; soak all the sheets and then rub gently when the skin has been well softened."

He cut the tough leather strips that ran in little grooves at the back of the binding, and pulled the boards apart. Dust flew as he slapped the loosened pages and piled them on the table with the others.

Hugh bent obediently over the first sheets and Brother John worked along with him.

"Did you say, Brother John, that these old manuscripts came from a vault underground?" he asked after a few moments.

"Aye," replied the monk, "from a crypt under the nave of St. Mary's."

Hugh tried not to sound particularly interested as he put the next question. "Are there many such storage places?"

"None that we know of save this one, though tradition has it that there was once a vault hidden somewhere between the abbey and the sea, where the brothers used to store their treasure in time of pirate raids. It must have been destroyed, or else it caved in, for no one has known of it for more than a century. Perhaps it never existed. At least it is gone now, out of the memory of all living." The monk breathed a little sigh and paused for a moment in his work as if thinking deeply.

"Did they—did the brothers in old times recover the treasure that they hid—or might it—some of it be still buried somewhere?"

Brother John turned and looked at Hugh keenly, a queer expression on his face. "Have any idle wits among the lay brothers been telling you aught?" said he. "What do you know of Glastonbury treasure, hidden or open?"

"Naught whatever!" Hugh assured him hastily. "I was but wondering; a vault caved in and forgotten somewhere on the moors—the thought makes the mind jump—and Glaston is so old—" he left his sentence unfinished. Brother John was still looking at him in that odd way as if he were half-minded to say something very important.

"Aye," said he again shortly. "Glaston is so old, it might indeed have the greatest treasure in the world hidden within it. True, my boy, but mark my words; if there be great and hidden treasure in Glaston, it is spiritual treasure, not such a thing as a man might hold in his two hands. To seek *that*—the material sort—would make a body restless, unquiet, yearning day and night for—" he broke off and plunged his hands vigorously into the tub of meal and warm milk where some of the sheets were already soaking.

"Go to! boy, thou art as idle as if there were naught to be done this day save to wag thy tongue! Fetch the pumice stone and bestir thyself! Scrape me this sheet clean and neat and, mind, not a hole scraped through or thou shalt rue it!"

Hugh said nothing further, but his mind was galloping. He must take care or Brother John would guess at Dickon's find. And what did he mean by that queer talk about treasure? He could scarcely bear to wait to go on with his explorations with Dickon! But he would not be free till this work was finished; that was certain. He fell to with a better will and more energy.

"This parchment has some scroll work on the margin," said he in a matter-of-fact voice, as if he had already forgotten the subject they had been discussing. "Seems as if it were a pity to destroy it." He held up the sheet he was working on for Brother John to see.

The monk glanced at it, then looked more carefully. Interlaced ribbons of design ran down the margin and adorned the top. The script was large and rounded rather than angular.

"Place it to one side," Brother John ordered. "I had not noticed the border. Perhaps our rubricator would find interest in the design, for it is ancient and unusual."

Hugh rummaged among the other sheets. "And here be pages with black and white drawings." He laughed suddenly. "Here is Our Lord God with His crown awry and His eyes too big for His head! By my faith, a child could have drawn better!"

"Saxon without doubt," said Brother John, without looking up. "They were clumsy artists, those Saxons of old, and knew naught whatever about beauty in a manuscript. Scrape it clean."

Hugh picked up his pumice stone, then hesitated. "Might I not keep that one, Brother John? I have never seen God look so funny!"

"Tut, tut, lad, be not blasphemous," reproved the monk. "Keep it if thou wilt, but pay for it with a little more nimbleness and speed in thy fingers!"

The boy returned to his soaking and scraping and before long the bell for Sext clanged demandingly. He began at once to dry his hands and put away his pumice stone, but Brother John motioned him impatiently.

"Nay, nay, Hugh, work on! The morning hath vanished like a will o' the wisp and naught to show for it! I would that Father Abbot would allow me to stay also, but he will not. Scrape me these—and these—and whatever more thou hast time for, and I will return directly after the office and see what has been accomplished."

With that he departed hurriedly and Hugh fell to examining the parchment sheets again. He had in mind the pages he had brought out from the secret vault and wondered if any of these might be of the same time and type. The one with the crude drawing of God on it had an odd and ancient looking script that might be similar. He would take it away with him and compare it. There were several more pages with sketches on them, but the script was not the same; looked more modern. One such sheet stuck stubbornly to its neighbor. He pried the two gently apart. The one that had been covered was distinctly like those he had hidden behind the loose panel of the Old Church. As Hugh studied it more carefully he realized it was written in the very same large rounded letters and stilted Latin. He slipt it under the sheet Brother John had told him he might have, resolving to compare them all more carefully later. Then he dipt the one that had been on top in the warm milk. The ink on it showed no signs of dissolving, did not even turn brown, so he left it to soak awhile and, taking his pumice stone, began gently rubbing the script of another that had come out of the same batch. After a few moments he paused, looked at the sheet more closely, then took it to the light. Under the script that he was so carefully removing was the faint impression of another, earlier writing. He wondered what it might be. It was very difficult, nay, impossible, to remove the top layer of lettering without injuring that which lay beneath it, but the little he could see bore again a distinct resemblance to the sheet that had been stuck to its fellow, and so also to the pages he had taken from the vault underground.

With infinite care he continued, softening with milk, scraping ever so gently. It was clear to him what had happened. The original script, written on heavy, durable parchment, had been very imperfectly removed before the sheet had been overwritten by some later hand, a fate that the page stuck to its neighbor had escaped, and also the one with the odd drawing on it. Evidently they had once been pages of a very ancient book of which Hugh's hidden sheets might just possibly have been also a part. He studied the script beneath the script more intently. There was one word he could make out quite clearly. "Glaston," and another, a name partly obliterated, "Joseph Arimath—"

At that moment the kitchen door opened and Brother John entered. Hugh started guiltily, realizing that he had accomplished next to nothing during the period of Sext.

"What art doing, Hugh?" Brother John's voice sounded stern. His arms were again filled with old manuscripts. "And what hast thou done during this hour?"

"I—Brother John, I have found something interesting. There is older writing under this, and one sheet was stuck to another and overlooked, and hath on it the same queer script."

He paused. Brother John, still frowning disapproval, advanced to the table on which Hugh had placed the sheets.

"I bade thee clean and scrape, not decipher, and —what is this?" He dropt his whole armful of manuscripts with a clatter on the floor, seized the parchment sheet that Hugh had been working over and stared at it with his mouth open. Then he rushed to the window where the light was better.

"Quick, boy, get me all the sheets that were with these! Hast scraped any others? Are any of them soaking? Fetch them out! Fetch them out!"

Hugh was too astonished to do anything but gape for a moment. Brother John, without waiting for answers to any of his questions, ran to a cupboard and got out a vial marked Tincture of Gall. Then he and Hugh rescued a few odd sheets that were being soaked. The monk dried them gently with a soft cloth and then applied the gall. It discolored the

sheets but brought out the original writing so that little by little the hidden, half-obliterated words could be read.

The lay brothers, cooks, and servers for the day came into the kitchen and began preparations for the noon meal. Brother John paid no heed to them at all, merely brushing them out of his way when they impeded him. Squatting on the floor, he examined every sheet of old parchment that he had brought in that day, scrutinizing some with breathless care, throwing some aside and placing others in Hugh's bewildered arms, saying merely:

"Hold on to them, boy, let not one of them fall to the ground or escape thee!"

The dinner hour came; Hugh fidgeted, looking hungrily at the caldrons of food cooking over the fireplaces. His mouth watered at the savory smell, but Brother John continued to fill his hands with manuscripts, ordering him again and again not to move or put one of them down until he was bidden.

The cooks clattered about, steam and smoke filled the air, but still Brother John paid no heed. The midday meal, the only large and substantial one of the day, was dished onto huge trenchers, the servers came and went busily to and from the refectory, and Hugh realized dismally that dinner was in progress, but Brother John showed not the slightest sign of relinquishing his task.

At long last every sheet of parchment, loose or in boards, which he had brought into the kitchen, had been examined and tossed aside or else given into Hugh's keeping, and the monk, puffing and groaning with the stiffness of his joints because of his long squatting upon the floor, arose and looked at the boy as if until then he had been ignorant of his presence.

"Good! Thou are still here!" said he.

"Why, Brother John, you bade me not move or let one of these fall," he answered, feeling justly aggrieved, "and it must be two hours, and dinner—"

"Two *hours?*" said Brother John, looking around

him with blinking eyes that were now smarting with long, close scrutiny and kitchen smoke. Then he laughed.

"I had forgot thine existence or took those arms of thine for a bench or press, most likely, and as for food, I knew not there was such in the world! No matter; we have work to do, boy, and when thou dost realize what thou hast found, food will not be of concern to thee either."

Hugh sighed a little and his glance turned involuntarily toward one of the great fireplaces, with dinner for the workers still simmering over it. The monk laughed again; he was mightily satisfied over something, and in evident good humor. Taking the pile of manuscripts he had placed in Hugh's arms away from him, he settled himself in the farthest corner of the kitchen, with knife, pumice stone, and tincture of gall. Then he motioned the boy away from him.

"Go help thyself! Fill up that young stomach to the full and then come and help me with a less woebegone countenance!"

Hugh did not wait for a second order. He fetched a slab of thick bread, by way of a plate, took the huge ladles hanging near the hearth, and helped himself liberally to everything he had a fancy for.

"I like this better than eating with the others in the refectory," said he.

"Aye," said Brother John, "I doubt it not! Here there be no reminders that one must serve one's body sparingly and remember the poor."

"And one does not need to listen to the Lector,"

added Hugh. "I like well to eat when I eat and listen when I listen, although in sooth, the brother who reads during meal times chooses such dull matter that most times I pay no heed to it at all."

"Aha," said Brother John. "Say you so? But what saith our good Father Abbot anent table manners:

" 'Eyes on your plate, hands on the table, ears to the reader, heart to God'; hast heard him?"

Hugh nodded, his mouth being too full of hot beans for a reply.

Brother John, moved perhaps by the good smell of the food, came to the table where Hugh sat and served himself somewhat to eat also. They sat there cosily enough and made a meal of it, while the servers and kitchen folk came and went paying no heed to them.

"Will you tell me, Brother John," Hugh at last asked hesitantly, well knowing the monk's ability to stop in the midst of a torrent of conversation and suddenly turn schoolmaster, "why this script beneath the script is so important?"

"I will not only tell thee but show thee," said the brother after a moment's pause, " 'tis but right."

He pushed aside his cup and the remainder of his bread, and left the table. Hugh, who had by now eaten his fill, followed eagerly. They took the parchment sheets which had already been scraped and treated sufficiently to show their original content and, leaving the others in a secure corner where they would be safe until their return, left the kitchen and entered the cloister walks. Brother John led the way straight to the Painted Aumbry.

"I am sure," said he, "and yet—there must be no shadow of doubt. These old eyes are dimming a trifle and I *might* be mistaken. But if I am not—! What a find! What a find!"

They reached the aumbry, the brother opened a panel at the side, took out some volumes far back, moved a false bottom, and then Hugh, peering curiously over his shoulders, saw a book lying by itself in the secret aperture thus disclosed. Brother John handed his parchments to Hugh that he might take two hands to lift with infinite care this hidden volume. It was brown with age, the rich leather over its board binding was worn through in spots and frayed at the edges. With reverent and gentle fingers Brother John opened the cover. Hugh could see that the pages were of thick parchment, deep cream colored, stained with soil, but adorned with exquisite lettering, heavy with gold and the bright scarlet minium dye. The script was the same character, rounded, large, as on the pages the boy held in his hand and, he was secretly sure, the same as on those others hidden in St. Joseph's Chapel. A few moments' careful inspection were enough to convince the two of them.

"This," said Brother John impressively, raising his head from the close scrutiny of comparison and indicating the ancient volume in his hands, "this book is the oldest in our abbey, doubtless one of the oldest in the whole world. It is the greatest treasure that we own, at least that we *know* we own. There may be others lost, hidden, forgotten—but of that no matter now. Whence it came none knows, nor aught of him who wrote it save that his name was

Blaise. Look you, the title page, scarce to be deciphered." He held the book open that Hugh might see more clearly:

The Book of the Seynt Graal.
Being the Record of Blaise, the Hermit

"And now, mark you," continued the monk, turning the volume carefully over and opening it from the back. Pages had been torn out, carelessly, ruthlessly, leaving a ragged edge here, half a sheet there, and none could tell how many missing entirely.

Hugh looked his question and Brother John continued:

"It is very ancient, as thou canst see, and the Latin is hard to decipher, yet it is not age so much as the matter it contains that makes this book a treasure beyond price." He paused. "I scarce know how to begin. Dost thou know, Hugh, that Glaston has been a sacred and a holy spot ever since Our Lord died upon the Cross, or since a few years thereafter?"

Hugh shook his head. The solemn manner in which Brother John spoke filled him with a sense of awe and expectancy.

"After Our Lord died, a rich Jew named Joseph of Arimathaea, took His body down from the Cross and laid it in his own tomb which was nigh unto Calvary. That thou knowest from the Gospel readings, and of the emptiness of Joseph's tomb on Easter morning when Christ had risen gloriously from the dead. But of Joseph the Scripture tells little more. 'Tis only in this book, this *Record of Blaise*, that we learn how he held in his possession the Cup out of which our blessed Lord drank at the Last Supper and in which, so the story goes, the centurion who stood at the foot of the Cross, caught drops of water and blood that fell from the pierced side of the Son of God at the end of the Crucifixion. That Cup is the most Sacred Hallow in the whole world. And I say *is,* not was, mind you, for I believe, nay I know deep in my heart, that it is still somewhere upon this earth, though men's eyes have not beheld it since the days of King Arthur. At that time it was known as the Holy Grail, and they who saw it bare witness that it was full of living light. Only those whose eyes were pure and whose lives were sinless might behold it openly, but even to those who caught the vision of it dimly, came wisdom, healing, food for the body and the soul, salvation for the spirit. But I am getting ahead of my story.

"Now after Christ's death and Resurrection, His friends and followers were persecuted by His enemies, and Joseph was imprisoned in a desolate tower, walled in and left to die. Some say that an angel appeared to him in his round-tower jail and gave him the sacred Cup, others that he had cherished it, hidden beneath his garments, and taken it with him. However that may be, the Holy Grail sustained him for forty long years, and he suffered no lack of anything that is needful to the body or the mind or the spirit. Then he was released and, still guarding that Sacred Hallow, he came, after much adventuring, at long last, here to our Glaston."

"Here!" broke in Hugh in amazement.

"Aye, to this very spot." Brother John closed the torn and ancient book as if the tale were finished, laid it carefully back in its hidden nook, slid the secret panel and replaced the other books over it.

"Know you not the low hill over beyond Tor?" he said. "We call it Weary-All Hill because it was there that Joseph and his eleven weary companions rested from their journeyings. And the thorn tree—surely thou hast seen the old thorn tree there on the side of the hill? That tree grew out of Joseph of Arimathaea's staff when he thrust it into the ground in token that he would remain here. Every year at Christmas time that thorn tree blossoms anew, when all other flowers are dead in the winter cold, a never failing miracle. And we, because our eyes are grown dim and our hearts careless, pass it by unheeding."

"And the Cup?" breathed Hugh eagerly, "what has become of the Holy Cup?"

"Ah, that is what I would be telling thee, boy," continued the brother. "But, mind you, prate not about these ancient sacred things, for it is all a great and solemn mystery, too sacred to be lightly discussed among the brothers and much less among unthinking novices. Thou art a good lad, and quiet, and hast kept thine own secrets well, and 'tis due to thy discovery—but come, I am overstepping myself. About the Holy Chalice, St. Joseph built a chapel for it, a small round chapel made of willow withies, and he put a simple altar within and placed the Cup upon it. And round about that chapel he built twelve huts where he and his fellows might dwell continually in the presence of that Hallowed Thing, worshiping

God and converting the heathen who were then living hereabouts. And knowest thou, Hugh, where that chapel stood, the first consecrated spot in all our England?"

Hugh shook his head.

"Where the Old Church now stands, hard by St. Mary's. Thou canst see the marks of the antique foundations on the floor within. It is still called St. Joseph's Chapel."

"And then?" urged Hugh, more eager about the Cup than the chapel.

"And then, though just how soon I know not, came evil days and much sin. Joseph lived to be an old, old man and, before he died, he hid the Sacred Hallow."

"Hid the Cup?" repeated Hugh. "But where?"

"No man living knows of a surety," declared Brother John. "Did I not tell thee it is all part of a great mystery? For long years there is no record of the Grail. Some said it had been reft away into heaven by the angel who had given it into the hands of Joseph, some said it had been taken to some sacred spot in the East, but our book, this book in our Painted Aumbry declares that it was hidden here, here in our Glaston, perchance in some chapel or vault under the earth, long lost and forgotten—Hugh, lad, what ails thee?" Brother John broke off in the midst of a sentence and stared at the boy who had suddenly paled and stood with wide eager eyes fastened so intently upon him that he was puzzled and amazed.

"Go on, Brother John, please, tell me the rest of it," urged Hugh, ignoring his question.

"What I have told thee, all of it, rests in yon book, and the end of the story must be there also, or was in it, before it was mutilated and nigh destroyed. The book goes on to tell how the Holy Grail appeared again before the eyes of men, many many years after St. Joseph built the little chapel of withies for it. In the days of King Arthur, when brave knights, pure and noble, more than in any other place or time, went about this realm of England and sought adventure and served God and the king in singleness of heart—then it was that the Holy Grail was seen again. Men gave up all they had, and sought it far and wide, knowing that if their eyes might once rest upon it they would have joy and peace such as is not found otherwise in all this world. But how they went upon the quest of the Seynt Graal, and who they were that found it and how and where, is lost with the lost pages of yon book."

"And what became of the Holy Grail at the end of the adventuring? Do you suppose the book told that, when it was whole and entire?" Hugh broke in eagerly.

"Doubtless," replied Brother John. "But we shall never know unless we recover the lost ending of it."

"And might it—the Grail itself—have been returned to its hiding place, here in our Glaston, to the very place where Joseph had once hidden it?"

Brother John nodded. "And now you know why the finding of those pages is a matter of such grave importance, lad. We must seek again, find every single sheet that may have been written over, scrape, recover, decipher, till every available word about our sacred treasure be brought to light, and the story told to the end."

Brother John looked again at the pages he had brought in from the kitchen to compare with the book.

"But however did the book get so torn? And whoever could have tried to erase pages from it and write over them?" demanded Hugh, still puzzling over the whole matter.

Brother John sighed. "Lad," said he, "there is much carelessness as well as sin in the world, now, as in the past. And there have been evil times even in our Glaston, times of ignorance and sloth when the monks lost sight of God and cared nothing either for the things of the mind or the things of the spirit. In some such period of decay, doubtless, our priceless book was mutilated. Indeed it is only by the action of chance, or more likely of divine Providence, that we are still in possession of a part of it." He was silent a moment, lost in thought, then he continued, "The broken book and the lost Cup; it may be that the time has now come, at long last, when God in His infinite wisdom and mercy is minded to restore to us both the Sacred Vessel and the one book wherein the tale of it is told. And then—and then, Hugh, dost thou realize what it would mean to our Glaston? It would become a place of holy pilgrimage for all the world. The sick and the sorrowful would be healed, here in our little sacred island, and those whose hearts were pure would be fed with the bread and wine of life and go forth to the ends of the earth and teach all men to love God truly."

Hugh listened, scarcely breathing lest he break the spell that again seemed to have fallen on the monk who stood with head uplifted and a light on his face that made the boy feel as if he were in the presence of something holy. In a moment or two it was gone and Brother John became his practical, busy self again.

"Give me those sheets, boy," said he, "we will stow them in a cubby hole here in the top of the aumbry. Then we will scrape and recover the others, all of them, and when I have deciphered them we will put them together and see."

Hugh reluctantly handed over the parchment sheets they had brought and saw them tucked away in the Painted Aumbry. It would be difficult for him to compare them with his find, unless perhaps that sheet with the crude picture of God on it, which Brother John had said he might have, should give him some clue.

"Shall we go back into the kitchen and work some more?" he asked.

Brother John looked at him keenly. "Thou art still pale, boy; nay, 'tis enough for now. Go you out into the sunlight and I will work alone for awhile. Young eyes must not be taxed over much."

Hugh was eager enough to be gone, to hunt out Dickon and tell him something of this find and, most of all, to get his pages again from their hiding place in the wall of the Old Church, and see if they also might be some of the missing ones. And if so—what about the chest in the underground vault full of ancient parchments?

He continued silently beside Brother John as he struck off across the garth in the direction of the kitchen. That sheet with the drawing of God on it might hold the key, might serve as comparison for further search among the loose sheets. Brother John had not realized the possible importance of that sheet when he had given it to him, had brushed it aside without noticing. Hugh must recover it before the monk pounced on it.

When they reached the kitchen, Brother John went directly to his stool in the corner and, in a moment, his eyes were scarce an inch from a half-scraped piece of parchment.

"I will gladly work over more sheets for thee now," said Hugh, not too enthusiastically.

"Nay," repeated the monk without looking up, "thou hast done enough for the nonce. Besides, I would be alone. Go outside—and lad, tomorrow morning, while the dew is still wet in the fields, gather me a goodly supply of cornflowers. I need them to make new dye for the Madonna's cloak in the title page of the abbot's missal. Mind they be fresh and unwithered. They boil down to a clearer blue if they be picked with the dew still on them. We must not neglect our other tasks because we have set out on a great adventure."

Hugh had been edging toward the cupboard where he had laid the page he wanted. Now he caught it up eagerly.

"Yes, Brother John, I will gather the cornflowers. The meadows near the grange are blue with them." (What a piece of good luck that he should be given such a task out of doors just when he wanted most particularly to confer with Dickon!) Bidding a dutiful good-by which Brother John was too absorbed to notice or acknowledge, he left the kitchen and turned at once in the direction of the Old Church.

ui. who goes there?

"IT IS THE same script, the same sort of parchment—it has the same *feel* to it; there can't be any doubt," said Hugh positively.

He and Dickon were standing in the ancient graveyard outside the Old Church a few days after the exciting discovery of the over-written pages in the kitchen. They had compared minutely and carefully the parchments they had brought from the underground vault with those Hugh had in his hand, the line-drawing one which Brother John had given him, and a few others which he had secretly slipt out of the growing pile of pages scraped clean of their over-writing and declared by the monk authentic parts of the torn volume in the Painted Aumbry.

"And you say that if the missing pages of that old book are all recovered they might tell where the Holy

Cup is hidden *now?* The very Cup that Our Lord Himself drank from?—faith it is unbelievable!"

Dickon's eyes were round with wonder.

"And the stories, Dickon," continued Hugh, "all the knightly tales of King Arthur's day, and how they searched then for the Holy Grail! The most marvelous stories in the whole world are in those lost pages! Just think, if we could find them again, restore the book to Glaston, whole, so that they could be read now—and forever!"

"That chest down in the vault has dozens of old yellow parchment sheets like these in it. I never thought to look a second time at them," declared Dickon ruefully.

"We wouldn't have known what to look for before, but now—come on, let's go and get a sheaf of them to work over!"

Hugh started ahead but Dickon held back. "Wait a bit," said he; "it would be fine to get that book all patched up and whole again, but it would be a lot more exciting if we could find the Cup itself! Let's get hold of some extra candles and a pick and go through that hole in the wall of my treasure vault. I've always wanted to explore further and now it seems as if we have just *got* to! We might come upon other treasures, whole vaults of them for that matter, and find the lost Cup in the midst of them!"

They stopped at the grange, found themselves a pick, and continued on toward the north gate and then out across the moor to the cleft in the ground which led into the underground passage. With little difficulty they made their way down through this to the mysterious room in which stood the three chests and the tall cupboard. Hugh wanted to begin at once to rummage in the chest which held the old, loose manuscript pages, and Dickon somewhat impatiently agreed to hold the candle while he saw what he could find. Hugh was just opening the lid of the chest when a cry of astonishment and terror broke from Dickon, making him drop it with a bang that reverberated loudly in the close walled space. He wheeled around and looked where Dickon, with an unsteady hand, was pointing. On the top of one of the other chests lay something that had not been there when the boys had left the place a few days before.

They went close, looking with pale, astonished faces from it to each other and back again.

It was a sword, huge, black-hilted, jeweled, and with steel blade as free of rust, as shining and polished as if it had but that moment come from the hands of a careful squire-at-arms.

"How did it get here?" breathed Dickon. "No man could get through that opening in the ground."

"Another boy like us could," suggested Hugh.

Dickon slowly nodded. His brows darkened as he thought of the possibility of someone else being in possession of his secret. "But the villagers would not dare, and besides, they would not know about this, it's so far out on the moorland. And the novices—there isn't a single one small enough to squeeze through."

Hugh put out his hands and touched the thing. "It's a noble sword; see, there are gems in the hilt, bedded in the iron of it. And the weight of it must be great!" He grasped it more firmly, to pick it up from the chest, but he found he must take both hands and then could only lift it with the use of all his strength, and it took Dickon to help him replace it.

"No *boy* would be dragging that through the passageway," said Dickon, still concerned with how it could have gotten to this place which he considered exclusively his. "That's a man's sword, and I tell you, a man must have brought it here, but how, *how?* And who?"

Hugh looked around him and up at the hole in the broken wall.

"Even one of *us* couldn't get through there," declared Dickon, following his eyes and his thought.

"It couldn't have *been* here somewhere, and you overlooked it?"

Dickon snorted in disgust. "Me, overlook a thing like that when I've examined every corner in this place? And even if I had been blind to such a treasure, it certainly wasn't here on this chest before; *you*

know that. It could not have walked in here by itself! How did it *get* here?"

Panic suddenly seized him again. "I don't like it!
Let's get out of here! Remember that bell we heard
last time? I tell you, I don't like it!" He started to
move away but Hugh caught his arm and pulled
him back.

"Don't run off now! Why, we're right in the middle of something big! And you wanted to be a knight
and seek adventure, didn't you?"

The words stung Dickon. His face flushed in the
pale light of the candle, but he was not angry.

"Brother, you are right," said he. "We will see this
thing through. But—aren't you scared, too?"

"Surely I am! I don't like the looks of it either;
but we haven't met anything yet that is dangerous.
Let's see if we can find out what is going on here.
Maybe the sword itself will tell us something."

The two boys fell to examining the ancient weapon
more carefully.

"Here are letters up near the hilt," said Hugh,
bending closer. "Hold the candle so I can read. 'Take
me' it says in Latin." He turned the sword over.
"And here is something on the other side. It isn't
Latin; it's a queer language. I think it is in runes, the
secret language the Britons used long ago. Dickon!"
He seized the boy's arm in his excitement. "Dickon!
I've a notion this is part of the whole mystery; the
broken book with the missing pages, the writing beneath the writing, the story of the lost Cup—and
now a sword sprung, as if by magic, from nowhere."

The candle flickered in the damp draft coming

from the hole in the wall. "Let's find out what's beyond this room," said Dickon uneasily, after an impressive pause. They climbed the rubble and broken stones in the corner and began to pick away loosened rock and cement around the hole, making it gradually larger. They had to work slowly and carefully, fearful lest they dislodge too much earth and the whole wall cave in on them. It would have been close and heavy with candle smoke, beyond endurance, in that low-ceiled room if it had not been for the damp current of air blowing in from beyond the hole where they were working. Hugh wondered where that could come from. Dickon's mind was evidently still figuring on how the great sword could have got onto the chest, for he kept looking back at it in puzzled wonder and uneasiness.

At last they had the opening big enough to crawl through. Hugh went first, then Dickon handed in the candle and followed him. The wall on the other side was rough and offered something in the way of a foothold, which was fortunate as the level of the floor was evidently much lower. As it was, Hugh, unable to trust his full weight on his lame foot, all but fell. Dickon took the candle again, as soon as he had got through the hole himself, and tried to help the other along. His admiration for Hugh was growing by the moment. That boy had courage! He could not run fast to get away if he were caught in a dangerous situation, yet he never let his lameness stop him—or his fear, if he had any.

When they had got down safely to the lower level they held the candle high and looked about curiously.

They were in what appeared to be a long, low, natural cave at the bottom of which ran a little stream. The walls and roof were uneven and seemed to close in closer at the opposite end. They gazed at the wall of the room down which they had climbed; it was rough but sheer and unbroken except for the hole which looked as if somebody had once tried to break through and then had abandoned it. The surface of the wall was covered with unevenly cut slabs of limestone from much of which the cement had worn away. The two ends of the wall were built flush with the earth on either side, and the underground stream which had evidently formed the cave, cutting through a softer stratum of rock, dropt out of sight in a narrow crevasse not far from where the two boys were standing.

"It's an old stream bed," said Dickon, after a long look around. "Up in the Mendip Hills to the north of Glaston, there are lots of these caves made by underground rivers."

"Whoever built that storage room must have made use of this cave," said Hugh, feeling along the rough wall, "or *did* they? I can't think the thing through. To bring those big oak chests and especially that tall aumbry in there must have meant a good sized entrance to that room. But where *is* such an entrance? One could not possibly have dragged those in through the passage from the moor that we came in by, nor through this cave. How did they get in?"

"Maybe those things were brought in through some entrance that was walled up afterward," suggested Dickon.

"But that doesn't make sense," objected Hugh. "If

that storeroom was used to hide treasures in, when there was danger of attack by enemies, the folk that hid them would want to get the things out again sometime, wouldn't they?"

To this Dickon could find no direct answer. "Well, one thing is certain," he said, "nobody could bring those big chests and things down this stream bed and up into that hole! Look how the cave narrows. Come on, let's explore that other end."

There appeared to be only one inlet to the cave and that was so narrow that the boys must needs climb along single file on hands and knees through the wet of the stream. It was hard going, at a slight incline upward, and it seemed endless, but it was fairly straight and had no branches or side caves to confuse them.

"If it goes on up," panted Hugh, close at Dickon's heels, "it ought to come out above ground sometime —or somewhere."

"Well, here's your somewhere," said Dickon, pushing his candle and then himself with a mighty wiggle through a particularly cramped spot. "But it certainly isn't above ground!"

He stood up straight and shook himself. In a moment Hugh was beside him. They found themselves in another cave, larger than the first. The stream still lay at their feet in a shallow depression of the floor, and it was flowing from a low, broken, circular stone wall which was built out from the side of the cave not far from where they stood. In silent amazement they approached it.

"Why, it's a well!" said Hugh, "an old, old well!

Somebody made it by digging down and then damm-
ing up the stream, and then the water must have got
away through this break in the wall, whenever there
was an overflow, and gone on carving that passage
through the earth down the way we came in. But
why a well here?"

"And how did folk ever get to it?" added Dickon.
This cave was not only larger in size than the other,
it also gave evidence of having been fashioned by
the hand of man as well as by the action of water.
Slowly the two boys inspected the four walls of it.
Three of them were lined with large irregular slabs
of stone very much like the walls of the treasure
chamber. The fourth, behind the semicircular well,
was of natural cave-bed material. It was uneven and
sloped back and, when Dickon held his candle high,
the light did not penetrate far enough to see where
the roof closed in to meet it.

"Maybe this is where the cave opens up entirely,
and if we could climb up here we'd come to daylight," suggested Dickon.

"You can't *see* any daylight, can you?" said Hugh,
peering up.

"No, but there's a draught of wind—and bats—
They must come in from here."

Several of the eerie little creatures darted close to
them, fascinated by the candlelight, and then swooped
about the cave, gibbering and confused.

"Look here," continued Hugh, "the stream that
feeds this well comes in from this direction. Let's
follow it as far as we can."

The water ran, a thin trickle, scarcely more, from
a break in the wall behind the well on the opposite

side from where it ran out. Once again the boys followed the line of water, climbing up a steeper grade
this time, through a rounded aperture and then a
passageway that was so relatively even and smooth
that it quickly became evident to them just what it
was.

"This is no natural water course," said Dickon to
Hugh's heels, for Hugh and the candle had gone
first this time. "This is a drain, man-made."

"Must be," said the other shortly. He was getting
very tired and, though he would not have admitted
it to anybody, least of all Dickon, this climbing down
walls and through caves and jagged underground water courses was much more difficult for him than it
would have been for another, on account of his feeble leg. He was secretly glad this course was smoother.

After they had scrambled on in silence for awhile,
Hugh exclaimed in delight and put out his candle.
A square of gray daylight pierced the darkness through
which they were progressing and the sight lent speed
to the aching bodies of both of them.

"We'll be on top of the earth again instead of under it in a minute now!" cried Dickon. "Where do
you suppose we will come out?"

Hugh had not an idea and saved his breath and
energies for the final climb.

In another few moments they were out of the underground stream bed, but not entirely above the
earth.

Once again they stared in stupefied astonishment,
first at their surroundings, and then back at each
other. They were standing on a ledge, in a niche or
recess of the wall of a round open well. The water

lapped over their feet a little, running down in the gentle trickle through the drain which they had been climbing. The back of the recess in which they were standing was the opening for the overflow; at their feet the well water stood reaching down deep and still. When the well was fuller, water would rush through the back of the recess, perhaps filling it, then down the drain to the well below ground whence the overflow would tumble through the broken wall, over the floor of that curious man-made cave and down its own naturally made bed, past the wall of the treasure chamber, and finally lose itself in the deep crevasse beside it. So much for the story of the stream, which was perfectly evident. But the boys at that moment were wondering how they were ever going to climb up the smooth inside surface of that well wall in the niche of which they stood, and get to level surface ground again.

"Think we can make it?" asked Dickon, looking uneasily at Hugh.

"We could go back the way we came, of course," he continued as the other hesitated.

"Seems as if we had come miles and miles," Hugh admitted with a weary sigh.

"If you could stand on my shoulders, maybe you could reach the top and pull yourself over."

"Then how would you get out?"

"I wouldn't like for either of us to fall into the water; it looks plenty deep," continued Dickon, looking down into it.

"And how *red* it is!" said Hugh. "Looks almost like blood."

They peered down into the silent depths, then up again at the blue sky above them.

Dickon suddenly began to laugh. "Here we stand between heaven and earth," said he, "and what have we got for our pains? Not a sign of a place where any treasure could be hid did I see."

"Nor I," admitted Hugh; "and what is more, we haven't got what we came in for! You know we planned to take a lot of those parchment sheets in the chest away with us to study more carefully—and they are still in the chest! Looks like we *can't* get up to heaven, whether we want to or not, so we might as well go back into the earth and fetch them."

Without another word they began to retrace their way down the long, wet, slippery drain into the cave of the broken well. It did not seem so long or hard returning as it had coming up and the strange underground room with its semicircular, low walled well gave them almost a feeling of familiarity as they came out into it again.

"There is just no place here where anything could be hidden, is there?" said Hugh, pausing a moment to rest and look about again.

"If *this* was ever a secret vault for treasure like that other room—my room," said Dickon decidedly, "the treasure is certainly all gone now. What I want to know is *why* is this here at all? Whatever could have been the use of it and, once again, how on earth could anybody bigger than us have got in or got out of here?"

"It's all part of the same mystery, I am sure it is," said Hugh impressively, "and some day we'll find the clue that makes everything fit together, the lost Grail and the broken book, the sword and—all this—" He waved his hand expressively, indicating the whole underground warren. "But now I want to get hold of those pages! Maybe we'll find the solution to the whole thing right there."

They were silent again as they made their way into the cramped stream bed that took them back to the little natural cave flanked by the wall of the treasure chamber Dickon thought of as his own.

When they got to the more open part, they stood upright with relief, stretching their aching arms and legs. Their second candle, which Dickon had managed to light again before they started back through the drain, was burning down all too fast; he looked at it uneasily and was just about to comment on it when a sound broke the underground stillness and fairly froze the words on his lips. It was a curious sound, a little like the drone of a gigantic bee, a humming, deep and throaty, then thin or muffled, and again rising until the echoes and reverberations rolled and thundered in the narrow confinement of the cave walls.

The two boys listened with hearts hammering in their throats. Dickon crushed out his candle. A dim light issued from the hole in the wall beneath which they were standing. Someone was in that treasure chamber—singing. For the hum had changed abruptly to a sort of chant in a man's voice, rich and full and clear.

Hugh put a meaningful hand on Dickon's arm and started to climb the wall as quietly as possible. Dickon followed and the two managed to find sufficient footing to stand, clinging with their hands also, where they could peer through the hole into the room. A man stood in the center of it, a man so large that he seemed almost to fill it, his head nearly touched the low ceiling and the sound of his voice made the very walls tremble as if it were seeking to push them out and get more space. He had sparse white hair and a scraggly white beard and he was dressed in a long, flowing, dirty, white garment, girdled with a rope from which hung an old metal bell. Beside him, on the floor, stood a stone lantern or cresset, which gave forth a dim, uncertain light and cast the shadow of his huge person upon the opposite wall, magnified and contorted and wavering. He stopped singing, and the bell jangled as he moved across the floor toward the chest whereon the black sword still lay. Grasping the blade near the hilt, he held the heavy weapon high, hilt up so that it looked like a cross, then he kissed it very reverently and laid it back, handling its great weight as easily as if it had been a child's toy. And as he replaced it on the chest he began to chant again, low at first and rhythmically, like devotional intoning, then his voice rose into a song as wild and triumphant as a pagan paean. The words were unintelligible, partly because of the reverberation in the close walled space, but even after the voice became lower again, they had a strange, outlandish sound. Dickon was too terrified to know whether they were Latin, English, or mere gibberish, but Hugh, whose mind had been trained in the study of other languages, realized at least that they were words, though in a different tongue from any he had ever heard before.

The singing stopt again as suddenly as before. The

old man turned to another chest. He muttered to himself, and the bell at his waist clanged as he opened the lid and bent over it. Slowly he drew out the jeweled altar. Dickon's fear gave place for the moment to indignation and an angry exclamation almost escaped his lips, but he choked it back, his eyes still fastened on the huge figure in the room. He had taken the altar out and now placed it carefully upon the chest beside the sword. Then he studied it minutely and in silence. Not a sound broke the underground stillness save the faint trickle of the stream running across the floor of the cave beneath the boys.

It was at that moment that Hugh's strength gave out. He had been clinging with both hands to a rough, protruding stone in the wall, easing thereby the weight on his lame foot which rested on an insecure foothold. His other leg and foot ached with the strain and his fingers were growing numb. Or perhaps the stone to which he was clinging slipped a little. However it was, he suddenly lost his grip and fell down onto the floor of the cave with a heavy thud and the clattering of loose rubble after him.

The man in the secret room gave a startled cry, then a shout. "Who goes there? Who goes there?"

Only echoes and then silence answered. Dickon had climbed quickly and quietly down to where Hugh was lying. They crouched there in the darkness, neither answering the cry nor daring to move.

Suddenly the light issuing from the aperture above them vanished, there was a rasping sound as of rusty, creaking iron, then stillness and dark.

"Art thou hurt, Hugh?" Dickon whispered huskily,

his ears still listening as acutely for any further sound that might come from the treasure chamber as for the boy's reply. Hugh could not be hurt, he just could *not*, or however would they get out of this place!

"Nay," Hugh whispered back stoutly, "not much anyway, I just couldn't hold on any longer. What has happened, think you? Has he put out his light and is he waiting for us in the dark? Or has he gone down the passageway with it?"

"He can't get out if he has done that," declared Dickon positively.

Again they both listened, scarcely breathing. Not a sound.

"Climb up and look through the hole again," whispered Hugh. "Here, I will get the candle lit."

In a moment Dickon, grasping the light, had climbed the wall and peered into the treasure room. It was empty.

"*Now* what shall we do?" said he, returning to Hugh. "You—you aren't hurt too much to go back to the well?"

The boy pulled himself shakily up. He was bruised and sore and his lame leg was aching painfully, but he squared his shoulders and set his lips. "I can get along all right," said he, "but Dickon, I could not get out of that well; we neither of us could, without help. We'll have to go back into the treasure room and out through the passage to the moor—even if we meet that queer giant of a man inside it."

Dickon said nothing for a moment, and Hugh continued. "There is really no reason to be afraid of him, is there? He looks like a hermit, and this place doesn't belong to him any more than to us, so why should he mind our being here?"

"Surely! it's the main highway from Glaston to the sea!" said Dickon sarcastically. "Why shouldn't one meet all one's friends and the world and his wife too?" The thought of his secret being in the possession of uninvited others still rankled in the boy's heart. "Anyway, I think he is mad," he continued after a pause. "Nobody who was sane would go on the way he did, chanting and all, down here in this queer place. It isn't natural."

Hugh could not but agree with him. However, there was nothing one could do about it. "Come on," said he, starting slowly and painfully to climb the wall to the hole. "We've *got* to go this way, anyhow."

Dickon followed close upon his heels, holding the candle which was fast diminishing. Once in the room they looked about more carefully. The sword was still on the chest, the sapphire altar beside it. Evidently the man had left in too much haste to replace the latter. With hearts beating more fearfully than either cared to admit, the two approached the arched entrance to the passageway and looked into it as far as the light from the candle would penetrate. No one was there.

They moved quietly. With every turn of the underground way they held their breath, expecting surely to see the large form of the mysterious stranger filling the cramped space, turning on them, possibly in a rage of anger or insanity. He must be without a light himself, for no competing glimmer shone ahead of their own candle. Slowly, cautiously, they advanced, saying no word, breathing deep with relief as each further turn of the passage opened up and showed itself empty.

At last they reached the cleft in the moor, extinguished their light and scrambled out. Hugh threw himself on the ground panting a little, as much from exhaustion as relief. Dickon's round eyes were fairly bulging.

"He isn't human!" said he. "There just isn't any way for him to have got out! He must be fey, or a devil in the form of a man, and have just vanished like a puff of smoke."

Hugh laughed. "Not *that* man," said he reassuringly. "He was as much flesh and blood as you or I, and there was too much of him to vanish!"

"But a devil could take any form," argued Dickon. "And, I tell you, there is not any way a man could have got out!"

"Well, he just didn't look like a devil, or anything but an old man. There *must* be some other way. Let's go in again as soon as we're both free and find out!"

Dickon crossed himself. Somehow the action seemed to give him more courage. "We will do that, Brother," said he.

Hugh got up and they started back in the direction of the abbey.

"I guess we don't have to wait to be errant knights to find adventure!" said Hugh. "We're right in the middle of one now."

"I told you anything could happen in our Glaston!" declared the other.

VII. The Mad Master
of Beckery

A FEW DAYS later, after the office of Prime, when the brothers were all walking from the big church of St. Mary to the cloisters, in their customary silence, Hugh suddenly found Dickon at his elbow. The boy was evidently much excited and bursting to talk, but the arm of the novice master, who was close behind them, would have descended upon him with unpleasant force if he had broken the rule of quiet, so he contented himself with making signs which only Hugh would notice and understand. They had agreed upon certain meanings and motions early in their friendship, for the daily occupations of each kept them far apart, Dickon being now consigned regularly to Brother Symon in the almonry and Hugh always at the heels of Brother

126

John in the north cloister, or at work in the kitchen. When they did come together, so often, as now, it was at a period when all talking was forbidden. So, when Dickon shook hands with himself, inconspicuously but firmly, as he was doing at that moment, it meant, "I shall be free this afternoon; meet me in the churchyard beside old St. Joseph's Chapel."

But Hugh with a downward thrust of his palm indicated the discouraging answer, "No, I can't possibly get off at all today."

Dickon choked in a vain effort to swallow his words and finally breathed between clenched teeth, "You've just got to! I *must* tell you about something!" He felt the eyes of the novice master burning a hole in his back, so moved away from Hugh entirely, but not before he had seen him shrug his shoulders and nod at the same time, signifying that he did not know how, but he would try to manage it.

Luck was with him. That afternoon Brother John, who had intended to set Hugh a task of copying

abbey accounts on a set of freshly scraped parchments, found some errors in them and bade the boy
leave him alone till he could get the matter straightened out.

Hugh ran gleefully off to the old churchyard. And
if he had been minded to think of the matter, he
would have been pleased and rather astonished at
the growing ease with which he *could* run. The Glastonbury atmosphere, the quiet and friendliness, or
perhaps the absence of the fear and unhappiness that
had so often overshadowed him at home, something
at any rate, was slowly working in his body toward
healing and strength.

He found Dickon waiting for him. "Let's go down
to the apple orchard beyond the grange," said he. "I
have much to tell you and we must not be interrupted."

Hugh nodded his agreement and they set off together.

"I have seen that mad giant of a man we found in
our secret treasure chamber," Dickon began at once.

"You *have?*" Hugh stood still in his astonishment.
"Where? Who is he? Where does he belong?"

"Wait till I tell you the whole thing." Dickon
moved on again. "He lives all by himself—a hermit—out in the marshes on a sort of island of firm
ground called Beckery. That's where St. Bridget once
stayed, and I've been there. I noticed a little tum-
bled-down sort of hut in among the ruins of an old
chapel, but I never thought of anybody living there
now. Well, he does live there, though just how nobody
seems to know. Once in a great while he comes to

the almonry and begs a little food, but scarce enough to feed a kitten, and then he is gone again for ever so long."

"The almonry!" Hugh broke in. "Then Brother Symon knows about him?"

"Yes, and he came to the gate only yesterday. He had a gash on his head; may have got it crashing into something when he ran away from that underground room."

"Do you suppose I scared *him* by the noise I made falling?" giggled Hugh. "I thought *we* were the scared ones! But go on!"

"Brother Symon made him come in and get the cut dressed, and I helped him put ointment on, and bind it up. His name is Bleheris, and he is mad all right. He kept muttering and talking or humming to himself, the way he did in the treasure chamber, the whole time. I could catch only a word or two now and then, for it was mostly in a language I could not understand—Welsh, Brother Symon said it was. But, Hugh, this is the exciting part—he wants to find something, wants it desperately! While Brother Symon was caring for his cut, he suddenly stood up—and he is so tall, you know, and the almoner is a little man—and he seized the brother by his two shoulders and fairly lifted him off the ground.

" 'Where is it?' he cried, and his voice sounded as if he would sob in a minute. 'Where is it? *You* must know, if anyone does. And it is *here*, it must be here, buried, forgotten, hidden away, under the ruins, under the earth, *somewhere!* They hid it because of the great wickedness of men; *he* said they did—he who

wrote the book. Here! Here in this sacred spot! I
must see it, hold it in these two hands before I die!
O God, let me behold it! Let me behold it!'"

Dickon, who had a natural gift for mimicry told
his story with a dramatic intensity that made Hugh
feel as if he were actually present at the scene in the
almonry.

"And then he did sob," the boy went on, "cried
like a child, great tearing sobs. I tell you, Hugh, I
was frightened when he laid his powerful hands on
Brother Symon, but when he broke down that way,
a big giant of a man, with tears running down his
face, I could have cried myself, I was so sorry for
him!"

"He must have meant the Sacred Cup, the Holy
Grail!" breathed Hugh.

"That is what came into my head, of course."

"Did he say anything more? Did Brother Symon
say anything?"

"Brother Symon was very quiet—he always is.
He looked up for a minute, the way he does, and
you know he is praying a little prayer for the person
before him, and then he soothed the old hermit as
one would a sick baby, his voice all gentle. Told him
that he must not grieve, for if it were God's will and
he asked in humility, his prayer would surely be answered and he would see his heart's desire before he
died. By and by the hermit went off, contentedly
humming, and I asked Brother Symon more about
him."

"And did you say anything about the Cup?"

"Not directly, but I asked if he knew what the old

fellow had been talking about; what he had lost that he wanted so badly."

"And what did he say?"

"He gave me a funny look as if he did not quite want to tell all he knew, or else was doing some wondering of his own. 'Not for a surety,' he said, 'but sometimes the good God hides things from the wise and reveals them to the childlike and foolish.' And that was all he would say, which does not mean much."

"Oh, but it does!" Hugh took him up quickly. "I think it *might* mean a great deal! Maybe the mystery of the hidden Cup is a tradition that some of the brothers hold among themselves; maybe they consider it too sacred a thing, too important a secret, to talk about to just anybody. And maybe Brother Symon thought he—the hermit—what was his name?"

"Bleheris."

"That Bleheris might be the one to find it; that God might even reveal it to him rather than to anybody else, just because he—his mind—. You know, folks think anybody whose mind is not right is especially beloved and protected by God."

"That might all be!"

By this time the boys had reached the orchard and were sitting under the shade of a gnarled old tree. Hugh continued:

"And, if *that* is what is so much on his mind, he might have been hunting for the Cup when we saw him underground."

"But how did he get into that room and how did he get out? That is what I want to know, first of all!" Again Dickon's thoughts went back to the impossibility of a large man going through an opening in the rocks scarcely wide enough to admit a thin boy.

"This whole thing needs thinking out," declared Hugh and they sat silent for awhile, chewing blades of grass.

"There just *must* be some other way into your treasure chamber," he continued at length. "It is not only the large man we have to account for but those chests and the big cupboard against the wall opposite the entrance. And what does it all *mean*, anyway? Take the well underground in the cave; that was certainly made—partly at least—by men's hands; and then that treasure chamber with no way into it except the small broken place in the wall and the long passageway coming out on the moor by the north gate? I just can't make sense out of any of it."

"And that well with the niche in the wall where we came out, you know?" Dickon broke in. "Do you know what that is, and where?"

Hugh shook his head.

"That is called Blood Spring and it lies between the monastery grounds and Chalice Hill, south of the abbey. That means, when we went underground near the north gate and came out, after all the climbing through river beds and caves and drains, into Blood Spring, we went from north to south of the conventual buildings and probably right under some of them."

"*Chalice* Hill!" Hugh caught him up. "Is that the name of it? Why, Dickon, whoever named that hill might have been thinking of the Sacred Cup, the Holy Chalice!"

They looked at each other silently as the thought struck home, then Hugh continued:

"It begins to fit into place a little! Look here now; suppose long ago the monks of Glaston were threatened by the Danes or heathen or something—and we know they were; and suppose they dug down into the earth, found where the spring water went down into a natural cave, the very cave we were in—"

"But why should they dam up the water and make a real well underground?" interrupted Dickon.

"So they could have a water supply and *live* under there if they had to, while the enemy laid siege."

"That might be—well, go on."

"They would take all their sacredest treasures down with them—the small ones they could carry—while the Danes hammered at the gates. Then, when they found how useful such a place could be, maybe the brothers later dug through to the north gate, so they could escape themselves and take stuff with them to a port on the sea."

Dickon nodded, but with a critical frown on his face. "But that means there must have been a man-sized way down to the Cave of the Well—and a man-sized way out near the north gate—and there just isn't! And that brings us right back to the original question; how did those monks in the old days get in and get out? How did Bleheris get in and get out? Do you realize that he vanished like smoke that day we found him there?"

"Look," said Hugh. "Let's draw a picture of what we have found so far."

He chose a spot of bare earth under the shade of one of the big apple trees and, taking a stick, began to outline a plan in it.

"Here's the cleft near the north gate; here's the Blood Spring, and here's the treasure chamber underground somewhere in between, with one entrance from the passageway. The other three sides have unbroken walls except for that hole which let us into a cave which is part of a river bed. Here is the stream— I'll draw it zig-zag—that comes from the Cave of the Well—much too cramped and narrow for the passage of a lot of monks with treasure to hide. Now, over here I'll draw the Cave of the Well with another stream bed behind it, a little to the right, leading back, and up to that queer niche in the wall of the Blood Spring."

"And where, by the saints," Dickon interrupted, "could there have been any way in or out of that whole underground business big enough for any man —let alone Bleheris?"

"Yet he did get down there and out again. If we did not know he had done that, I'd say simply that there must have been some way down under, from the monastic grounds, and it got blocked up and forgotten long ago. But there is Bleheris." Hugh sat back against the tree, thinking deeply.

"There just *must* be a hidden passage, and we've got to find it!" declared Dickon positively, after a pause. "Come on, let's try again!"

Hugh hesitated. "Yes, but that hidden passage is

only part of the whole thing; we want to solve the mystery of the way into the underground room, of course, but most of all we want to find some clue to the hidden Hallow, the Holy Cup. Maybe finding the lost way into the treasure vault will help us in that much greater search, and again maybe it won't. There's the name 'Chalice Hill,' that should tell us something—and the *Blood* Spring, with that strange deep niche in the wall. Do you suppose *that* might once have been the hiding place of the Holy Grail and that it was taken away somehow, by someone, long ago, and now only the names and the tradition are left?"

Dickon regarded him, round-eyed and wondering, but made no reply other than a grunt admitting that it might be so.

Hugh continued, thinking aloud, as it were, and scarcely expecting any comment. "And there's the book, Dickon, we mustn't forget that broken volume about the Seynt Graal in the Painted Aumbry. If we could only recover all the lost pages of that book, we might be able to read the whole story from beginning to end; how the Grail came to our Glaston, why it disappeared the first time, what happened when it was seen again and where and how one might search for it now. It seems to me those missing pages are even more important than the passages underground."

Dickon did not look convinced. "That's such a slow way," said he impatiently, "reading and poring over stuffy parchments. What I want to know is how Bleheris—"

"Bleheris!" Hugh had a sudden idea. "Why not go directly to Bleheris and see what we can find out from him? If there *is* a different way into that treasure vault, he is the one who knows it! And what is more, he may know a lot more about the Holy Cup itself, if he wants so much to find it! Come on, let's go to Beckery this minute!"

"But Bleheris is mad," demurred Dickon. "He might fly at us and kill us! He could snap us in two with one twist of those big hands of his!"

Hugh was considering directions. "Where is Beckery from here?" said he. "We have two quick working brains to get away with if he begins to act dangerous. I tell you, Dickon, this is an important quest we are on, not just a play adventure. Think what it would mean to our Glaston and the brothers if we could restore to them the sacredest treasure in the whole world!"

They turned west in the direction of the sea and were soon deep in the salt marshes, floundering about among the reeds and mud, stepping from a bit of firm ground into ooze and water, and then climbing again onto tussocks or low banks. Gulls and marsh birds screamed overhead, a great heron lumbered out of the tall grasses near them and went flapping away, and something alive and frightened splashed into a pool behind them.

"Do you know just where the place is?" asked Hugh, panting in his efforts to keep his footing.

"Not exactly, from this direction, but I believe there is the remnant of an old road out here somewhere, on a ridge that is above water and dry. If we can find that and get onto it, we'll be all right, for it leads straight to Beckery. Brother Symon said it did."

And soon they could distinguish it, a ridge of higher land and the vague suggestion of a road, scarcely more, upon it. At one time it had probably connected the abbey grounds with the seashore, but it had long since been abandoned and fallen into ruin and decay. However, even in its broken and dilapidated state, the old road made walking much easier than cutting their way directly through the marshes, and the two boys moved on quickly and easily enough for the space of nearly a mile. Then they saw what must be the island; a plot of ground not very large, roughly circular in shape, but higher and dryer than the reedy marsh land which completely surrounded it except for a broken, half-sunken old stone causeway which joined the ridge to it. Willow trees grew on it and as the boys approached they could make out some stone walls, evidently the ruins of some ancient building, and near that a hut made of mud and willow withies, old and small and sagging out of shape.

"There it is," said Dickon, pointing.

"And there is Bleheris, the hermit himself, sitting in front of his hut!" added Hugh.

They both paused, hesitating to go straight up to the old man, uninvited as they were. If his madness should suddenly make him turn ugly, getting away over the broken causeway and rough ridge road would not be altogether easy.

"What shall we say?" queried Dickon.

"Oh, just be friendly," said Hugh with a confidence

he was far from feeling. "Just tell him we were out this way and—"

"And stepped in? Yes—being a hermit who chooses to live apart from all the world, we thought he'd like *us* to be neighborly! Sounds natural and pleasant, doesn't it?"

Hugh chuckled at his sarcasm. "Well, come on, anyway!" he said. "If he knows anything about that Holy Cup, I want to hear it!"

They started forward again, making their way carefully over the jagged stone remains of the old causeway, which was partly sunk and almost hidden by overgrowing willows. From this a path straggled up toward the hut and the ruins behind it.

The two boys were almost upon the hermit before he saw them. He was sitting on a large stone which had evidently once been part of the broken walls, his hands folded in his lap, his head bowed, deep in thought. The sound of their near footsteps roused him and he looked up. For a full moment he gazed at them in astonished silence while they gazed back, ready to turn and run for their lives if he proved dangerously hostile.

He rose slowly to his feet, bowed with great dignity and composure, then lifted his two hands with a motion that was both welcoming and apologetic.

"Ah," said he, "so the young sirs have deigned at last to visit the old Master of Beckery! My lords, you are welcome indeed to my poor castle. Alas, the drawbridge is broken, the moat dry and blistering in the sun, the walls of the donjon fallen and grown over with ivy. But enter, enter, good my lords. The feet of the best knights in all God's world have trod these stones, the noblest and the highest born among men have sat before my hearth and knelt in yon sanctified and holy oratory."

The boys stood speechless. The hermit with another gracious, sweeping gesture indicated the door of his hut and evidently expected them to go in.

Hugh led the way, hesitantly, and Dickon followed. The lintel was so low that even they must bow their heads to enter, and the tall hermit had to bend almost double until he had got into the middle of the hut. Inside were a bed made of willow branches partly covered with a rough blanket, a block of stone standing upright with another thinner block on top of it, thereby making a table, and a chest, a great black oak chest much like the three in the underground chamber. On the top of this chest stood two iron candlesticks with half burnt candles in them, and a plain iron cross. On the floor near it rested the bell and stone lantern the boys had seen when they had come upon the old man in the underground treasure chamber.

Bleheris noticed how their gaze rested on the chest which stood against the back of the hut, the eastern end, which was the proper place for an altar.

"Mine oratory," said he, with a wave of his hand. Then he sighed heavily. "Since the old and sacred chapel of Beckery, the Chapel Perilous, hath fallen into decay, I do my humble best to maintain the sanctuary, to keep the light burning until such time as the ancient splendor shall come again; until that which is lost and hidden shall be found, and a glory not of this world shall shine forth once more upon all the earth."

He seemed to forget his visitors for a moment; he lifted his face, his lips moved as if in silent prayer, and there was a light in his eyes as if they beheld, not the blackened walls of the low, sagging little hut, but some shining inner vision.

Suddenly all fear of the old man slipped out of Hugh's heart. It seemed as if he himself had caught a tiny gleam of that vision, or at least of that light which illumined the hermit's face.

"Sir," said he humbly, in a tone he scarce recognized as his own, "Good Master Bleheris, we would see that shining glory too. Therefore are we come."

They might have been magic words, the formula of a mystic spell, for the effect they produced. The tall hermit wheeled around and fastened his eyes upon Hugh as if he would bore holes into his inmost being and behold all that lay within.

"Dost thou know aught of it?" he whispered, his voice husky. "Hast thou seen—? But no, thou hast said as much—thou, too, art seeking—seeking—! Lad, who art thou? Whence comest thou?"

Joy had been flooding Hugh, joy and a deep thrill of wonder and expectancy, as if he were on the very brink of something that he had been waiting for all his life, and that would mean to him more than all else in the world. And now, with that old question he so dreaded to hear, about himself, who he was, whence he had come, all the joy vanished and he hesitated, stumbled, dropt his eyes miserably as though he had done wrong and were ashamed.

Dickon came to the rescue. "This is Hugh," said he, "he is of our Glaston. He can read and is learning to be a scribe and a maker of books."

"Ah," said the hermit, nodding his head slowly and approvingly. "Books; there is a Book, lost also—but no matter now. You shall hear of that anon—if you prove worthy. And who are you, young sir?"

"I am Dickon, the oblate. We came here to see you because—because—" It was his turn this time to stumble and hesitate.

But, astonishingly enough, the hermit seemed to need no further explanation for their presence.

"I know why you have come," said he, nodding wisely. "The word has been spoken, the secret word; we are one, all three; Hugh the young master, Dickon the oblate, and—" Here he paused and straightened to his full height, so tall his head barely escaped the thatched roofing. "*And*," he repeated impressively, "Bleheris, now hermit and seeker for that which is lost—once Master of Beckery, minstrel and teller of the noblest and loveliest tales in the world."

A little smile, not of complacency but of wistfulness, played across his face. "But come! I must entertain my young guests fittingly. Beckery is so old, it is nigh forgotten of men; years upon years and there comes no knightly visitor riding to the Chapel Perilous upon adventure bent. And now two young sirs—so young, so untried. . . . Messires, I crave your pardon for an old man's garrulousness. I will fetch my lute directly. Sit you down before my hearth and I will tell you of brave deeds and men-at-arms."

There was, of course, no hearth whatever in the

bare cell-like hut, but Bleheris was off on a new trend of thought, picturing, no doubt, his surroundings as they used to be in his minstrel youth; a tapestry-decked hall with a huge fireplace under a projecting canopy, and many knights and ladies sitting and standing about, eager to hear his minstrelsy. He began to hum like a great droning bee, ran to the black chest and, after carefully laying the candles and cross on the floor beside it, he lifted the lid and took out a minstrel's lute of antique design.

The boys had a glimpse of the contents of the chest which was apparently filled with all sorts of metal objects and bulky looking bundles wrapt in white linen. The hermit closed the chest at once, replaced the cross and candles on the top of it and, running his fingers over the strings of his instrument as if all impatience to begin, he motioned the two to follow him and stept out of the dingy hut into the sunshine.

With a wide, gracious gesture he bade them be seated, bowed to right and left as if in the midst of an audience of people, moved toward the bole of a big willow tree and took his stand. He drew his hand, large, old, wrinkled, but perfectly steady, across the strings of his lute in a fine ringing chord and began:

> *"Listen, lords and lordlings,*
> *Give ear for a little stond—"*

There was nothing for it but to settle themselves at his feet. At first the boys looked at each other uneasily, wondering how long they would have to

stay and listen, but in a few moments they were en-
tranced, their eyes fastened upon the hermit's face,
their ears attentive to every word as he chanted in a
sing-song minstrel voice, clear and strong as any young
teller of tales, a story, which he called—

SIR GAWAIN AT THE CASTLE OF THE GRAIL

viii. the hermit's story

"NOW IN THE days of King Arthur, in the times called adventurous, many a good knight and true rode forth upon a strange quest. Only the best knight in all the world might accomplish that quest, and many there were that sought it and failed, and some few others who traveled far and achieved much, coming at long last upon the outer fringes of success. Even they, beholding for a moment that which their hearts longed for, found blessing beyond all that they had dreamed.

"For the quest was a Sacred Hallow, the sacredest in all the world, even the Holy Grail, the Vessel wherefrom the Lord Christ drank at the Last Supper and into which the water and blood fell from

His riven side what time He hung upon the Cross
on Calvary."

The hermit paused and looked keenly at the two
boys who had exchanged glances of understanding
at the mention of the Holy Grail.

"Do you know whereof I speak?" he asked sharply.

"Somewhat we know, Master Bleheris," answered
Hugh. "Of Joseph of Arimathaea and of the coming
of the Sacred Vessel to our Glaston and how it vanished—or was hidden away."

"Who told you?" The great hands of the hermit
were clenched upon the lute as if he would break it.

"Brother John," replied Hugh quietly. "But go on,
good master minstrel, we know only of that first
hiding. Tell us of its coming again among men, in
the days of King Arthur."

Bleheris relaxed a little and drew his fingers over

his instrument again, playing chords that were strong, vibrant, exciting at first and then quiet and dreamy.

"Listen, lords and lordlings," he repeated the conventional minstrel chant, "ye who love a true tale and adventurous, give ear to the strange story of Sir Gawain, nephew to the king." He seemed to sink himself deep down into the well of his memory as he swung into the rhythm of his telling.

"Now Guenevere, King Arthur's queen, would make a tryst with her lord, one summer's day, out in the meadows where the air blew sweet and the field daisies blossomed and the sun lay glad and warm and bright. For Arthur, coming back from the wars, would pass that way. So she let pitch pavilions of silk, heavy and rich and gay, out in the fields. And all the court folk gathered about her to play at games, and feast and make merry, aye, and to laugh and chatter the long hours away until their liege lord should ride into their midst. There were highborn ladies and young damsels and brave and courteous knights more than I can tell, and they all wandered to and fro about the meadow or else stood or sat hard by the queen as she played at chess. In the crimson silk pavilion which stood nigh upon the road she sat, playing her ivory chessmen, with her ear attuned so that she might be the first to greet her lord, King Arthur, when he should come pricking along the way.

"Suddenly men heard the thud of hoof beats and a knight came riding down the road. Armed was he to the full, with visor down, and he rode in haste, looking neither to the left hand nor to the right.

Squires ran to hail him, knights stood astonished, and the queen raised up her eyes and queried:

" 'Pray, who is yon discourteous knight who doth not pause to pay his devoirs unto me? Of a surety 'tis an act most unmannerly that any knight should so pass me by ungreeted and ignored.'

"Then spoke Sir Gawain, most truly courteous of all King Arthur's noble knights. 'Liege Lady,' said he, 'I know not either the name nor the station of yon knight but, if thou wilt give me leave to do so, I am minded to follow him instantly and bring him back, willy-nilly, to ask thy pardon for his rude folly and to pay thee the greeting he doth owe.'

"So Sir Gawain, after he had got leave of his lady, bade a squire fetch him a horse and armor, and set forth with all the speed that he might, in the direction taken by the stranger. But so great had been the haste of that other that Gawain did not overtake him for some hours. At last, however, he drew near enough to hail him.

" 'Sir Knight,' he cried, 'draw rein and hear what I would say to thee, else will I ride against thee to slay thee in combat for a most ungentle caitiff.'

"At that the knight stayed him and, turning his steed, awaited Sir Gawain's approach, showing neither fear nor anger. 'Sir,' said he, 'what would you?'

" 'I am a knight of King Arthur's court,' said Sir Gawain, raising his visor, 'and I come even now from the queen whose pavilion, set nigh unto the road, thou hast most discourteously passed by, without so much as a greeting to her nor a word to pay thy devoirs. Nor will I countenance such disrespect unto my lady; wherefore I bid thee come with me now, upon the instant, and kneel before her, asking her pardon for thine offence.'

" 'Of a truth,' declared the knight gently enough, 'I was never minded to do offence to any lady. I would indeed have paused, save that I ride upon a quest which brooks no delay. Already I am awaited long and I may not tarry.'

" 'But, Sir, there is no quest nor no adventure so demanding that a knight may not pause even so long as to give reverence to his rightful queen.'

" 'In that thou speakest true,' replied the knight reluctantly.

" 'Then come, good Sir, and by my troth, I promise thee safe conveyance to the pavilion of the queen, and after thou hast greeted her thou mayst ride again, without let or hindrance, whithersoever thou wilt.'

"So the two, Sir Gawain and the stranger knight, rode back along the road whence they had come. When they were nigh unto the meadow where the gay pavilions flaunted themselves in the sun, lo, suddenly, from no hand that man could see, from no copse or thicket or hedge, for there was none hard by, came a lance swift as the wind, sure and true of aim, and it pierced the side of that stranger knight, so that he fell forward on his horse's neck with a cry.

"And immediately a press of folk came running from the meadow, and they marveled greatly, for not one among them knew the knight nor whence he came. They laid him softly upon the ground and

Gawain bent over him, his heart torn with wrath and dismay that one to whom he had promised safe guidance should be thus traitorously done to death.

"The stranger knight made as though he would speak and all kept silence to hear him, though it was to Gawain only that he addressed his words.

" 'Sir,' said he, 'by the honor of thy knighthood I do adjure thee to take upon thee the quest that of necessity I now give over. When I am dead, take thou my armor and my horse; mount quickly, for there is need of haste, and let my good steed be thy guide to take thee whithersoever he will, though it be a long journey. Alas, my breath faileth; I cannot tell thee more save to ride quickly, and for the adventure thou shalt meet with at the end of thy riding—the Lord be with thee. Farewell.'

"With that the stranger breathed his last and Sir Gawain, looking upon his dead face, vowed that he would not rest till he had fulfilled that unknown quest and avenged this knight of the foul deed that had been done him.

"And so it was that Sir Gawain, armed with the mail of the mysteriously slain knight, and mounted upon his horse, set forth that very afternoon, when the shadows of the trees lay long across the highway and the fields hard by, and rode with bridle loose, letting the steed take him whither he would.

"All that night he rode and the next day and, when the dusk of twilight gathered again, he found himself in a strange country. The air had grown still and sultry and thunder reverberated round about him.

The sky darkened suddenly and, ever and anon, lightning flashed from cloud to cloud. Sir Gawain would fain have turned aside and found some shelter from the oncoming storm but his horse had another mind to the matter. As often as the knight laid pressure upon the bridle, the beast shook his great head, increased his speed and took, as it were, the bit in his teeth, refusing to be guided.

"The storm came on apace; black clouds piled one upon the other until the whole face of the heavens was darkened. A moment of intense, quivering silence was followed by a roaring rush of wind in the treetops, then the rain came, torrents of sheeted rain; the thunder roared and crashed, lightning leaped from cloud to cloud and, in forked fury, stabbed the earth. Great limbs of trees came hurtling down and the force of the wind was so great that Sir Gawain and his horse must pause, whether they would or no, for they could make no headway against it.

"Then Gawain spied a light, a faint small glimmer, shining to the right of him, and he turned him toward it, the steed for the nonce being willing. So, with wind and rain lashing against their sides, they made their way slowly toward what the knight hoped would be some kind of shelter. Nor was he wrong in his surmise. As he drew nearer he found that the small gleam he had seen in the dark issued from a chapel, the door of which stood open wide and high to wind and weather. Mounted as he was, Sir Gawain rode within, thankful to be out of the fury of the tempest.

"Inside the chapel it was as if no storm raged anywhere, for there was silence, utter and profound. Upon a plain bare altar stood one candlestick and the flame thereof neither moved nor flickered in the draft. And below the altar stood a bier with a dead knight thereon, the half of his body covered over with a pall of heavy silken stuff, black with a cross upon it broidered in rich gold. Long time Sir Gawain sat motionless upon his horse, gazing upon that dead face palely lit by the single taper upon the altar. And he marveled at the unnatural stillness and the unwavering flame, and wondered what all this might portend. Then, suddenly, out of the blackness behind the altar came a hand, a man's hand with long strong fingers, though Sir Gawain in nowise beheld the figure of the man, only his hand as it were alone and bodiless. And the hand seized the candle upon the altar and extinguished the flame and at the same time the heavens broke loose again and the storm shrieked in a thousand voices. The wind rushed in at the open door, lightning flashed in livid brightness, showing for a moment the bier and the dead knight and the altar with the candlestick prone upon it; then darkness—deeper, thicker, more ominous than before—covered all, and the thunder roared itself out over the hills, growing at length fainter and fainter. When the noise of wind and rain and thunder had somewhat abated Gawain heard a new sound, a human voice wailing now close above his head, now farther off as if borne upon the wind itself.

" 'Woe! woe!' it moaned. 'Woe to that knight who

rides unworthily upon the quest whose end is secret and sacred beyond all others!'

"Now Gawain's horse which had been growing ever more restless and uneasy seemed to take sudden panic from the sound of that strange bodiless voice. He reared and backed, then dashing from the door of the chapel, made off in great leaping bounds. Gawain could neither control him nor see, by reason of the darkness of the night, whither he was going. He gave him his rein and, gripping with his knees, rode on as if upon the back of the tempest itself.

"All through the night he rode thus and when the first gray of dawn broke the blackness of that strange night, the horse slackened his speed and moved jauntily and seemingly without fatigue over a springy turf. As the light of day grew brighter, Gawain saw that he was in a desolate country hard by the sea. A narrow path ran along the shore and the waters were so high and so tempestuous from the storm that they washed over it and threatened to tear it away. But the horse trotted on in seeming confidence, splashing through the foam of the waves, thudding over the harder ground with steady and unwearied gait.

"After a great while Sir Gawain spied a castle ahead of him abutting on the sea, and the path that he rode ran through a marshy land and over a causeway and an ancient bridge and brought him to the portcullis of that castle, which was straightway raised to admit him. As his horse clattered into the courtyard there came many young squires who greeted him in friendly, eager fashion, as though he had been expected. And many more folk gathered about him, both knights and ladies, and bade him welcome, some of them saying, 'Sir, we have awaited thee long,' or 'May the Lord bless thee, good sir, that thou hast come at last.'

"Then was he led away to the bath and given fair rich clothing of fine linen and silk and vair and, when he had washed and refreshed himself and was clothed in the new apparel, he came forth into a great hall where all those people were gathered. But when they saw Sir Gawain's face more clearly and that it was not the face of him whom they expected, a great moaning cry arose among them and with one accord they withdrew, vanishing behind arras-hung doors and out beyond the hall into the outer courtyard until Gawain found himself alone in an empty silence.

"It grieved and offended him sorely that he should be thus discourteously treated, though he minded him that he had come clothed in the armor and upon the horse of that strange knight who had been riding on this quest and doubtless was the one expected. While he was thus pondering upon the strangeness of the whole affair he noted that, at the far end of the hall, tapers were being lit upon a high altar-like table. Dark robed figures lighted them and, when they had done, they departed into an inner room whence they soon issued again, carrying a heavy couch which they placed beside the table. Sir Gawain drew nearer and, by the light of the candles, he saw that a man lay upon the couch, a man incredibly old and wrinkled, his eyes sunk deep into their sockets, his scanty beard white, his face and his two hands, lying gently upon the rich coverlet that was over him, as wan and pale as death itself. Yet was the man not dead, for Gawain noted how the light breath came and went and the fingers moved now and again. And upon the coverlet, just beneath those thin pale hands, lay a sword, broken at the hilt.

"Anon into the silence of the hall came the noise of many feet and all those folk who had greeted Sir Gawain were returning, yet they looked never a one at him but only on the old man upon the couch, and they wailed and lamented bitterly, so that the sound filled the hall. And after they had wept awhile they ceased and stood silent and expectant. Then from that inner chamber, whence the bed had been borne, came a tall knight clad in scarlet vesture, very rich and costly, with a crown of red gold upon his head, and he approached Gawain and made to him gestures of greeting, yet said not a word. The eyes of all were fastened still on the doorway of that hidden room and so complete was the silence that lay upon all that press of folk that Gawain could hear the feeble, tremulous breathing of the old man and the occasional sputter of the candle flames. There followed a faint stir, a little sigh that ran around the great hall among all those people, and then, out from the inner chamber, came a strange procession; six damsels wondrous fair in face and figure and clad in heavy samite, scarlet and gold, and behind them a young page with fair curling hair and noble countenance bearing in his hands a spear, the point held downward, and from the point ever and anon, drops of blood ran down even to the hands of the lad so that they were dyed red with it. And behind the boy, at a little distance, came a maid more beautiful than any on this earth. In white she was clad and her long yellow hair, in two braids, fell over her shoulders to her knees, and about her brows she wore a narrow fillet of gold. Something she held aloft as she came, a vessel like a cup or shallow dish upon a golden stem; it was covered over with a thin white veil, and there shone light from within it and about it so strong and dazzling that the eyes of Sir Gawain could not bear to look upon it, but must close. When he had opened them again, the Holy Vessel was gone and the spear and the damsels, but the air was sweet with perfumed incense and on the table lay food for every man. Scarcely did Sir Gawain know how he was fed nor what manner of food it was, yet was he soon replenished and satisfied.

"Then did that kingly one beside Gawain lay his hand lightly upon the knight's shoulder and lead him out of the hall and into a small room where they two were alone.

" 'Sir Knight,' said he to Gawain, 'well I know thou art not he for whom we have waited but it may be thou art come, directed by God, to rid our land of its great sorrow and to make whole our maimed one. Wouldst thou know the meaning of these mysteries and what it was that passed thee by in light and glory?'

"Now Gawain fain would ask about these things and question all the strangeness of this passing strange adventure, but he had ridden for long hours without food or rest, and a bodily heaviness fell upon him which he could not overcome. Sleep like a pall folded over his mind and spirit and, even while the knight beside him spoke, his eyelids drooped and his knees and shoulders sagged with weariness. His tongue clave to his mouth and he answered never a word, but fell upon the ground and slept and knew nothing.

"When at length he awoke Sir Gawain found himself in a marshy meadow hard by the sea. Gone was the great gray castle in which he had beheld so much of mystery and marvel. Gone were the knightly knight and all those many people, and he was alone, clad in the armor in which he had come upon this curious quest. Beside him grazed the horse he had ridden and the path he had followed ran back along the sea. But the land about him lay desolate, without sign of human life or any mark of cultivation, a place for sea birds and wild creatures of the shore.

"Into the heart of Sir Gawain swept a sudden fierce longing. He must find again that shining thing upborn in the hands of the maid in the vanished castle. He must see with his two eyes the Holy Grail, though the search for it should take him his whole life and lead him to the ends of the world."

Slowly the hands of the hermit Bleheris dropt from his lute, the instrument slipt from his knees, his shoulders drooped and his eyes became glazed and unseeing. The boys stirred restlessly. He seemed to have forgotten their presence and be lost in some inner world of dream. Hugh approached him slowly and gently touched his arm.

"Master Bleheris," he said, "we thank you, Dickon and I, for that noble tale. But—you have not told us the ending of it, and we are eager to hear. Did Gawain find the castle again? Was it indeed the Holy Grail that he beheld? And—and—what happened to it?"

At first they thought the old man had not heard them. He made no answer, gave no response to the touch of Hugh's hand. They looked at each other, wondering if they had best slip quietly away without disturbing him further. Then, suddenly, he turned to Hugh, reached out his arms and seized him placing him directly before his face. He stared at him with eyes that kindled with an inner fire, held him thus and spoke to him, his voice trembling with intensity.

"Who art thou, boy? But, no matter; I care not what thy name or state. There is something within thy spirit—I can feel it—I can see it shining! Thou art one to whom the hidden glories may be revealed!" He paused, still keeping his burning eyes on Hugh's face, his strong hands gripped on the boy's shoulders.

Then nodding his head slowly twice, he continued, "Aye, that was indeed the Holy Grail that Gawain beheld; that was the Castle of Corbenic to which he went. But whether he found it again, saw once more that Sacred Hallow and achieved the quest—I have forgotten. Once I knew, and sometimes those old, old stories that I learned in Wales come back to me. And then again, they drift away in mists and shadows." He sighed and dropt his hands and, when he spoke again, it was as if he were thinking aloud, speaking to himself, rather than to Hugh.

"It is lost," he said, "all lost; the book of the Welsh bard, the old, old book that a hermit got from an angel out of Paradise. In that book are all the stories written about the Seynt Graal and those who sought it. And the book is lost, lost." He swayed back and forth moaning as if in bodily pain. "And that Holy Thing, the Chalice—gone, too—but hidden—not lost. I tell you it is here, here in Glaston, in Avalon, hidden away from the sight of sinful man. Marked you not in the tale as I told it—a waste and desolate land, a low, half sunken causeway—and a castle by the sea?"

He rose and spread his arms in a wide gesture that took in the marsh land, the line of the ocean out beyond the water meadows, Tor in the distance and the lower hills, Weary-All and Chalice.

"It was there," he repeated solemnly, "that the Castle of Corbenic reared its gray walls beside the sea, right over yonder; and the Holy Grail itself; it *must* be here—not lost, but hidden. Dear God, if I could but recover it, behold it with these old yearning eyes, hold it in my trembling old hands! If I could only find that hidden Hallow before I die!"

"Couldn't I—couldn't we help you look for it?" breathed Hugh.

The old man paid no heed to him but brushed by him and entered his hut without another word, closing the low door of it behind him.

ix. the sword and the quest

THE BOYS HAD plenty to think about and discuss after their visit to the mad hermit of Beckery.

"You heard what he said about the book, didn't you?" Hugh reminded Dickon, a few days later, when they met in their usual spot near the Old Church. "It must be our broken book in the Painted Aumbry, *The Book of the Seynt Graal,* and Bleheris just does not know it is there. Now you see how important it is for Brother John and me to find and work over the missing pages. I almost think we ought to tell Brother John right now about that chest of manuscripts in the treasure chamber."

Dickon shook his head decidedly. "No, not yet. It wouldn't be our secret any more if we did. It is bad

enough having Bleheris know about our underground vault. If we told Brother John we would have the whole community rooting around down there in no time."

Hugh suddenly giggled. "How would they get in? You are forgetting there isn't any way in or out of those underground passages big enough for a man to go through—"

"Except Bleheris!" interrupted Dickon, making a wry face. "And he is bigger than any two ordinary men! And that brings us back to exactly where we started—and stopped. With all that long yarn he told us, the old hermit never dropt a hint as to how he got in that underground room, which was what we went to him to find out about."

The two were silent for a few moments. They had started aimlessly across the grounds in the general direction of the grange.

"It sets me crazy to think about it!" Dickon continued irritably. "Bleheris just could not get into those passages, and yet he was there. Hugh, I have got to find out or I'll go madder than the old hermit himself! And I don't want Brother John or anybody else interfering. It's our puzzle, and I want to solve it!"

"Well then," said Hugh, "it seems to me there are two possibilities—maybe three; we could try again to get some information out of Bleheris, or we can hunt and hunt for some other passageway."

"What is your third possibility?" asked Dickon as Hugh paused.

"There might be something in our broken book, as I suggested before, or in the pages we are finding, or the ones we're scraping clean."

Dickon snorted impatiently. "Too slow. Let's look again for ourselves. If Bleheris got in, he certainly must have got out—through some place bigger than a mouse hole!"

"All right," agreed Hugh. "Let's go down and have another look around right now, though I declare I don't see how we *could* have missed anything the last time."

Dickon had already turned in the direction of the north gate.

"And I'll collect some more pages from the chest to work over," Hugh added. "I want to solve this puzzle of the hidden passage as much as you do, but I also want to keep right on in that other matter."

They studied the walls of the passageway from the entrance on the moors to the arch leading into the treasure chamber, with careful scrutiny. There was one place that looked as if a land slide might have occurred at some time, blocking a possible side passage, but if there had been any such, it was effectively and completely cut off now. Inside the treasure vault everything looked exactly the same as when they had left it, the huge iron-hilted sword still lay on top of one of the chests, the other, containing the books and loose pages, stood open. Neither Hugh nor Dickon could remember positively whether they had closed the lid when they had last been there or not. Probably they had not. Hugh halted for some moments before the large aumbry against the wall opposite the archway, in thoughtful silence.

"Let's move that," said he, "there might possibly be something behind it."

But with all their strength the boys could not budge it an inch. They tried to pry the doors open but were unsuccessful in that also.

"Bleheris couldn't have come out of a locked cabinet or through unbroken walls," said Dickon gloomily; "he couldn't have dropt from the ceiling or come up out of the floor—or could he? Let's examine this floor more carefully."

There was no sign whatever of loose flooring or a possible trapdoor. Dickon sat down on the chest beside the sword and gazed at the hole which he and Hugh had made bigger and which led into the stream bed beyond. That certainly gave them no further clue.

"It's either enchantment or the devil or maybe both," he declared with finality, and crossed himself as a matter of protection. "Bleheris just could not have got in here—and yet he did."

Hugh was rummaging among the loose manuscripts and made no reply for the moment. Suddenly he cried out excitedly, straightened up and held a single page near the candlelight. "Dickon! Look here! What do you call this?"

The boy glanced over Hugh's shoulder. "Just a funny design, isn't it? No, it isn't! It's a chart or map of something! Let's see it closer!"

They both studied the page in eager silence. Very evidently the faint, half-obliterated lines and squares were meant to represent a chart. Latin words, by way of explanation, ran beside some of them and short phrases in the corner, which were unintelligible to Dickon but yielded their meaning to Hugh. He translated: " 'The Cave of the Well'; 'The Hidden'—something—I can't make out; 'The Old Church'; 'Passage to North Gate.' "

"Dickon!" he whispered, almost too excited to speak. "Dickon, do you realize what we have found?"

It was at that moment that a strange sound caught their attention. They wheeled around toward the great aumbry whence it came; a noise of rasping metal, unmistakably the sliding of a rusty bolt. The two gazed in fascinated terror at the doors of the great cupboard which moved and shook a little and then were thrust open. Through them emerged the giant figure of the mad hermit of Beckery, with the customary bell at his girdle and the antique lantern in his hand.

And there was no mistaking his madness either! His face, dead pale, was working with emotion; his eyes blazed, his great hand gripped the handle of the lantern with a power that whitened the knuckles.

"Thieves! Caitiffs! Villains!" he screamed. "Away with you, lest I fling you against yon walls and shatter your feeble bodies! Be gone! Be gone or I will—"

He was looking directly at Dickon, then his gaze shifted to Hugh; a flash of recognition passed over his face, and his rage lessened.

"How came you here, boy, and for what purpose? Tell me! Tell me quickly, ere the foul demons that govern my passions let loose upon you, to slay you! What are you seeking?"

Hugh with a mighty effort got control of his panic, steadied his shaking voice, and answered quietly:

"Master Bleheris, we are seeking what you seek— the Holy Cup, and all such things as may pertain to that sacred mystery—"

"Aha!" the hermit took him up eagerly. "Now I remember! And hast thou found it? But no, thou art but a foolish lad. Thou canst not succeed where I, Bleheris, have failed."

His anger seemed to have softened and died down as suddenly as it had blazed up. He looked about the room and then back at the two boys. "How came you here?" said he again. "None save I knows of the hidden way and I—'twas scarce a month ago that I came upon it, following the direction of a dream."

He forgot that he had asked a question, apparently,

or cared not for the answer. Going over to the chest whereon lay the huge sword, he picked it up as lightly, as effortlessly as if it had been a child's toy.

"Excalibur!" he said reverently. "King Arthur's sword! After that last great battle, Sir Bohort took it, he who had borne the wounded king upon his shoulders from the field of war. And it was here that Arthur bade him fling it from him, here in our marshes hard by the Island of Beckery. He flung it with all his mighty strength out into the water. And they say a hand reached out and drew it under, and no man saw it after that day. . . . But that is not true."

Bleheris, who had taken on the sing-song monotone customary to minstrels, and whose eyes had become glazed, unseeing, as if fastened only on some inner vision, changed suddenly. His voice sounded harsh, combative, his eyes fixed themselves upon Hugh with fire and intensity as if the boy had contradicted him. "It is not true!" he repeated. "I found it myself, hidden in the marsh grasses, dull, rusted. I polished and cleaned it. See you, how it shines? King Arthur's sword! It is mine now, mine! Mine!"

"King Arthur's sword, Excalibur," exclaimed Hugh in awe. "But, Master Bleheris, how know you it is indeed that sword?"

"The old stories tell of it," said the hermit, "and that which is inscribed on the two sides of the blade, up near the hilt. Look you—look you—'tis just as the records say."

The boys drew closer and watched him trace with his finger the words on the one side. "Take me."

Then he turned the great blade over in his hands and pointed to those other words in the language Hugh had not been able to read. "Runes," said he, "the hidden, secret language that the Druids wrote and some few master magicians among the Welsh still understand." He laid the sword back on the chest with a great sigh.

"But what do they say, those runes?" pursued Hugh eagerly.

" 'Throw me away,' "said the hermit, sighing again. "Alas, I cannot! It is my greatest treasure, Excalibur; often and often I carry it with me as I wander about the fens and ancient roads and among the hills— Chalice, Tor, Weary-All Hill, sacred, mysterious, ancient places that lie round about our Glaston. It whispers to me, tells me again the stories of those brave old days, stories of knightly deeds and high romance. It led me here, here to this long lost treasure chamber of the Viking times. And it may be—lads, lads, it may well be—that, holding Excalibur before me thus—" he picked the sword up again and held it, hilt upward before him, so that it looked like a cross— "it may be that Excalibur himself will lead me to that hidden Hallow, holiest of all in the whole world—"

"The Holy Grail," finished Hugh as the old man paused, his lips trembling in emotion.

"Aye, the Holy Grail," he repeated solemnly.

A long silence followed. The boys could hear the trickle of the stream beyond the hole in the wall. Dickon fidgeted; Hugh watched the hermit intently, eager to urge him on, yet fearful lest, by breaking in upon his mood of reverie, he start the flighty, unstable mind into an entirely different channel.

" 'Throw me away?' " Hugh repeated softly after a few moments. "Might that not have been written for the men of King Arthur's day and not for us?"

Bleheris nodded his head. "Those words have meaning for all time, like all great words. King Arthur read them aright—for himself. For me they have perchance a different meaning—and for you. Take heed, boy, that you read them aright."

To Dickon this conversation made no sense whatever, and he was growing restless. Those two could moon around and get emotional over an old black sword, but as for him, he wanted a look in at that passageway! He moved over to the huge aumbry and was about to go through the doors when a long strong arm caught him by the shoulder and flung him back against the wall. The hermit, his eyes blazing again, had evidently not been as oblivious to Dickon's thought and actions as he had appeared to be.

"Stand back," he cried harshly. "Who gave thee permission to tread my secret way? I tell thee, it is *mine* and thou shalt not enter it until I bid thee!"

"But, Master Bleheris," said Hugh, touching his arm gently, and making unmistakable motions to Dickon from behind the old man's back, to hold his tongue, "we are in the mystery, too. We found this treasure vault—maybe before you did—at least Dickon found it and brought me here. We be searchers, too."

"True," agreed the hermit, mollified. "How did

you get in?" He eyed Dickon keenly but no longer with anger.

"From the moor—a cleft near the old north gate. But you couldn't get in or out that way; you are too big!" Dickon laughed as he said it.

Bleheris nodded slowly. "The ancient way," said he, "blocked by a cave-in, forgotten for many centuries. It once led from the monastic grounds to the village, and in the days of the Danish raids, the brothers took their treasures underground, left many here—or so it seems likely—and carried what they could on through to a port whence they might escape, inland or overseas."

"That is the way we figured it out," said Hugh, "only we can't imagine how they got in and wherefrom."

A shrewd look came over the hermit's face. He turned from Hugh to Dickon and then back again. "How know I that yon oblate is worthy of trust? As for thee, there is something about thee that makes me sure—"

"We be sworn brothers," said Hugh proudly. "It was here in this very spot, beside the jeweled altar, that we mingled our blood and swore that we would be true brothers in all things until the end of our lives."

"The jeweled altar? I had forgotten; show me!" The old man's interest swung off to another turning again.

Hugh and Dickon opened the chest where they had left it, and drew forth the portable altar with its gold base and marble top and the large shining blue sapphire set in the center of it. Bleheris looked long and appraisingly at it, touched it reverently with his strong fingers, and then spoke.

"Aye, it was here the day Excalibur led me to this place. I remember now, Saint David's altar, given him by the Patriarch of Jerusalem. It floated across the seas, men say, straight to our Avalon, drawn as by a lodestone to the sacredest spot in England. For a long time the brothers used it in their services for the dying and then it was lost. How came you upon it, boy?" He turned to Dickon again.

"It was here, right in this treasure vault, when I first got in and explored this place."

"Then there may well be other things hidden— that Other Thing, most holy of all." The old man caught up the sword again which he had left standing in a corner while they had talked. " 'Tis a good notion truly, to swear brotherhood. Now, by this sword of mystery and magic, King Arthur's sword, Excalibur, let us three swear that we will not speak of this thing nor cease to seek till we have found the Grail, the Holy Cup, if so be it still rests hidden in our Glaston."

It was a solemn moment. Bleheris thrust the mighty blade into Hugh's hands. "Take it," said he, "swear by it—secrecy, brotherhood, the sword and the quest—forever and ever!"

Dickon as well as Hugh must hold the sword and repeat the words. Then Bleheris laid Excalibur gently down, walked to the aumbry and threw open the doors. The two boys stepped eagerly forward. Now, at last, the mystery of the hidden passage would be laid bare. But the hermit held up an imperious hand, his eyes half-closed, and regarded Dickon inscrutably.

"Not yet," said he, "not yet, my young friends." And with that he stooped, entered the aumbry and closed and bolted the doors after him!

It was *too* much! Dickon lay down on the floor and laughed hysterically, the sound reverberating oddly from the walls and passageway. Hugh stood as if rooted to the spot.

"The crazy old bird!" sputtered Dickon, sitting up. "Of all the fool performances! All that gibberish about the sword and just as we are about to stick our noses into the heart of the mystery—bang goes the door in our faces, and we are scarcely one step further along than we were when we first got in here!"

"Oh, yes, we are—*much* further!" corrected Hugh. "We know this end of the secret way out, and we've got our chart; don't forget that!" He waved the piece of parchment with the map on it before Dickon's face.

"That's true." Dickon scrambled up. "But of all—" he laughed again. "If my face was as blank as yours, when he shut that door on us, we must have looked like a couple of pie-faced loons! Come on, let's get away from here before our candles give out."

For awhile after that things moved with discouraging slowness. The chart was indistinct, almost impossible to decipher. Day after day the two boys studied it minutely, carefully, and Hugh made a copy of it with a piece of slate on a flat stone in the old monks' cemetery near the two ancient pyramids outside the Old Church, where they were accustomed to meet.

"Here's our treasure vault," he said, pointing with a stick while Dickon kept his finger on the corresponding square marked on the chart. "The secret passage goes from the aumbry quite straight, according to those dotted lines in the map, to the Cave of the Well. That's clear enough—on paper—but there's no sign of *any* break in the walls of that Cave of the Well where an opening might come through."

Dickon grunted. "All lined with flat limestone, one slab as like its neighbor as two peas in the same pod."

"Never mind, let's leave that question for a moment and go over here to the well. See, here is the well, marked on the chart with an arch over it, and something that *might* mean a stairway to the left, behind it. The Latin is rubbed out so I can't read it. And then, over here are the words, 'Old Church.' Dickon, I think there must be stairs up from the Cave of the Well to St. Joseph's Chapel!"

The next time they went down into the underground vault, they climbed at once through the hole in the treasure chamber to the stream bed and thence, crawling along with more certainty now that the way had become familiar, came directly into the Cave of the Well. They scrutinized the walls once again, always hoping that the flat limestones that lined it would give some indication somewhere of a break or hidden doorway.

"The passageway from the aumbry, the way Bleheris came, *must* open out into this cave," Hugh said, for the hundredth time.

"Maybe not," said Dickon. "For all we know it may lead back through the marshes to Beckery and the hermit himself."

"But the chart indicates a line straight from the treasure chamber here, and up and out by a stairway to the Old Church; at least it looks that way."

The two boys climbed behind the arch over the well. To the right was the trickling stream coming through the overflow drain from Blood Spring which they had climbed before. They turned to the left. Here the wall was irregular and unlined, the natural rock substance of the cave. Holding their candle high they peered about and soon made out a darker recess behind a jutting promontory. With hearts beating high, they soon found it to be indeed the entrance to another passageway, high and broad and definitely man-made. They entered, followed it a few yards and came upon a stairway, rough hewn out of the rock substance, broken and worn away in places, but still firm and whole enough for them to mount without difficulty. It led upward at a slight curve and came to an end abruptly under what was very evidently a trap door, large, heavy, sunk solidly into the walls on either side. Dickon handed the candle to Hugh and pushed with all his might. The door gave no evidence at all of yielding. They found a rough place in the wall where they could wedge the candle so that it would be held upright. Then they both pushed against the door with straining shoulders. Useless; not so much as a crack did the great door open.

"Only Bleheris himself could move that!" declared Dickon, panting after a final effort.

"Well then, it's back to Bleheris we go," asserted Hugh, picking up the candle. "There's no use trying any further at this end unless we have him with us. If we can only keep his mind on the fact that we three are bound together now in our search, maybe we can get him to show us the rest of the puzzle down here himself."

Dickon grunted disgustedly. "Seems to me," said he, as they emerged again into the Cave of the Well, "that every place we go we come flat up against Master Bleheris. And he's crazy as a hoot owl and can't be counted on to stay in the same mood or on the same subject for fifteen minutes on a stretch, so—"

"But he's a grand old minstrel, anyhow!" Hugh interrupted, "and I like him!"

"Well, why don't you go over to Beckery without me?" suggested Dickon. "You seem to have a good effect on him and maybe he would talk more to the point if I wasn't there to get his old wits all bothered—if you're not afraid."

"Oh, no, I'm not afraid."

So Hugh began going to Beckery alone. On his first visit he was a bit uneasy. Would Bleheris remember the scene with the sword Excalibur and accept him as a friend and fellow-worker, or would he blaze at him again in one of his sudden and terrifying fits of wrath? He need not have worried, but also he might as well not have made his visit, or so Dickon thought when he was told about it. The old man acted as if he had expected him, greeted him with lordly courtesy and started at once upon a long, wandering story of knights and ladies and romantic adventure. Much as Hugh loved a good tale, he found it hard to sit through this one with patience, eager as he was to ask questions and probe more into the mystery that absorbed his mind.

And when at last the minstrel came to the end, twanged his lute in a final chord and then rose, bowing right and left to an imaginary courtly audience, the boy wondered whether he dared break into his mood at all.

Somewhat hesitantly he began, "Master Bleheris, you remember Excalibur? You left it in the treasure vault after we three—you and Dickon and I—had made a solemn pact together to go on searching—"

The old man's brows darkened, then cleared. "Oh, aye, aye, the sword and the vow. 'Take me' and 'throw me away.' Well, what have you done about it?"

"We have tried to find the other end of the passage," said Hugh more boldly. "You locked us out, you know, from the aumbry way. Good Master Minstrel, I pray thee tell me one thing. How didst thou get into the passage that leads to the treasure chamber through the doors of the aumbry? We *must* know that if we are to be comrades in our quest!"

Bleheris turned away from him with a look of disappointment. "Thou art impatient—and stupid," said he. Then he picked up a sharp stone from the ground and began drawing with it on the surface of one of the flat building stones near his hut.

Hugh moved over and watched him, thinking perhaps if he waited a few moments, the crazed mind would focus again upon the subject about which he was so eager. Bleheris was outlining crudely a design and, as the boy saw the form it was taking, he began to wonder whether there could be method and purpose in what he was doing. It represented an even cross, curved at the ends. When it was finished Hugh recognized it at once as one of the odd figures in the border of the chart he and Dickon had been so carefully studying.

He raised his eyes questioningly to the hermit's face.

"Search for *that*," said Bleheris quietly. There was no sign of madness in his face at the moment. He looked kind and wise. "Search diligently, Hugh, lad. You will find the passage, but it is empty—nevertheless seek—seek for yourself in your own way. . . . The words on the sword Excalibur, dost remember, lad? 'Take me?' We *have* taken it, we three, thou and I and yon round-faced oblate, Dickon; we have taken upon us the sword and the quest, but we must each one seek in his own way, and perchance throw away all that we find at the last. There is something that whispers to me thou art not following faithfully *thy* way. But mark now, the clue, a fresh clue to thy young eyes—a cross, even, the ends curved outward. Where that leads thee, follow."

x. in the marshes of avalon

HUGH WALKED SLOWLY back to the ab-
bey buildings lost in thought. The design which
the hermit had drawn so crudely was familiar enough
to his eyes though not, as far as he knew, as a "clue"
to anything. It had been used as decoration and background for many of the capital letters in the ancient
Book of the Seynt Graal, both in the volume itself and
in the loose pages he had been deciphering. That
had been one rather easy way of proving that a ques-
tionable sheet belonged to the broken book. Small
copies of that special cross were also in the four corners of the sheet with the map on it. He and Dickon
had taken it for a mere conventional decoration. Could
it have any other significance? And just what did
the old minstrel mean by searching, each in his own

way? Bleheris might be mad, was indeed unmistakably mad, but sometimes his utterances had not merely obvious meaning, but a hidden meaning as well. It occurred to the boy that *his* way of seeking for the Holy Grail, his very own way, was through the broken book and its missing pages. Bleheris did not know of the book at all, and Hugh felt instinctively that it was wise he did not, for the present at least. Dickon could not read and obviously had little interest in that line of approach anyway. Brother John? Hugh felt a bit uncomfortable whenever he stopt to realize that Brother John really ought to be in on their secret and possibly could help them more than anybody else. But he had no right to tell the good armarian until Dickon agreed to it, and what was more, he had an eager desire to wait until he had himself recovered and replaced all the missing pages that it was possible to recover from the chest under-

ground. Brother John, and everybody in the monastery, for that matter, had been so good to him. It
would be a wonderful thing if he, a boy whose whole
family was living exiled and accursed, especially in
the eyes of the Church, could restore to Glastonbury,
by his own effort, the long lost pages of the greatest
treasure book they owned!

When it came to recounting his Beckery visit to
Dickon, he found it difficult to make any sense out
of it, yet he himself felt that he had definitely gained
something. He told about the design, how Bleheris
had sketched the even cross with the curved ends
that adorned the map and some of the pages in the
chest, but Dickon only snorted in disgust.

"I'm about ready to stop," said he. "I've thought
about the whole thing till I'm turning circles, and
just when I think we can really *do* something, Bleheris
appears and talks gibberish, or you do. Let's forget
the whole thing for awhile." He turned a cartwheel
with precision and stood on his head, by way of
clearing it, perhaps. When he stood upright again
he was grinning.

"You go on with your books and your Beckery
and when you have got a brand-new idea, or I get
one, we'll go at it again together."

Hugh did go on. He hated to give up and the
whole mystery of the Holy Grail fascinated him from
every angle; the tantalizingly incomplete old book, the
strange underground hiding places that might once
have contained it, or a way to its hiding place, even if
they did not now, and the stories that were connected

with it. He threw himself anew into the study of scripts with an intensity that surprised Brother John, learning to copy and imitate different kinds of lettering, as well as to recognize types, and to date manuscripts fairly accurately.

There were the large, square books that came from the Irish monasteries of the sixth and seventh centuries. They had round, big letters, much scroll work, and exquisitely clear gold leaf backgrounds to their initial letters. Then there were the later, more carelessly written, smaller scripts, with crude pictures rather than intricate designing of capital letters, and the more modern books bound in smaller boards with French enamel inlays and, frequently, little round separate pictures in them called miniatures from the lavish use of minium, the brilliant red dye. The most up-to-date manuscripts of all were tending toward a pointed style of handwriting and varied greatly in size. Brother John complained that no two books fitted the same shelves in any aumbry any more.

The broken *Book of the Seynt Graal* was in a class by itself, having the scroll work and soft coloring of the Irish school, also some figures, and the tall title letters of the Anglo Saxons. Hugh soon became able to recognize at a glance a loose sheet that had belonged to it, even when mixed up with countless others of a later date. There was something distinctive also about the twist of the S's, the quality of the ink, and the texture of the gold and blue and scarlet of its illuminated title letters. He spent long hours, when the monks were dozing or busy out in the fields and the cloisters were deserted, poring over the ancient mutilated volume and fitting in the pages he had recovered from the chest underground. He would climb into a far corner behind the aumbry, where no one happening to pass by would notice him, and read, decipher, compare, with furious intensity. And gradually his mind became filled with the lore of the Holy Grail; the story of its coming to Britain, of Joseph of Arimathaea, his companions, the later guardians of the Sacred Cup, and its first disappearance because of men's sins. That was in the first section; the second took up the tale in the days of King Arthur when the Seynt Graal, as the book called it, appeared again and was sought by many through adventures of wonder and marvel so enthralling that Hugh followed them with bated breath and high beating heart. It was in the very midst of these stories that the pages broke and the tedious piecing together of the scattered and recovered sheets became necessary, a confusing and almost mountainous undertaking. There were the few that Brother John had added, some of them consecutive, others not so. They were kept in the secret drawer in the Painted Aumbry along with the book itself. The ones Hugh was struggling over gave him pieces of a story here, a few unrelated incidents there, dialogues broken off, scraps of description or meaningless paragraphs in another place. But the boy was immensely proud that the pile of extra pages which he kept behind the loose board in the wall of the Old Church had already grown much larger than those of Brother

John. With every fresh sheet that he picked up, his hope was renewed that he would find some hint as to the final resting place of the Holy Grail and that that place might indeed be Glaston. But no such hint did he discover. Only the word Avalon appeared again and again, and Avalon was the name used by all the peasant folk for the marshy land between Tor Hill and the monastery.

Sometimes Hugh grew discouraged. It was rather wearing work, the more so because Dickon did not share it and seemed, indeed, to have lost all interest. He continued going to Beckery, not only because he still hoped to get some further clue to the mysteries of the Grail from the old hermit minstrel, but also because he had become strangely fond of the man himself and was happy and contented in his company; and he began to feel that Bleheris really looked forward to his coming. The hot days of midsummer saw him frequently striking out across the marsh land in the direction of the island, and there he would stay until the shadows of twilight began to fall and he knew that the bell for Vespers would soon be ringing. He could not have explained it even to himself, but he felt in the hermit's presence a sense of tranquillity, a sympathy and understanding, that were apparently mutual. Sometimes he found him silent, depressed, or querulous; sometimes almost like a child, needing to be amused and comforted. Hugh was quick to catch his mood and play up to it and the strange friendship between them grew deep and was completely genuine. But as for any actual information about the possible hiding place of the Holy Grail in Glaston, Hugh gleaned nothing whatsoever. The hermit seemed to have forgotten entirely the pact that the three had sworn on the sword Excalibur.

September brought mist and fog. Hugh could often see it rolling in across the marshes from the sea when he sat with the hermit at Beckery. It would come suddenly, like a ragged wool blanket, blotting out land and water. Bleheris seemed to have an uncanny foreknowledge of its coming. He would grow restless, uneasy, stride up and down his island shore, peering off to the horizon before even a wisp of fog had appeared, sniffing the air like a great dog. Then he would hustle Hugh off, bidding him make all haste back to the conventual buildings.

"There be uncanny things abroad in Avalon when the mists hang low," he would say. "See, over yonder where Tor Hill lifts out of the valley? When the fog sweeps in from the sea and covers the land, there be strange forms riding in the air and over the marshes. Along forgotten roads they come—from the gray Other World."

Hugh would have liked to stay through a fog on the island but Bleheris would not have it.

"Go back quickly," he would say again and again, his voice tremulous and anxious. "Promise me, lad, delay not on your way."

"But why, Master Bleheris? The mist won't hurt me!"

"Nay?" said the old man, regarding him question-

ingly. "Fog in the eyes may give them power to see
more than is permitted. Besides," he added in a more
matter-of-fact tone, "you might lose yourself. In a
thick ocean fog one cannot see to place one foot after the other. And there are quicksands and treacherous bogs and, very like, evil spirits to entice you
into them."

There came a day when Hugh remembered these
warnings, though he had discredited them, when he
heard them, as merely the fancies of a mind that
was not sane. He had set forth for Beckery in mid-
afternoon, later than was his wont. The day had
been uncertain, muggy and hot, cloudy at first, then
partly clearing, but with no wind to lighten the atmosphere, and with a look and feel in the air of im-
permanence, change, and increasing damp. He had
scarcely got beyond the monastic grounds when the
fog enveloped him. So swiftly it came that he scarce
noted its approach before it was upon him, a thick
greenish fog, heavy and low, completely shutting him
within itself. First the Tor vanished, then its foot-
hills, Chalice Hill, Weary-All; the monastic buildings behind him were gone, the marshy way ahead,
and soon even the uncertain ground beneath his feet.
Doubtless he ought to turn back; Master Bleheris
would certainly not receive him cordially if he reached
Beckery out of the very mists which he had been at
such pains to warn the boy not to trifle with.

But there was a fascination about the eerie dim-
ness. Hugh liked the feel of the salt wet on his face,
the sense of hiddenness in the walls of gray about

him, and the mysterious quiet. Once a sea bird called above his head, invisible though near him, and a fish plopped in a pool near by, though he could not see the water. The marsh grasses stood tall and strange, wet and motionless; his feet, as he moved slowly through them, gave forth an oozy, sucking sound.

The boy paused frequently to listen and gauge his distance. It was impossible to distinguish the grasses a yard ahead of him, and he had only a vague sense of direction to tell him how to proceed. Before long this left him and he realized uneasily that he had no idea whether he was heading toward Beckery, or back in the direction of the abbey, or going around in a circle. He had certainly best go back and not try any longer to feel his way blindly to the island. But which *was* back? He turned about and started out hopefully, only to come upon open water, and when he tried to skirt this he went further and further in what he realized must be territory over which he had never been before. The ground became more boggy and soft, the hummocks of higher ground and stretches of marsh grass less frequent. Hugh turned his back on the water and struck inland, or what he hoped was inland, but the water seemed to follow him and he found himself wading up to his knees over a spongy sea bottom. He turned again, trying a different direction. At first the ground under his feet seemed more solid and he made better progress, though the baffled sense of walking almost completely blind, not knowing whether he faced unlimited sea or treacherous bog, the old broken road to

Beckery, or the safe friendly abbey grounds, made his heart beat fast with anxiety and real fear. Suddenly he plunged knee-deep into an oozy pocket of ground; the soft mud sucked at his feet and he had great difficulty climbing out onto a relatively dry hillock of marsh grass. He found himself trembling all over, partly with fright, partly because of the damp chill of the air which seemed suddenly to strike into the very marrow of his bones. He was in real peril now and he knew it. Had not the hermit spoken of bogs and quicksands? And this horrible cold seemed to have taken the strength and courage right out of him. He struggled on, moving with less care because of his panicky fear. The fog grew thicker still. He could scarcely distinguish water from reedy land and could not tell whether the next step would rest on firm ground or plunge him into deep water again. Then for a little while things seemed to go better; he found himself upon a low bank of fairly solid earth with slow flowing water apparently beside it. Once he stept off it and down so abruptly that he would have lost his balance and fallen in completely had he not grasped at the tough reeds and pulled himself up. He increased his speed, panic again driving him, and suddenly lunged forward, sprawling full length into mud and ooze. He attempted to stand up but a sharp pain ran like fire up his leg from his ankle, and the unstable earth gave him no footing. He struggled, groaning, only to sink deeper into the treacherous bog. Then, summoning all his strength, he wrenched himself free of the clinging mud, and pulled himself to the bank again. On hands and knees he managed to climb along it, and felt its firmness beneath him with incredible relief. He tried again to stand, but could not bear the pain in his ankle and leg; even crawling on hands and knees was agonizingly difficult, yet anything was better than staying near the quaking bog, so he struggled on. The bank rose gradually and the earth became firmer; marsh reeds gave place to clumps of low willows; and finally he made out the dim outline of a sizable tree, its upper branches lost in the mist, the bole of it hearteningly substantial to the touch.

The boy crawled close to the tree and leaned against it, utterly exhausted. Chills wracked him, giving place now and then to feverish heat. He must be ill, and it became plain to him that he could go no further; he must stay where he was until the fog lifted. At least he was on firm ground and as dry as any place could be in the drenching mist. He might call and shout for help; possibly some peasant would hear him and come to his aid. But no, the village folk went mostly in another direction, to the peat bogs. Still, he would try. He shouted with all his strength, then listened. No sound at all; even his own voice seemed muffled in the woolly gray air. The cold shook him so he could scarcely think; when he tried to consider his position clearly, fear gripped him again.

"God and Mother Mary come to my aid!" he prayed. "Help me, bring somebody to me! I can't do anything more myself."

As so often happens, prayer quieted him. He relaxed a little and huddled closer to the tree trunk as
if it might warm him. The intense chill was giving
way to waves of heat and he began to feel drowsy.
Then he must have slept for a little while.

When he awoke the fog still lay thick about him
but the silence of the swamp was broken. Perhaps it
was the sound that had awakened him. It seemed at
first to drop out of the air above him and at the
same time be round about him, breaking in upon
him from all sides; a noise of wailing and lamenting,
women's voices, now low and sobbing, now high,
wild and keening. Hugh sat up from the bole of the
tree against which he had been leaning, and peered
searchingly into the fog. He could see nothing and,
for a few moments, could hear nothing. Then it
came again, the wailing of many voices, more distinct now and nearer, seeming to come from down
the stream. He made out another sound, distinct
from the wailing, the rasp of oars in rowlocks and
the rhythmic dip of blades in quiet water.

Suddenly, as if brushed away by a giant hand, the
fog lifted and Hugh saw the low afternoon sun slanting through willow branches and lighting up the water below the bank at his feet. It was a broad, slow
moving river or, perhaps, an estuary of the sea, and
on the opposite side a soft, well-tended greensward
sloped down to the water's edge. The voices and the
dip of oars grew louder, nearer, and around a curve
in the stream came a low barge. Men in dark clothing plied the oars and on the deck was a company

of women making lamentation. In the midst of them was a bier with rich crimson coverings, and on the bier rested the form of a man, large, clad in shining chain mail, with a golden crown on his head. The ladies, too, were richly clad in long gowns of blue and purple, green and scarlet, and their white veils and wimples moved softly in the breeze caused by the moving boat. The hair of each was long and plaited with gold, hanging over the shoulders and down to the knees, and they all sparkled with rich gems on hands and wrists and girdles, and on the head of each rested a thin fillet of gold.

The barge grated on the shore of the opposite

bank, the dark men left their oars and, taking up the
bier with the dead king on it, they carried it onto
the greensward, the queenly women following after.
Slowly the sad procession moved across the grass
and the slanting sun fell upon them, making a pattern of long lights and shadows through the tall
trees beyond the bank. The wailing of the women
rose higher, clearer, wilder, and then began to die
away as they went further and further from the river.

Now a strange thing happened to Hugh. It seemed
as if he shook himself loose from his sodden, aching
body, stept out of it, as it were, and walked with
light and easy step down the bank to the water's
edge. And, as if the water of the river had been
glass, he moved easily across it and ran with feather-
light step after that strange procession. He caught
up with it in the midst of a wood of tall trees, and
the light was dusky because of all the interweaving
branches and the cover of leaves. The wailing of the
women took on a muted note, sorrowful, rhythmic,
but no longer wild and high. They moved on and
on, and Hugh followed, scarce seeming to touch the
forest path over which he passed. Oak and ash and
thorn tree and tall sycamores gave place at last to
apple trees, all blossoming and a-buzz with bees. It
passed through Hugh's mind that this was strange in
late September, but no matter, the trees were pink
with bloom and the air sweet with the scent of them.
The wailing ceased as the company advanced under
the laden branches, as if sadness, even grief in the
presence of death, could not abide in the midst of
such a miracle of loveliness. And then, suddenly, the

orchards vanished and Hugh found himself standing on the edge of the abbey grounds. The procession of women and the men bearing the bier were going on directly toward the Old Church, but something stayed Hugh so that he could no longer move. He watched them and heard again the lamenting of the women and then an answering chant coming from the cloisters, the rich intoning of the funeral service as a company of monks came into view, strange monks whom he had never seen before. He remained where he was, his legs and body grown suddenly so heavy that he could not stir. And then the fog came folding down again; rough-edged gray wool, moving silently, swiftly in from the sea, blotting out trees, conventual buildings, and all that group of folk, queens and monks, and the dark dim figures that carried the bier. It enveloped Hugh, pressing down upon him, covering him till he could see nothing but an impenetrable mist.

He stirred and moaned as a stab of pain ran up his throbbing leg. The marsh was alive with sound; frogs boomed, a night bird cried, and myriads of insects buzzed and droned and sang about his head. He was leaning against the bole of the willow tree, twilight had fallen and night would come on apace. Hugh was on fire with fever, his head swam, his body ached, yet, strangely enough, he felt neither anxiety nor fear. A voice seemed to be ringing in his ears and the words held him as of being infinitely important.

"Between the two pyramids," it seemed to say,

"outside the Old Church, between the two pyramids. Dig there."

He must have slept again for he awoke with a start, hearing a bell very faintly in the distance. Listening intently, he thought he heard his name called. Yes, someone was shouting, hallooing. It was pitch dark; a night without stars, and, though the fog had lifted somewhat, it still lay thinly damp upon the earth. Hugh roused himself, listened again. A man's voice calling, then a higher, shriller voice that might be Dickon's. Summoning all his strength he shouted back. "Dickon, Dickon, I am here." His voice sounded hoarse and weak. Would they hear him? He cried out again and yet again. The jangling of the distant bell ceased for a few moments and then came an answering cry.

"Hugh, lad, keep on calling! We are coming."

At last, straining eyes and ears, he spied a light through the willow withies and reeds along the bank, heard the bell clanging nearer, the crackle and swish of broken underbrush, and there was Dickon beside him! And another figure was towering above him, Bleheris, with his stone lantern in one hand, the bell which he had been ringing in the other.

Hugh found himself crying with relief and weakness, like a sick baby. And he was sick, no question about it. His teeth were chattering again with chill and his head was dizzy and confused. When he tried to stand up his knees gave way as much from weakness as from the pain that shot up from his ankle. He would have fallen had not the hermit caught him in his strong arms. He felt himself lifted tenderly, firmly and, clasping his arms about the old man's neck, he suffered himself to be carried, scarcely realizing what he did or why.

Dickon took the lantern and led the way. The buzz and whir of night insects blended in Hugh's ears with the swish of withies as they pushed their way through them. The light in Dickon's hands flashed and winked and trembled. He kept his eyes on that with a grim, determined fascination, as the world reeled and tilted up and down about him, and he clung to the warm, strong, supporting shoulders of Bleheris. By the time they had got him to Beckery the boy had lost consciousness and was muttering incoherently in his fever. Carefully and tenderly the hermit laid him on his own straw pallet in the corner of the hut, and spread the rough blanket over him, adding two ancient and torn, but warm sheepskins, as the boy alternately shivered and burned.

Hugh never knew how long the old man nursed and tended him without a place of his own to sleep, and almost without rest or food. Dickon told him something of those days and nights of his illness after it was over, but in his memory it remained an indefinite period of aching limbs and thirst, of fierce burning fever and gruelling chills, of restless tossing sleep and confused dreams that were as real to his mind as they were fantastic and impossible in actuality.

There came a day when he opened his eyes with a feeling of stability, of being his actual self again, and looked at his surroundings in mild curiosity and wonder. He was too weak even to feel surprised, though he had no recollection at the time of having been carried to Beckery and put into the hermit's bed at all. The old man was kneeling beside him crooning and humming like a comfortable tea-kettle. When he spied Hugh's eyes upon him, he put a large, gentle hand on the boy's forehead and then nodded with satisfaction.

"Good!" said he, "the fever hath abated. Here, child, drink this healing brew and then sleep again. Praise God and His blessed Mother, thou art at last on the mend!"

Hugh drank the bitter potion uncomplainingly and slept again. When he woke a second time he felt distinctly better. He even tried questioningly to move a leg a little, and found that it was not too heavy as he had fancied. One ankle twinged with pain occasionally and he realized that the reason it was heavier to move than the other was because it was thickly wound about with bandages.

"What happened to me?" said he, surprised again at the weak sound of his own voice and the effort it took to say anything.

"Thou hast been sick, grievous sick with the swamp fever, but thou art better now."

Hugh smiled up at the gaunt old face above him. A sudden peace and security seemed to have descended upon his mind, and the feeling of mutual understanding that had always existed between him and the hermit, flooded over him in a wave of affection. He said nothing but Bleheris caught the sense of what he was feeling. Tears came into his eyes and the two looked long at each other, without need of words.

At that moment the doorway of the hut was darkened by a figure and Hugh heard the familiar voice of Dickon outside. Brother Symon, the almoner, entered with a basket on his arm, followed closely by the boy carrying another.

They were overjoyed to note Hugh's improvement. Frequently, Dickon told him, Brother Symon had come with food and medicines, and he himself had not missed a day, but this was the first on which Hugh had recognized him. They had wanted at first to carry him back to the infirmary, where he could have better care, but Bleheris would not hear of their doing so, and had become so wild when they had urged it that they had given it up. Also, it did seem risky to them to try to carry the boy so far when he was so acutely ill.

"And now," finished Dickon happily, "you will soon be back in the cloisters again. Brother John has been desperate without you—and—Hugh," he bent down to whisper, so that the two men would not hear him, "I've a new notion about our search for the hidden treasure—"

Suddenly there flashed into Hugh's mind the memory of his strange experience out on the marsh in the fog and those words ringing in his ears. "Between the two pyramids, outside the Old Church—dig there." Had it been only a sick dream or was it a vision that meant something? Or had it really happened? Master Bleheris had suggested that when the fog lay thick upon the valley below the Tor, shapes and forms not of this world might be abroad, riding in the gray mists. He must tell Bleheris about it, and Dickon, but not now. His eyes were already growing heavy with weariness; he was too tired to speak further.

XI. here lies Buried

THE NEXT DAY Hugh told Master Bleheris of his curious dream out in the marshes of Avalon. Or was it a dream? It had seemed so real. As he thought back over the experience he could hear again the dip of the barge's oars in the water and the wailing of the women, he could see the glint of gold in the crown of the dead king and the outline of his large body half-hidden under the crimson pall on the bier. He could even smell the damp earth of the greensward at the edge of the abbey grounds and feel the springiness of it under his feet. A thousand small details came to mind as only happens when one passes through an experience intensely real and never to be forgotten.

Yet now, in the light of common day, Hugh tried to tell himself that it must have been only a dream.

The hermit listened as he recounted it with increasing intensity of attention. He had carried the boy out of the airless hut and laid him in the shade of the big willow, for the day was unseasonably hot. Now he leaned over him as if he feared lest a single word escape his ears. His eyes burned with eagerness, his pale gaunt face flushed, and his long powerful hands clenched and unclenched themselves as the narrative proceeded. When Hugh came to the end he drew a great sighing breath.

"Between the two pyramids," he repeated, "outside the Old Church; we must dig there. Aye, it is most right and fitting!"

He began to stride up and down restlessly and Hugh, watching him, felt his own excitement grow keener.

"But what do you think it all means, Master Bleheris?" he asked, raising himself on his elbow. "Who was the old king and why should it be so important to dig in that particular spot—unless—unless—?"

"That was King Arthur, undoubtedly." Bleheris paused in his restless striding and spoke with awe and conviction. "None has ever known where Arthur, the greatest king in the world, lies buried. There is a saying in the ancient Welsh tongue which goes thus:—

" 'A grave there is for Mark, a grave for Uther,
A grave for Gawain of the ruddy sword;
But for Arthur's grave—only a mystery.'

"For a long time folk believed that he had never died at all and that he would come again from some hidden fairy world to succor England when she had special need; or to usher in again a time of vision and adventure. To Avalon they bore him, the old stories say, to be healed of his wounds, or else to die, if so God willed."

"To Avalon!" repeated Hugh. "And that's what the peasants call the country round our Glaston, especially the marsh land between Tor Hill and Beckery, the very place where that strange vision came to me!"

The hermit nodded his great head solemnly. "Exactly," said he, "Avalon; and mark you, lad, how things are shaping toward the solving of our sacred mystery."

"The mystery of the lost Holy Grail?" whispered Hugh as the old man paused.

He nodded his head again. "First the sword," he continued, "Excalibur. Think you it had lain in the mud of the salt marshes all those centuries since it was cast away? Lad, it would have rusted into nothingness long ago. There be those who know, both in this world and in the land of spirits and fairy folk, angels and demon powers; those who know when the time is ripe for the unveiling of great mysteries, for miracles—"

"Miracles?" said a voice behind him, and Bleheris turned with a start to see Dickon, his eyes round, his face eager. Hugh had seen him coming up the path from the marshes for his daily visit but the hermit had been so absorbed in his own thoughts and words that he had neither heard nor seen him. "Miracles?" the boy repeated. "Who is talking about miracles? Has anybody seen any hereabouts?" He looked around as if he expected to find a very real and tangible one lying on the ground at his feet.

Somehow the matter-of-fact way in which the boy spoke changed the atmosphere. In spite of his joking habit of thrusting his cap on a sunbeam to see if it might by any chance stick, things that were not solid, that you could not see and hear and feel, were not real to Dickon, and a miracle would have to be a very obvious one before he could see it. This practical side always seemed to jar a little on the visionary old hermit. Hugh turned again to Bleheris, a little uneasily. He was staring wordlessly at the boy, his face showing all too clearly the conflict of his emotions, annoyance at having his world of wonder and dream and mystery broken into, and a sense of loyalty and even affection, which had been growing in him as the two had shared daily their anxiety over Hugh.

"Tell him," said he at last, addressing Hugh. "Tell him your adventure in the world of fog and shadows out yonder. And tell him, Hugh, that we must take up the quest again, the sword and the quest. Because of my negligence, boy, it has been too long neglected; aye, I will confess it, and because there is something about yon oblate that is—" He seemed for the moment unable to find the phrase which would express what he wanted to say, but continued before either of them could speak. "Yon oblate hath always the effect of bringing my soaring spirit back to earth, he hath nothing in common with dreams and shadows and other world creatures—he is of this earth."

Dickon grinned and Hugh burst out laughing. It was so true! Yet were they not seeking that which *was* real and solid, a Holy Cup that actually existed? And, if so, Dickon certainly might be more valuable in the search than the mad Master of Beckery himself. But was the quest indeed for something that one could hold in one's two hands? Vaguely, uncomprehendingly, yet surely, Hugh felt that the Holy Grail was something infinitely greater, more meaningful than any object fashioned by man's skill out of wood or stone or metal. And that dream adventure of his in the fog out in the marshes of Avalon, was that perhaps a hint, an indication of the otherworldly side of the whole thing?

Bleheris and Dickon had seated themselves on the ground beside him and were waiting for him to begin. He told the story again, and this time it seemed to him in nowise a dream but an actual experience.

When he had finished, his listeners both kept silent

for a long moment, each thinking his own thoughts. Characteristically Dickon was the first to step from thought to action. He jumped to his feet.

"By all the saints, what are we waiting for?" said he. "You get a dream—all about King Arthur and Avalon—the time and place where your books says the Grail once was, and the dream tells you to dig, and where! Let's go to it!"

"Wait a bit, boy, wait a bit!" Bleheris held up a detaining hand. "All must be done in a way fitting and proper or the vision will leave us. It must be Hugh who puts pick into the earth first."

"That's so," agreed Dickon, sitting down again. "And, of course, we must tell Father Abbot. We can't go digging by ourselves and without permission in the monks' cemetery. How soon will you be well, Hugh? And shall I tell folk, or shall we keep this secret till you get back to the abbey?"

"Tell them about the dream," said Hugh, "but don't say anything about what we hope to find buried there between the two pyramids."

"You mean the Holy Grail?" said Dickon.

"Aye," said Hugh. "That is what we are hoping for, isn't it?"

"Buried with King Arthur, as indeed it might well be," added the hermit. "Not only the place but the time is fitting. The sword, Excalibur; King Arthur's sword. Did I not tell thee, my finding it was but a short time back—and—other things."

"Aye, Master Bleheris, you were speaking of the sword when Dickon came in. Tell us more. Surely now there must be no secrets between us three."

The old man nodded but could not suppress a hesitant and doubtful look at Dickon.

"You said that your finding the sword was near a miracle," Hugh prodded him on.

"The dreaming mood was upon me." The hermit leaned his big frame against the willow tree close to Hugh and, keeping his eyes upon him and away from Dickon continued, his voice growing softer, more reminiscent. "My mind teemed with memories of old tales, of romance and brave deeds in the days of King Arthur and his knights. I was wandering in the lowlands over by the sea when, suddenly, my foot nigh trod upon it, the sword with its iron hilt all brown and rusty, and its great blade broken at the edges, dull and blunted. I picked it out of the ooze where the low tide had left it and brought it here. I cleaned and polished and sharpened it; I slept with it beside me; I loved and cherished it almost like a live thing. And then the dreams began to come to me again thick and fast, dreams of Arthur's day all mixed with the memory of stories that I told in Wales in my minstrel days, stories that I had forgotten, and forget again as soon as the dream leaves me."

He sighed, lost in thought for the moment.

"And then? What happened next?" urged Hugh quietly.

"And then," continued Bleheris, rousing himself. "I began to wander again far and wide, the old stone lantern in my hand, the bell at my girdle to ward off evil spirits, and frequently the great sword in my other hand, held high like a cross. It seemed to lead me out over the marsh lands and to the hills, Chalice, Weary-All, Tor, and back again to St. Joseph's Chapel. I could not guess why my steps were drawn over and over again to the Old Church, deserted for so long. And then, one time, I found the entrance to the passage down into the Cave of the Well."

Dickon started and opened his mouth to say something, but Hugh made violent signs to him to keep still. The old minstrel was sinking into one of his absorbed, dreamy moods in which an interruption would startle and annoy him and be fatal to the continuation of his narrative.

"Inch by inch, not once but many times, I explored that cave for hiding places, for chests of treasure. I knew what it must be, a stage in the underground way where precious things must once have been hidden. And then, not many months since, I found the passage from the Cave of the Well to that stone-lined room with its entrance cunningly concealed by the aumbry doors. And along that passageway were niches and alcoves that must once have held treasures beyond count! How I hoped and prayed and hunted, my heart in my mouth, for that Sacred Vessel, the Holy Cup—but it was not there, it was not there."

Dickon could contain himself no longer. "What *was* there? By the saints, I wish *I* had come upon that passageway! Maybe there were all sorts of relics and saints' bones and things I could have added to my collection!"

Bleheris slowly and meaningfully nodded his head. "Aye," said he, "there was much. The great quest was closing in closer all about me, though I knew it not. My heart failed me, grieving that I had not found that one treasure—but—look you!"

He rose, moved swiftly into the hut and dragged from thence the ancient black oak chest that Hugh had been wondering about ever since he had first seen it. Throwing open the lid he began to take out its contents, handling each object with infinite care and laying it beside Hugh so that both boys might see. There were a hauberk of linked mail, silvered, that glinted and shone in the sunlight, and a long, strong lance of tough ash-wood, its iron tip blunted as with many battles, a mailed gauntlet set with gems and a helmet of metal shaped like a peaked cap with a bit of frayed silken cloth tied to it, a scarf maybe, or a belt once worn by some fair and noble lady and given by her to her knight. Only shreds and tatters remained, yet one could tell from these the texture of it, heavy and rich and finely woven, and in the knot close to the helmet a glowing red gem still clung to it.

Dickon whistled softly. "And these must once have belonged to some knight who rode about adventuring, doing great deeds of valor," said he, his gay matter-of-fact boy voice subdued and awe-filled for once.

"A knight indeed, and very like a knight of the Round Table, for all these things be of King Arthur's day." The old hermit's great powerful hand touched first one object, then another, with gentle carefulness.

"But how do you know these things had anything to do with King Arthur?" asked Hugh a little skeptically.

"It is because of *this,* I know," said Bleheris, taking from the chest a final object wrapt in soft linen.

The boys watched breathlessly as he unwound it and, laying the wrappings aside, held in his hands with infinite care and tenderness a crystal cross about a foot and a half square, even, with spreading ends, transparently clear, unblemished, lovely beyond words.

Hugh and Dickon both exclaimed in astonishment, not only because of its beauty, but because both recognized at once that it was the cross Bleheris had drawn on a stone for Hugh, and the very cross the picture of which had adorned the chart and some of the other pages belonging to *The Book of the Seynt Graal.* Dickon seemed even more excited than the other.

"It's the same!" he whispered. "Hugh, I found that figure cut in the stone of—"

But Hugh nudged him to be quiet, for the hermit was speaking again.

"This crystal cross was there among all these things," said the old man, "and it is the one that was given to King Arthur by Our Lady Herself. It was in the days of great adventuring when all the knights of the Round Table had gone forth to seek the Grail." He paused for a long moment, then shook his head sadly. "The story, once I knew it well, but alas I have forgotten it again. Only I know She gave it to King Arthur, after a vision—"

"Why, *I* know that story!" said Hugh, sitting upright as the truth flashed upon him. "It is in the broken book! I know! I pieced the ending of it together a long time ago. He went to a chapel in an island surrounded by marshes—"

Bleheris, with a great sweep of his hand, indicated the marsh meadows all around them.

"Beckery!" cried Hugh. "It *could* have been Beckery! The book said 'The Chapel Perilous'—"

"Aye," declared the hermit, "and so was this chapel once called; the stones lie scattered, the walls are down, the altar vanished, but the very spot whereon we are now sitting was once called by that name. But go on, boy, what happened to King Arthur here?"

"He had a vision," continued Hugh, "not here but some place else, and he was bidden to go, in the dead midnight, to the Chapel Perilous, and there he found a Mass being said by an old, old priest. And Our Lady appeared out of the shadows and assisted in the celebration, and after the service was over she gave Arthur an even cross of clear crystal. I had forgotten the story and a good deal of it was missing—still is, in fact—and I never did understand why She gave him the cross or what it signified."

"And this is it!" Dickon touched it gently as it lay in the hermit's lap. "And you found it with those other things, in the passageway to our vault?"

"Yea, I told thee it was so," Bleheris impatiently brushed the boy away, his mind having caught upon something else. "But there is something hidden in thy speaking, Hugh. The story, where did'st *thou* come upon it? No minstrel knows, no one in all the world knows those stories of King Arthur and the Grail save I, myself—I, alone. A *book,* saidst thou?"

Hugh told him then, impulsively, all about the broken book in the Painted Aumbry, how he and Brother John had found some written-over pages belonging to it, and then how he and Dickon had found more in the chest in the treasure vault.

Bleheris listened with eager intentness and, when Hugh had finished, still sat gazing down at him with eyes wide in his pale face, his lips parted in astonishment.

"The lost book!" he cried at last. "The lost *Book of the Seynt Graal!* And now the vision of the burial of King Arthur. Boy, do you not see how all the hidden forces are working together? The time has come! It must surely have come, when the mystery of the vanished Holy Grail will be revealed!"

He wrapt up the crystal cross carefully again, and then gathered together the other treasures he had spread out for the boys to see and replaced them in the chest, muttering the while, half to himself, half to the two, who were silently watching him.

"I must see that book," he said again and again, and then, after he had dragged the chest back into its accustomed place in the hut, he stood in the doorway looking first at Hugh, then at Dickon.

When he spoke again his voice sounded as if he were on the defensive, as if they had been arguing with him.

"They are mine," he said positively, "all of them, mine! I found them; I have cleaned them, cared for them, cherished them, these treasures of King Arthur's

day. The book should be mine also—and the Cup—
the Sacred Cup—if ever the saints permit us to see
it!" He sighed wearily.

Hugh felt almost as if a cold wind had blown
over his spirit. He had grown to love Bleheris, to
feel intimate and companionable with him, to understand his wavering moods and to have faith in
the fine and tender side of him that lay like a rocky
foundation underneath those flighty and tempestuous seizures. But now he knew, somehow, that the
old hermit had struck a false note, that he would
never find his heart's desire if he sought it selfishly,
possessively. He thought of the Benedictine rule that
a monk should consider nothing, even the clothes he
wore and the bed he slept in, his personal property.
In spite of the fact that the idea was carried to an
extreme, he sensed a humility and idealism in the
way the brothers avoided the use of those little words,
my, mine, my own. He said nothing, only looked at
Bleheris wistfully, hoping he would change his mood.
But the old man seemed to have turned definitely
glum and irritable. He dismissed Dickon with little
ceremony and carried Hugh back to his straw bed in
the hut without another word.

When Hugh at last went back to the abbey, fully
recovered, he found, to his surprise, that the monks
regarded him with curiosity and interest. The story
of his vision in the marshes had been spread abroad.
Brother John almost immediately asked him to repeat the whole of it in every detail, and then he
must tell it over and over to other monks, among

them to Brother Symon, who listened with shining eyes but said nothing; and finally even to Abbot Robert himself. The good father summoned him to his own quarters and questioned him minutely, coming back again and again to those final words so unforgetably written on Hugh's memory:

"Between the two pyramids outside the Old Church; dig there."

The abbot gave orders that digging should be begun as soon as possible. Hugh was given the honor and privilege of first breaking the sod, and then two strong lay brothers from the grange went to work at it. Nobody seemed to have time to think or talk about anything save what the busy picks and shovels might unearth.

The monks surrounded the space between the two pyramids with screens, that their labor should not be under the continual view of the curious. But Hugh was allowed to watch the proceedings whenever he had a mind to, and nobody seemed to object to Dickon's being with him. The two were permitted to lend a hand with the digging whenever they wished. It was curious to see how the different monks took the matter, and listen to the buzz of gossip among them. Most of them were as vague in their ideas as they were superstitious. Relics, the bones of some saint—no? A king then? Arthur? Some of them apparently had never heard of King Arthur. But they expected a miracle of some kind. There had been instances in other abbeys.

Tongues wagged and clacked, but Hugh noticed

that the few to whom some hint of the story of the long lost Holy Grail had been vouchsafed said little, yet carried in their faces an eagerness, a barely masked fire of desire and wonder. Brother John, Brother Symon, and Bleheris, most of all, hovered over the diggers impatiently, tirelessly, and the boys knew that they were looking for something infinitely more important than the discovery of the tomb of a king, be he ever so famous.

The diggers had got down fifteen feet or so and nothing more interesting than a few bones had been uncovered. One late afternoon, just before Vespers, only Hugh and Dickon had remained, watching and giving an occasional hand at the work, when things began to happen. The picks of the diggers struck something hard, metallic. The workers cried out excitedly, the two boys scrambled down into the hole, and all began feeling about in the damp earth with their hands. Dickon got hold of it first, something large, cold, heavy. With a huge effort on the part of all four, they overturned a great iron cross which was lying face downwards. Dickon climbed out of the hole and ran to get more aid; monks and lay brothers came hurrying from all directions. The news spread like wild-fire; something had been discovered at last between the two pyramids! Someone brought strong hempen rope and extra shovels. The cross was hauled up out of the excavation and laid on the ground. Eager hands brushed the dirt from the inscription which was on the underside of it. Brother John pushed everybody aside so that he could kneel close and bring his nearsighted gaze to bear upon it.

An expectant hush followed as he read and translated the half-obliterated inscription:

" 'Here lies the great King Arthur, buried in the Isle of Avalon.' "

Then came a rush of talk, more excited than ever. Abbot Robert, who had been summoned, bade the diggers climb down into the hole again and dig further. They did so at once and with feverish haste, their picks flying and falling in quick alternation. The onlookers watched, tense, eager, silent again. No one spoke a word and only the dull sound of iron cutting into soft earth broke the stillness. Then a fresh tremor of excitement ran through the crowd. One of the picks had again struck something solid. Hugh and Dickon who had managed to keep their positions in the forefront of those at the rim of the hole, though they were not permitted to go down into it again, never let their eyes wander from the diggers for a moment!

Slowly, very slowly in spite of the eagerness of the workers, a huge, rough hewn, long box of oak came into view. Without waiting to get it entirely out of the earth in which it was embedded, the diggers set to work to pry the lid from it. With relatively little effort they got it open and all gazed down at the contents with silent astonishment. Inside reposed the bones of a human being, large beyond those of an ordinary man, the skull pierced as if with many wounds. Beside it lay a heavy golden crown rich with inset gems, and at the feet were the bones of another figure, small, delicate, the bones of a woman; and a long thick strand of human hair that glinted as yellow as buttercups in the sun, and as fresh and living.

"Arthur, the King," murmured Brother John in an awed whisper, "and Guenevere, his queen. Peace be unto their souls!" He crossed himself as in the presence of something holy. A solemn silence lay over the company standing there. Dickon broke it by suddenly scrambling down into the deep excavation.

"A miracle!" he cried huskily. "Her golden hair! See how it shines!" He reached over the edge of the rough, hollowed, oak coffin as if to touch it, and immediately the gleaming tresses dulled and there was naught but a little pile of gray ashes. Or had it been only a trick of the sun caught by a gem in the fillet of gold that lay half-concealed by the ashes, a thin little jeweled crown?

It took many hands, strong cords of hemp, and much labor to get the huge coffin out of the ground and beside the iron cross that had been buried face down over it. Then the brothers formed themselves into a great procession with a cross-bearer and Father Robert at the head, and novices with incense following after. They bore the relics and the iron cross with chanting and singing, in all solemnity into the Abbey Church of St. Mary and there laid them down in the north transept, to await a special day which would be set apart for the shrining.

The delayed Vespers followed immediately. Afterwards, during the short period before Compline, when talk was permitted, the whole community burst into excited conversation.

The bones of King Arthur and Queen Guenevere!

Found miraculously through the vision of a boy, lost in the fog out in the marshes of Avalon!

Yes, Hugh—*their* Hugh, the lad Brother John was turning into a scribe!

The bones would probably be enshrined, with great pomp and ceremony, under the floor of the chancel near the High Altar.

The king must be told! Couriers must go at once with the news to the royal court in London Town.

The record must be written down in full detail, how the grave was found, and of the miracle of the shining strand of Guenevere's hair, and how it turned to dust before the eyes of them all.

A miracle truly!

A costly shrine!

Honor and glory for our Glaston!

Dickon heard it all, never missed a sentence, as he milled about among the brothers in the common room. He was so interested in everything that was said that he did not notice for some time that Hugh was no longer beside him. Stepping out into the cloisters in search of his friend, he soon came upon him sitting disconsolately on a bench near the Painted Aumbry. Twilight was fast slipping into evening, but there was still light enough for Dickon to note the dejected droop of Hugh's shoulders and, as he drew closer, he thought he saw tears on his cheeks.

"What aileth thee, Hugh?" said he. His voice was gentle and the arm that he threw around the boy's shoulder was warmly affectionate, though the gesture was awkward.

"Oh, Dickon, it was not there!"

"The Cup, you mean?"

Hugh nodded.

"But there is so much to be excited about!" Dickon paused for a moment, then added shyly. "Do you care such an awful lot about—just the Holy Grail?"

Again Hugh nodded. "It isn't the Vessel itself," he tried to explain. "It's—it's—what it means—all the sacredness and wonder—and—and what just seeing it might do to a person's life, as it did to the knights who found it in King Arthur's day. Seems as if I never wanted anything in all my life so much as to see the Holy Grail with my own eyes."

Dickon's hand on Hugh's shoulder poked him in affectionate raillery. "You and Master Bleheris! Seems to me the one is near as loony as the other!"

"Bleheris!" cried Hugh, jumping to his feet. "Why, the old hermit never put in an appearance at the finding of King Arthur! Maybe he does not know yet! Maybe he is sick! I was thinking so hard of my own disappointment I quite forgot him! Come on, let's go over to Beckery now and see what ails him!"

"Now?" repeated Dickon, aghast. "Why, we can't! It will be dark in a little while, and black as a monk's habit going through the orchard and marshes."

Hugh looked up at the sky. Twilight was already darkening into night but across the garth, climbing up over one of the lower buildings, he could see the moon, pale still, but almost full, the harvest moon. It would grow bright and brighter.

"Look!" said he, pointing. "It will be plenty light; the moon will be high over the marshes and we can see as well as by day. Bleheris may be needing something or somebody. I don't want to wait until tomorrow."

Dickon shrugged his shoulders but moved along after Hugh who had already started across the garth, headed in the direction of Beckery. "What will Brother John do to you if you don't turn up in the dorter at the proper time?" said he. "I'll be all right if I just tell Brother Symon I was off on an errand of mercy, which, goodness knows, this is! And anyway, he doesn't thrash people. I don't believe he *could* intentionally hurt anybody. And it's a funny thing how he affects one. I've never been so good and obedient for so long in my life as I have been since I've been under him."

Hugh grinned in the dark. "You'll be hanging your cap on a sunbeam yet! As for Brother John, I can't picture his thrashing anybody either, unless some harm came to his precious books! If ever I let anything happen to that broken *Book of the Seynt Graal—!*" He left his sentence unfinished, and the two continued walking in silence for a few moments.

"Maybe we'd better tell Brother John about those pages pretty soon, all the ones we found in the chest and you have been working over."

Hugh stopped short in astonishment. It had always been Dickon who wanted most to keep the whole matter of their search, and the hidden passages underground, secret.

"But that would mean telling him the whole business," said he, "and I thought you—"

"Yes, I know, I wanted not to let anybody into those passages till I had worked out the puzzle of how Bleheris got in there myself."

"Well?" said Hugh as the other paused.

"Well—I *have* found out!"

"Oh, Dickon," cried Hugh reproachfully, "you've gone on hunting without me!"

"Just while you were sick; I couldn't put the thing out of my mind, Hugh. And you remember that day when you were getting well, I told you I had a new idea about it?"

"That's so; well, what was the idea?" Hugh felt distinctly hurt that his friend had pursued his exploration of the underground passageways without even telling him, but in a moment he realized that, even though he and Dickon were sworn brothers, this search must of necessity be carried on by each in his own way, separately at times, together at others. Hugh, for instance, could not include Dickon in his painstaking work over the pages of the broken book and perhaps, though he hated to admit it, Dickon could get along farther and faster without a lame companion in the caves and passages underground.

"You—you don't mind, do you, Hugh? I knew you would not be strong enough to go with me for some time and, anyway, the passages are empty, all of them. There just isn't any Holy Grail."

"Oh, yes there is, there must be, *somewhere!*" Hugh caught him up eagerly. "But, anyhow, I don't mind your going ahead without me. We're just that much further along. Tell me about your new idea."

Dickon hesitated. "I can show you better," said he.

"Then show me the whole thing tomorrow."

"I will!" Dickon's voice sounded relieved and he quickened his step.

The marshes were lovely in the moonlight; soft and mysterious and very still, for birds and insects had flown south or sought their winter quarters by this time. The air was snappy and chill and the smell of salt tingled in the nostrils. When they had reached the old road, higher than the surrounding salt meadows, they could see the moonlight glimmering in a long golden path far off across the ocean. A pale luminousness hung over the water meadows and the dim outlines of Tor and Weary-All looked ghostly in the distance.

At length they reached the broken causeway, crossed it single file and, stepping carefully, soon set foot on the firm ground of Beckery. They saw Master Bleheris almost at once, sitting on his customary stone outside his hut. The light of the moon shone on his white hair and beard, turning them to silver. He sat motionless, his shoulders and head drooping, and there was something on his lap that caught and reflected the light with a mirror-like brightness. So absorbed in thought was the old man that he did not hear the boys approach, and sat there so utterly still that they scarcely dared to speak to him, lest they startle him. For a long moment they stood silently, close beside him. Dickon nudged Hugh and pointed wordlessly to the object in the hermit's lap. Hugh nodded back but said nothing. It was the crystal cross that had been given to King Arthur by Our Lady Herself.

At length Hugh very gently touched the old man's shoulder and slowly, without a start or sudden motion of any kind, he came out of his reverie, looked at the boy and smiled.

"We feared for thee," said Hugh softly.

Bleheris drew a deep breath as if pulling himself back from far depths of slumber. "There was no cause for fear," said he. "I have been dreaming."

"But thou didst not come to the grave of King Arthur. They found—"

"I know very well what they found," interrupted the hermit, "the dead bones of a dead king and his queen, not the living Cup. Hugh, lad, the dreaming state came upon me and I knew, past any shadow of doubt, that the Holy Grail would not be buried there and is not buried anywhere."

"Well then, where *can* it be? Or isn't there any, really?" Dickon's matter-of-fact voice cleared the atmosphere. Bleheris put down the crystal cross at his feet and got up, stretching and shaking himself like a great dog.

"I know not," said he shortly, "but this I do know, to search further is useless—without sacrifice. Lads, when they sought, the knights of the Table Round, they gave up all that was dear to them and sought in purity of heart and singleness of purpose—and to some the vision was vouchsafed at long last, to a very few."

He picked up the cross and took it into the hut.

In a moment he came out again and stood in the doorway.

"The moon will soon be hidden in clouds," said he, "make haste while there is light. We three shall meet again—perhaps in an hour of sacrifice. Pray God that we may have eyes to see the vision when it stands before us."

It seemed to be a word of dismissal, so the two turned homeward.

"What did the old codger mean by making haste while there is light?" said Dickon as they picked their way across the ancient causeway again. "There isn't a cloud in the sky and the moon won't go down for hours yet."

"Bleheris almost always means two things when he says one," replied Hugh. "That's one reason why I like him so much; he keeps me always guessing. I'm sure I don't know at all what he meant just now, except that he is off on a new line of thought. 'Sacrifice,' he said, and 'in an hour of sacrifice.' Well, maybe it will come clear after awhile."

"Come clear!" repeated Dickon disgustedly. "How can anything come clear from such a loony?"

"Don't call him that!" Hugh objected. "I—I love him."

Brother John raised himself up on his elbow as Hugh, some time later, crept softly into the bed next to him in the hushed and sleeping dorter.

"Where hast thou been, boy?" he demanded in a stern whisper.

"I've been to Beckery, Brother John, to see Master Bleheris. I feared for him, not having seen him at the grave of King Arthur."

"I feared for *thee*, Hugh. My heart was very anxious. I am glad thou art back safe."

The monk settled down under his rough blanket with a sigh of relief.

A warm feeling flooded Hugh's heart. Brother John must be truly fond of him, else he would not have worried. It was good to be loved, even to be worried over! And good to love, and there were several now: Bleheris, Brother John, Dickon, yes, and Father Abbot in a more distant way, and Brother Symon. One could not even look at Brother Symon without loving him.

"I am sorry I caused thee anxiety," he said, not too sincerely.

Brother John grunted.

"Bleheris was all right," Hugh continued after a few moments, still whispering. "He was just daydreaming, I guess. . . . Brother John, I think I must tell thee something—the broken book in the Painted Aumbry—" He paused, raised his head and leaned closer to the little monk beside him. "Brother John, are you awake? Are you listening? I want to tell you what Dickon and I found, what I have been working over—"

A faint, uneven little snore settled into a long, rhythmic one. Brother John had not heard him. Hugh settled back in his bed with a sigh. He must tell Brother John soon—and then he, too, drifted into sleep.

If he could only have known! If he had only shaken Brother John broad awake and forced him to listen, then at least the responsibility would have been shared, and Hugh would not have felt that he alone held the fate of the broken book and its recovered pages in his own hands!

XII. WINTER AND SPRING

THE NEXT DAY Hugh and Dickon met, as by agreement, at the door of St. Joseph's Chapel. "You remember those stairs and that trap door we came up against?" said Dickon. "You know we couldn't get the thing open, but you were quite sure from the chart that the stairs led up to the Old Church."

"Yes, I know. Then I began going over to Beckery by myself. But I never did learn anything from Master Bleheris that would open a trap door or clear up the puzzle."

"Oh, but you did!" Dickon assured him. "Don't you remember how he drew a design on a stone, a cross just like that crystal cross he showed us later, even, and spread at the ends, instead of the usual

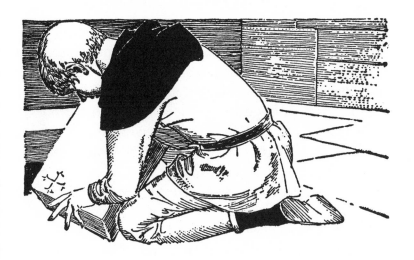

straight plain Latin cross? He told you not to be stupid, or something like that."

Hugh smiled ruefully. "And I guess I went right on being stupid! That special cross is on lots of the loose pages of the broken book—and in the unbroken part too—and I thought he meant for me just to go on plugging away at salvaging pages."

"Yes, but that is on the chart too—don't you remember? And it is somewhere else! Hugh, it is the sign, the key to the whole thing! Come on in and I'll show you!"

They opened the heavy wooden door of the Old Church and went in. Once inside, Hugh paused and looked about him. Often as he had stept into it, to hide or take out sheets of parchment from behind the loose board, he had never given the church itself much thought. The monks had not used it for generations, not since the spacious and beautiful modern

edifice of St. Mary's had been built. It was typically
Anglo Saxon in form, rectangular, without transepts,
instead of the cruciform Norman church architec-
ture, and now it was bare, empty, unadorned. At the
far eastern end, opposite the door by which the boys
had entered, was the chancel, separated from the
nave, short though that was, by a low rough stone
wall with a broad arch in the middle. Through this
arch the altar could be seen standing well away from
the back wall, with a canopy over it, a square altar of
old and darkened wood, topped with an altar stone
of rich grained marble with nothing whatever on its
dust covered surface. The walls of the Old Church
had originally been wood, over which a lead substance had been laid, a curious alloy no longer understood. The roof was still composed of it, and one
might see the edges of it around the narrow, glassless
windows. But interior as well as exterior had, at some
long past date, been covered again with wood which
had weathered with age into a rich hue; no furniture
remained in the church at all, nothing save that plain,
ancient altar.

Hugh felt suddenly and unaccountably moved, as
he stood there looking around at the little empty
building. A sense of its great age filled him with
awe, and the thought of the countless human beings,
long dead, who had knelt on the worn cold stones
of that floor, turning their eyes, sad, eager, radiant,
full of fear, adoring, as the case might be, toward
that square altar set behind the chancel wall, and
only glimpsed through the archway, impressed upon
him a feeling almost as if they were still kneeling

there at that moment. And there was something more; the boy could not have described it or explained it, but in that quiet, empty place, he suddenly felt as if he were in the actual presence of something holy, as if he must kneel down himself reverently and bow his head.

Dickon nudged him impatiently and the spell broke. "What are you gaping at?" said he. While Hugh had been daydreaming he had got the chart out of its hiding place behind the loose board and now he was pointing to an indistinct mark on it. "See that?"

Hugh looked closer. It was the even cross.

"And now," continued Dickon, his voice taking on the pride of a show man, "see what we have here!"

He moved quickly down the nave, Hugh following him, in through the arch and behind the altar. There he knelt down, scanning the worn blocks of stone with which the floor was paved. Hugh leaned over him and exclaimed in surprise at what Dickon pointed out. In the corner of one of the largest stones, almost obliterated, was the indistinct outline of the same even cross. Dickon was feeling under the edge of this slab of stone. Using both hands he forced a latch of some kind, cleverly concealed.

"Here, give me a lift," said he. "I managed it by myself once, after I'd discovered the latch, but it's 'most too much for me."

Hugh's fingers felt around the edges of the stone slab also, and then the two of them, bringing all their strength to bear, pulled it up, displaying beneath rough-hewn stone stairs leading down into darkness.

These they recognized as the steps in the wall behind the well that they had climbed before from the other end. When they had gone to the bottom of them Dickon paused, reached into a small recess beside the bottom step and drew out some rushes dipped in wax, and some flint.

"Candles are hard to come by," he said, "but I've still got two hidden in the cave by the moor entrance way, and these rushes will have to do for here."

"Then you haven't given up searching entirely?" questioned Hugh.

"Well," answered the other dubiously, "there does not seem to be anything else mysterious and hidden that we can find down here, now that we've discovered the whole way from that cleft in the moor to the interior of the Old Church. But I like the feeling that I can come down here to a place nobody knows anything about—"

"Except Bleheris," interrupted Hugh. "Funny he should be the only one to have discovered all this."

Dickon had been leading the way across the Cave of the Well as they talked, and now he paused before the wall opposite the well and scanned the flat stones that lined it. Again the faint carved outline of the even cross showed him which one covered the hidden doorway, though the stones themselves were so skillfully set in the wall that no one could possibly have guessed any single one was any different from any other.

Together the boys pulled at the slab of limestone which was held in place by a hidden latch like the one above, and when it finally swung in on creaking, rusty hinges, a large, apparently straight passageway opened up before them, leading off into the darkness. It was in good repair and high and wide enough for the big chests in the treasure vault to have been dragged through it, and every few yards there were niches in the walls where treasure might have been stored. But they were completely empty.

"Here are two passageways," said Dickon a moment later, moving on. "The right hand one goes straight to the aumbry doors, this one bearing off to the left ends shortly, blocked by a cave-in."

"Let's see it," said Hugh, taking the one indicated. It did not extend far and, as Dickon said, ended abruptly in a pile of loose earth and stones. "Maybe this once led on to the sea. Here it is on the chart extending a long ways."

Dickon merely grunted. They returned to the place where the two passageways had come together and followed the right-hand one to the doors of the aumbry. The bolts stuck badly but were finally drawn, and the two boys stepped out into the treasure vault they had originally found.

"So that is the end," said Dickon with finality. "No mystery any more to unearth, but a wonderful hideout from Viking pirates, if there were any Vikings left these days. But there aren't. I kind of wish there were."

Hugh sighed and, lighting a fresh rush candle from the stump of the one he was holding, turned back toward the aumbry doors and the way they had come.

When they emerged into the Old Church again and had managed to close the heavy trap door, they heard footsteps moving down the nave toward the chancel. Hurrying through the stone archway to see who it might be, they were surprised to see Bleheris, carrying Excalibur. His face was alight, his eyes shining, and he greeted the boys as if he had fully expected to see them there.

"Ah, my friends," said he, "well met! You have reached this sacred spot before me. You have been underground, but you have found the hidden chambers and passageways empty—empty. All that was left in them I took to Beckery. I wanted them—and I wanted more, that Other Thing. But all is as it should be. It is not hidden in the dull earth, that we shall find the Shining Wonder. Lads! Lads! After bitter disappointment and long wondering, this old heart of mine is full of joy! There are forces at work, great forces, good forces! And I know beyond question that I shall see my heart's desire before I die. But first, I have a duty to perform, a great sacrifice to make."

He moved past the boys and, with quick, determined step, went through the archway and to the foot of the altar. There he knelt and, taking the great heavy sword in both hands, he raised it aloft, his lips muttering a prayer, then laid it before the altar and bowed so low that his forehead nearly touched the ground. Then he rose and turned to the boys again, leaving the sword behind him.

"And now, Hugh, lad, the book! *The Book of the Seynt Graal.* Where is it? Show it to me!"

"The book is in the Painted Aumbry," said Hugh, "the main part of it. The pages I found in the chest and have been working over, are here."

"It should all be here," said Bleheris decidedly, "the book, the whole of it, and the sword. Also the crystal cross, all my relics and yours; St. David's altar and those other things down yonder! This is the spot most hallowed in all England. They should be here, all of them; they are not yours or mine to keep and hold."

There was an undertone of excitement in his voice, a certainty and conviction. Hugh warmed to it.

The three moved to the front of the Old Church, and Hugh took out his pile of manuscript pages, showing Bleheris the ones he had worked out and those still to be done. The old man looked at them keenly, then drew a deep sigh.

"I cannot read the script any more," said he shortly, "my eyes are grown too dim. Dost thou say truly this is part of *The Book of the Seynt Graal?*"

Hugh nodded.

"And when thou hast read it all and got it all in shape, what then?"

"Then I will take it to Brother John," the boy spoke eagerly, "and with what he has found, the pages written over, we'll be able to piece together a good part of the whole thing. And then we'll rebind, or maybe we'll make a fresh copy, and it will be the loveliest book in the whole world! We'll have blue enamel set in the binding, and maybe gems, and a clasp of gold. I know Brother John will want to make it beautiful."

The hermit grunted impatiently. "What matter the outside of the book, boy? But the inside, the story of the Grail, nobody in all the world knows that story from beginning to end! I did once, and the ancient bards of Wales who told me knew, but they are dead now, all of them, and my old memory has failed. Hugh, lad—"

He laid his large hands on Hugh's shoulders and held him, gazing passionately down from his great height into the boy's eyes. "Hugh, lad, whatever comes to pass, let *nothing* destroy that book. It must be given, dedicated here upon this altar, and then be handed on, not only to Glaston but to generations still unborn. And no one can do that now but you, *no one!*"

The winter months came on apace. The cloister walks grew bitter cold, the abbey church struck chill to the very bones in the early morning services; dorter, chapter house, refectory, all felt damp and cheerless as the low sun shone more palely through the shortening days. Only in the warming room, the calefactorium, where the monastic family gathered between Vespers and Compline, did a comfortably blazing brazier take the chill from the atmosphere. And the kitchen, of course, with its huge open fireplaces, felt heavenly warm by comparison with the other buildings. Hugh was glad indeed when Brother John's work kept them both busy in the kitchen.

There were, apparently, no more parchment sheets with the precious old writing of *The Book of the Seynt Graal* under the more modern script. Brother John sighed with disappointment whenever he commented on the very few they had recovered, and Hugh's heart warmed with secret satisfaction, thinking of the surprise he was going to give the good armarian as soon as he had completed deciphering his cache of pages from the chest in the underground vault. He had gone back to his original idea of keeping his discovery of them to himself until his work on them should be done. It would seem then like his very own gift to Glaston and, anyway, no fitting opportunity to talk to Brother John about it seemed to present itself. There was always so much to be done. They made their own glue by boiling down scraps of old vellum with oil and wax. A little cinnabar ground upon a stone with water, mixed with the pure, brilliant red dye called minium, and then beaten up with white of egg, made a base in constant demand for the backgrounds of capital letters. The rubricators added a very little liquid glue to their gold when they were ready to apply it, and after it was quite dry, burnished it with an agate or a dog's tooth. Hugh and Brother John must also keep on hand a supply of clear blue made from boiled down cornflowers gathered in the summer, and other colors from vegetable roots and powdered stone such as lapis lazuli and cinnabar. The work of the scriptorium seemed to increase daily and the two found almost more than they could do to keep the writers, illuminators, and book binders supplied with the materials they needed. But in spite of long hours over his prescribed tasks, Hugh managed to work by himself at odd times, hidden away in a corner behind the Painted Aumbry in the north cloister walk, and his pile of deciphered manuscript pages grew steadily larger. Although the cloisters were practically out of doors, his chosen nook was more sheltered as well as more secluded than any other spot he could find, so he continued to bring a handful of pages to work on there, and then return them to their hiding place behind the loose board in St. Joseph's Chapel. It was too dark inside the little Old Church to see the pale, half-obliterated script, so he only stayed there long enough to fetch a fresh supply of parchment sheets and put his completed ones at the bottom of the fast growing pile. If he had thought to look again at the chancel, half hidden by the ancient wall, and at the odd square shaped altar, he would have been as-tonished beyond measure, but it did not occur to him; nor did he ever notice the footsteps that, even while he was in the building, moved occasionally with soft tread over the uneven flooring, back there in the dim light at the east end of the building.

Hugh had grown taller and filled out. He limped still, but held himself so well that one was scarcely conscious of it. He never mentioned his infirmity, of course, but once in a while, when he grew weary be-cause of it, or watched Dickon with his two sturdy legs and his immense activity, he sighed a little to himself. It would be good to be free of handicap, to be able to walk and ride, wrestle and climb, without thought of pain or incapacity, like other lads. But he was happy enough, far happier, as a matter of fact, than he had ever been. He had often heard that life in a monastery was monotonous and dull, but he

found it not so at all. He loved his work with Brother
John, and each day brought its variety and interest in
the tasks he had to do. And whenever he was free to
roam about, there was usually Dickon to keep him
company.

The oblate still served in the almonry with Brother
Symon, work at the grange being definitely lighter
through the winter season. He had more time to
himself now, and loved to tramp through woods and
meadows with Hugh; or the two boys would amuse
themselves with the various artisans or workers connected with the abbey, for the monastery was a whole
and self-sufficient community in itself, with plenty
of activity going on all the time. Dickon never seemed
to mind the cold. The one extra woolen garment
given to every member of the conventual family suf-
ficed him, and his red cheerful face under its customary borel cap always looked pleased, contented,
and interested in everybody.

The search for the Holy Cup was, of necessity,
laid by for the time being. There seemed to be nothing more to find in the passages underground and
the increasing cold made further visits there unap-
pealing. Every now and then Hugh would wrap his
cloak tightly about him and face the winds that swept
icily over the salt marshes to visit Master Bleheris at
Beckery. But he no longer went to seek information,
only out of friendliness and concern for the lonely
old man in his self-imposed exile, and because of
the strong bond of congeniality and genuine friendship between them. Hugh liked to sit with him beside his smoky peat fire in his dingy little hut. He

liked to tell of the small daily events of the monastic community, and the hermit liked to listen, often making astonishingly shrewd or wise observations. Sometimes he seemed completely sane and would talk long and interestingly about his minstrel days, or his boyhood in Wales; sometimes he would drop into a knightly tale which would hold Hugh in fascinated attention. And once in a great while some story would come forth out of the depths of the old man's clouded memory, that had to do with the solemn, adventurous days of the Holy Grail. Then, indeed, Hugh would hang upon each word, scarcely daring to breathe lest he break the spell and stop the telling. As for the actual search, however, Bleheris said nothing at all, and when the boy tried to egg him on by hints and questions, he only looked at him with a strange light in his face. "Not yet," he would say, "the sacrifice is not complete, the hour has not struck, we are not ready —thou art not, Hugh, lad, nor yet am I."

The long cold weeks of midwinter passed at last. Lent was early that year and gave little promise of spring in spite of its name. Forty days seemed a long stretch for meager fare, much actual fasting, and the cold stormy days of late February and March. Tempers became edgy among the brothers and an air of gloom and depression settled down upon the whole monastic community, except for Dickon who kept his buoyant good spirits as unchanged and unsuppressed as the wide and always ready grin on his round, cheerful countenance. Perhaps working with Brother Symon was partly responsible for his continual happiness, for the good almoner went about his daily tasks among the poor with a tranquillity and radiance in his face that never seemed to leave him and was quite contagious.

The gloom of Lent was temporarily lifted on Palm Sunday when all the villagers poured into the monastic grounds for the ceremony of the blessing of the palms. Then the abbey church was bright with candle lights again, the music was glad and triumphant and, after the long service of High Mass, dinner was plentiful and satisfying!

But Monday morning plunged the conventual community into an even deeper heaviness and gloom. And on Thursday the altar was stripped of its beautiful carved and gilded frontal, and nothing was left upon it save the cross, still heavily veiled in purple. A plain wooden cross, painted red and with no figure upon it, was used in the processionals. Twenty-four lights set in a triangular candlestick in the sanctuary gave forth the only light in the huge dark church; and when Matins and Lauds were sung, they were put out one by one at the end of each of the psalms, making the atmosphere darker than before. Bells were muted and the hours for the offices were struck by a wooden mallet beaten on a board by one of the novices. The Still Days, people called the period between Thursday of Holy Week, and Easter Sunday.

Very early on Good Friday morning a strange ceremony began, a kind of liturgical drama which did not end until Easter morning. Before the entire monastic body, assembled in the abbey, Father Robert, clad only in the simple black robe of his order, unwound the altar cross from its veils of purple silk and laid it in a fine linen cloth, swathing it carefully as if it were a dead human body. Then he carried it to a wooden sepulcher which had been set up in the chancel and covered with rich palls of samite embroidered in gold. In an opening made for the purpose he placed the crucifix, closed the small door and knelt before it. Two tall candles were lighted at the head and foot of this symbolic tomb, and then all other lights were extinguished and the monks filed out in almost total darkness. Not a sound broke the stillness save the soft padding of furred boots, and the abbot was left alone, his tall figure motionless and bowed in prayer. Others would come to relieve his watch, and there would be no moment without its praying soul there beside the cross as long as it was buried in its wooden sepulcher.

The Lord's Day of Joy, the monks called Easter. It began in the chill of earliest dawn, but even as Hugh, with the brothers, in the big dorter, hurried into their boots and drew on their winter wraps over their habits in the shivering cresset lights, they seemed to expand with a feeling of inner joy. Down to the church they marched as usual and found a thousand candles burning. The oldest brother among them all went, with feeble, tottering steps, to the sepulcher wherein the cross had been placed, took it out, laid aside its linen shroud and bore it triumphantly to the altar. Then he went to the door of the south transept where Abbot Robert met him with two choristers bearing lighted candles.

"Whom do you seek?" intoned the old man in a quavering voice, and clear and strong rang out the three voices in reply, representing the three Marys at the tomb of Our Lord.

"We seek Jesus of Nazareth."

And then the choir in the chancel, the great company of monks behind them, and all the lay people and village folk who filled the nave, took up the exultant, triumphant song, singing until the high rafters of the roof re-echoed.

"He is not here! The Lord has risen! He is not dead, He is alive and will live forevermore! Alleluia! Alleluia!"

XIII. ROYAL GUESTS

AFTER EASTER THE whole universe changed, or so it seemed to Hugh. The dreamy quietness, the sense of the closeness of the world of the spirit which had so pervaded the very air of the monastery, especially through the happenings of Holy Week, vanished suddenly and completely, and material matters became important again. It began when a richly caparisoned horse and messenger came clattering up to the main gate and announced that King Henry, his queen, and his court were even then upon their way to Glaston and would spend two days as guests of the abbot. His Majesty wished at that time to witness and take part in the shrining of the bones of King Arthur and Queen Guenevere, and to discuss many and sundry matters concerning the abbey with Father Robert.

240

The whole place was at once thrown into a state of preparation and confusion. It was like King Henry to give them so little warning! People who knew his ways said he frequently went to bed giving no hint of any intention of moving elsewhere and then, in the early dawn, would suddenly issue orders for his court and servitors to wake up and prepare instantly to move to another spot, even to another country! Hugh remembered more than one occasion when his father had left home with barely an hour's notice, because the king had suddenly taken a notion to go off somewhere, north, east, south, or west, and desired Sir Hugh de Morville to accompany him. The boy smiled rather grimly when Dickon fell upon him, all excitement and anticipation at the news that the king and his court would be riding into the grounds of Glastonbury within two short days.

"It will be like a plague of locusts!" said he. "They

242 THE HIDDEN TREASURE OF GLASTON

came to our house once, our castle of Knaresborough. Such a stir-about and hullabaloo, such a clatter and fuss, and then when they were gone, there was nothing left—nothing in the larders, nothing in the wine cellars, nothing, literally, that wasn't too heavy to carry off! What we had not given away was just taken by the king's servants and hangers-on. I can't see why anybody should get so excited about His Majesty, Henry the Second!"

Dickon looked thoughtful for a moment. "Why, he's *king*, that's why it's so exciting. He isn't just a man, he stands for things—knighthood and deeds of honor and courage and—Oh, just everything adventurous."

Hugh grunted, but made no further comment. At the moment he had more sympathy with Brother John who was restless and irritable because his orderly routine was all upset by the confusion in the kitchen. His special corner, where he stretched his parchment skins and mixed his dyes and boiled his herbs and roots and made his glue, was swept over by cooks and stewards who paid no more attention to him and his work than if he had been a fly. After being scolded by pastry cooks, dripped on by syrup makers and bumped into wherever he went, he gave it up and retired to the cloisters, where he walked up and down, as uneasy as a duck out of water.

The guest house must be got in order for the most unusual presence of ladies, the wine cellars must be inspected carefully and replenished where necessary, tons of meat, fowl, game, and fish must be got in, and as much pastry as could be cooked beforehand must be prepared and set aside for the great days.

At last they came; outriders and heralds first, in gay clothing, with plumed caps, waving pennons and sounding trumpets. Then the knights, with the king and queen in their midst, their helmets shining in the sun, their chain armor glinting, their horses splendid in trappings of blues and greens, reds and yellows, with bridles jangling as they tossed their spirited heads. Queen Eleanor rode beside her lord on a snow white palfrey. She sat tall and easily on her red Spanish leather saddle, looking older than the king and much more regal and commanding, her scarlet, fur-edged cloak falling gracefully about her shoulders, her hands gloved in jeweled gauntlets which rested with firm grace on the slender bridle. Behind this noble company rode damsels and ladies-in-waiting, and many pages, squires, and lesser knights, and then servants, a long retinue.

Hugh and Dickon stood with a crowd of monastery folk and villagers just inside the gate, and watched them ride by. Everybody doffed his cap and gave a little ducking bow as the king and queen passed. Dickon's sharp eyes missed nothing; the strong, stocky build of the king, his thick neck, wide shoulders, and the vigor with which he rode his powerful steed; the pride in the queen's beautiful face, the long hair braided with strands of scarlet ribbon, the fillet of gold that held her white coif in place, and the smile which was both condescending and coldly gracious, as she looked out over the crowds gathered on both sides of the road to watch her pass. He noted the curled locks of pages, the rich brocaded and fur trimmed tunics and cloaks of squires and courtiers, and all the dazzle, pomp, and splendor of the whole cavalcade.

"That is Maurice, the king's minstrel," whispered Hugh, nudging his companion as an especially gaily appareled gentleman rode by, with a page close at his heels, bearing a lute and a leather book satchel. "And there goes Walter Mape, the archdeacon, the one in scarlet cloak and black cap. He is a great friend of the king's and he writes clever verses—and chronicles, and stories, too, so they say."

"That page boy looks too proud to notice his own belly button," commented Dickon rather vulgarly as a curled and gorgeous youth rode by, his nose in the air. "And there are some girls, quite *little* girls! That one on the dappled pony with the long brown hair looks younger than we are. Looks saucy, too. Know who she is?"

"No," said Hugh, following the other's unabashed and pointing finger. "Must be one of the queen's wards. Why she's got a *dog* under her arm, a little white dog—see him?"

They were all in through the gates at last, and such a chattering and laughing, such a stamping and neighing of horses, such issuing of orders and such bowings and courtly greetings! Hugh and Dickon promptly got themselves into the middle of it all. The abbot was there at the king's bridle and His Majesty dismounted and kissed him on either cheek, a formality permitted only to the great. A courtier in a blue and white tunic, fur-edged, was assisting the queen to dismount and now Father Abbot approached her and she bent gracefully to receive his blessing and kiss his hand. Lay brothers were leading horses toward the stables and squires followed with their masters' mounts. Brother Arnolf, his cowl bobbing on his shoulders and his black habit winding itself about his ankles, ran hither and yon, bowing a greeting here, issuing directions there, apportioning this group to the guest house, that to the abbot's quarters, and the servants and retainers to a little-used dormitory over the infirmary. It was all delightful, colorful, and exciting. Hugh helped the guest master in telling folk where to go. Dickon hung about the horses, fascinated by the splendid steeds, the bright trappings and gay saddle leather. He also managed to keep within sight of the young damsel with the dog and when, in the confusion and crowd of dismounting and being greeted, the small beast slipped from his mistress's arms and ran off, barking and yapping, it was Dickon who recovered him and bore him back to his owner.

The little lady's blue eyes were large with tears when Dickon bashfully approached her, but she broke into a radiant smile at sight of her pet.

"Oh, *thank* you!" she exclaimed, "thank you a thousand times! My Kenny must have been so frightened! He might have got away entirely if you had not caught him, and then my heart would have been broken, I verily believe."

Dickon, finding nothing to say, stood awkwardly

on one foot, then on the other. Luckily, at this moment Hugh came up to them.

"Greeting, fair lady," said he with a sweeping, courtly bow, "and welcome to our Glaston."

The girl smiled and curtsied in return. Dickon, suddenly realizing that his manners lacked something in the way of knightly courtesy, snatched off his round cap and imitated Hugh's bow, albeit he was ill at ease in the process. Then the three stood looking at each other, unable to get started in conversation.

It was Hugh who saved the situation by saying with courteous formality, "It is a great honor to us of Glaston to receive Her Majesty, Queen Eleanor, and all her fair ladies, of whom you are surely the fairest." (Not for nothing had Hugh been instructed in troubadour ways and manners of speech!)

The young lady thus addressed colored and then giggled. "Faith!" said she, "I be not so fine as all that! I be just Eileen, ward to the queen. I come from a castle in the north and am sent to my lady, Queen Eleanor, to be nurtured and taught manners." Suddenly her blue eyes clouded and the tears started. "I be mortal tired of being stiff and proper all day long, and sore homesick. If it were not for Kenny that I brought with me from home, I think I should die!"

All the courtly, artificial manner slipped out of Hugh like starch from wet linen. "I know what it feels like to be homesick!" said he in quick sympathy.

"And I'm—I'm so glad I found Kenny for you,"

Dickon added heartily. "If you lose him again, just tell some one to find Dickon the oblate, and I'll get him for you, if it's the last thing I do in this world!"

"So you're Dickon—and I'm Eileen—and you—?"

"Hugh," said the other, then after a moment's hesitation he added, "Hugh de Morville—you—you probably know of my father?"

The girl shook her head. She was smiling again now, a wide friendly smile that showed her even, white young teeth and brought a dimple into one cheek. "No, but I don't know many people yet, even by reputation. I'm new at court, you see."

At that moment a large scolding woman bore down upon them and whisked the Lady Eileen away.

"Watch for me after dinner," said she over her shoulder; "if I can, I will talk to you. Good-by, Dickon and Hugh; see, Kenny is waving to you!" She waggled the dog's paw in their direction and then hurried on, in the train of the large woman, toward the guest house.

The two boys watched her out of sight. "By the bones of St. Crispin," declared Dickon emphatically, "if I were a knight, I should not rest until yon damsel were my lady! One does not realize, mewed up in a monastery as you and I are, that ladies *are* good to look at and to be with, does one?"

"One does not!" agreed Hugh, "and one forgets. I thought my sisters were silly, with their troubadours making big eyes at them, and always laughing and giggling and fiddling with their hair, but the Lady Eileen—" he left his sentence unfinished.

"Let's show her around the place," suggested Dickon. "We might even take her down to the treasure vault and let her see the sapphire altar."

Hugh shook his head dubiously. "She would not be permitted to go—and besides, she would probably be afraid. Girls are not very brave, you know."

"I guess Eileen would be!" Dickon defended loyally. "Well, come on, let's see what else is new and exciting. The shrining begins well!"

The rule of silence at the dinner table was laid aside because of the important visitors, but the guests were so distributed that they seemed to stand out less conspicuously among the monastery folk than when they had arrived in a body. The king and queen and their immediate followers were entertained in Father Abbot's own quarters. The rest of the women folk ate in the guest house, and the men went to the monks' refectory, where they mingled familiarly enough with the brothers.

Neither Hugh nor Dickon caught sight of the Lady Eileen after dinner nor yet during the long afternoon, though they kept bobbing around in the vicinity of the guest house between their various tasks, always hoping they would meet her. After supper most of the guests and all the brothers gathered together on the lawn hard by the abbot's quarters, to chat together and, perhaps, be entertained by a song or minstrel's tale, for this was the time of day and the place where such things were customarily permitted.

King Henry, Queen Eleanor, and the abbot sat on carved wooden chairs that had been dragged out

from the chapter house for them, and the knights
and ladies stood or strolled about, talking to one another or, occasionally, to some of the brothers, though
most of the monks were so unaccustomed to small
talk, especially with ladies, that they held back modestly, content to watch the unusual picture of the
gay world disporting itself pleasantly in their do-
main. The twilight seemed long and the air mild for
the season, though it was cool enough for the ladies
to don their cloaks which fell so gracefully from
shoulders to ankles and displayed edging or lining of
vair, marten, or, in the case of the queen at least, soft
white ermine. The king fidgeted incessantly, crossing
and uncrossing his stocky, scarlet-clad legs. Father
Robert, sitting beside him, seemed by contrast to
hold himself unusually still. The queen sat in lan-
guid ease, not talking much, although several courtiers, in gay cloaks and tunics and modish pointed
shoes, hovered about her. Among the ladies gathered
together a little apart from the queen, stood the young
maid, Eileen. Dickon and Hugh noted her as soon
as she appeared and both stared at her in uncon-
cealed admiration as much as they dared. She was a
small person but she made the most of the inches
she had, standing straight with head held high. Her
hair, the boys noticed, had a touch of red in the
brown of it, and the long green cloak falling from
her shoulders and caught at the throat with a clasp
of gold, became her well. They wondered what she
had done with her dog; perhaps she had left some
servant to care for it. She looked tranquil enough
and smiled in frank pleasure when her eyes rested

on their eager faces. They managed to work their way around through the crowd until they were near enough to speak to her.

"Where's Kenny?" said Dickon, by way of starting the conversation.

"In the guest house, shut in. I only hope nobody will let him out!"

Dickon privately hoped he *would* get out and run away so that he could have the pleasure of finding him and returning him again.

Before Hugh could say anything there was a sudden hushing and quieting of voices and the faces of all turned toward the center of the terrace whereon the king and queen sat.

"Maurice, the king's minstrel, is going to tell a story," whispered Eileen, "and it will be so long— and I would rather go about and see the grounds and talk to you two, the way the other ladies have been talking to the knights and courtiers."

"The ladies are talking to *one* knight each," Dickon whispered back significantly. "Why don't you slip away with me a little while and we can walk and talk in the cloisters back yonder, while Hugh listens to the story."

Hugh grinned. "Go to it," said he good-naturedly. "The cloisters have plenty walking about in them already, folk who like talk better than a story! I prefer a story!" And he stuck his nose in the air in very uncourtly fashion, though he would have much preferred to join them.

But in a few moments nothing could have dragged Hugh out of the sound of Maurice's voice. The minstrel had plunged at once into a knightly tale, an odd story of Sir Gawain the Courteous and his encounter with a misshapen, "loathely" lady, who asked him to be her knight. The tale was interesting enough in itself, but what caught Hugh and caused him to hold his breath and gaze in fixed absorption on the teller, was the fact that it was a story told almost word for word in the broken *Book of the Seynt Graal.* Indeed, it was in the middle of that very story that the break came, that pages had been torn out and lost. Hugh had wondered how the tale came out; now he would hear. But what was more important to him was the realization that here, standing before him, was a minstrel who knew one of the collection of Grail stories. Perhaps he knew more, perhaps he knew the end of the whole and could tell what happened to the Grail finally, where it had been hidden, or if it had really been snatched away into heaven to be seen no more by sinful men. He could scarcely wait for Maurice to come to a close, and when he did, the king summoned him to his side to talk to him, and then others gathered around him. Hugh hung about, waiting his chance, and at last it came. Maurice strolled off in the direction of the cloisters with only the archdeacon, Walter Mape, beside him. The boy followed, hurrying to overtake him, then gently touched his arm. The minstrel paused in the middle of whatever he had been saying to Walter Mape, and the two turned and looked at Hugh questioningly.

"Good Master Minstrel," said the boy with a courteous bow, "that was indeed a goodly tale about the loathely lady. May I—sir, pray be not offended if I ask thee—I would fain know where it came from?"

For a moment Maurice did not answer and the boy wondered whether he had committed an unpardonable fault in courtesy by asking such a question. Then the minstrel spoke, graciously enough.

"It *is* a goodly tale and I am glad it liketh thee. I had it out of Wales, long since. Why do you ask?"

"The story is the same as one I read in a book," Hugh answered hesitantly, "a broken book. Half of the tale is torn away and it was right pleasant to hear the ending of it."

"What book was that?" broke in Walter Mape abruptly.

"It is a very old book, sir, *The Book of the Seynt Graal.*"

Maurice and Sir Walter exchanged meaningful glances. "And where saw you that book, boy?" continued the former.

Hugh began to feel uneasy. How much should he tell these men of the hidden treasure in the Painted Aumbry? They seemed extraordinarily interested. "It is a volume we have here in Glaston, noble sirs," said he, not knowing how else to answer them.

"*The Book of the Seynt Graal,*" repeated the minstrel thoughtfully. "Surely it could not be *the* book— the lost volume of which we have heard! Boy," he continued after a moment, "we must see that book. By my faith, I would rather set these two eyes upon it than on anything else in the world—if indeed it is *the* book!"

"It may be Brother John, our armarian—" began Hugh, but Sir Walter interrupted him.

"Nay, we would not bother the good brother with our idle curiosity. You must know, lad, that in Wales there is a tradition of a book long lost and mostly forgotten, containing the whole history of the Sacred Cup which men called, in the days of King Arthur, the Holy Grail."

Hugh nodded his understanding.

"Now and then an ancient minstrel tells a tale concerning it, such as this our Maurice has just repeated, but the sense and source of them all is not to be found either there or, so they of Wales would have us believe, in any spot on God's earth."

"Saving it might be in Avalon," added Maurice.

Hugh started. Avalon! The misty meadows between the abbey and Tor Hill, the place of his vision of the funeral barge of Arthur, and of strange tales and uncanny traditions of which Bleheris had told him.

"And so," the archdeacon was continuing, "to see that ancient book would mightily please us, being minstrels both, of a fashion, for I too create verse," he smiled wryly, "and likewise tell tales, though of an order quite different from the romances of King Arthur!"

Hugh smiled back, for he knew the reputation of the clever Walter Mape for cutting personal satire and gossipy tales of court scandal!

"But some day," the other went on, "I, too, intend to write a tale that is lovely, perhaps a story culled from the history of the Grail and its seekers. Who can tell? Come, boy, if thou knowest where the book lies, let us look upon it now, this very moment. By tomorrow we shall all be busy with the shrining and after that it will be too late."

Surely there could be no harm in merely showing them the book, thought Hugh. He felt a sudden pride that Glaston should possess a manuscript that these two men, so world-traveled and important, desired greatly to see. And yet, he felt uneasy. If Brother John were only there. He looked hastily around at the thinning crowd. The twilight was deepening.

"It will soon be too dark," urged Maurice.

"Over in the north cloister walk," said Hugh. "But if you would wait until tomorrow Brother John could show you—"

"We will ask the good armarian more about it on the morrow, if it be indeed the real thing," said Sir Walter. "A glance should tell us."

They had walked on while they were speaking and now, led by Hugh, they stood in the alcove before the Painted Aumbry. Deftly and swiftly Hugh drew out the books that covered the secret panel, opened it and, with the reverent and careful handling that he always used for it, lifted out the broken volume of *The Seynt Graal.*

Walter Mape took it in his hand while Maurice looked over his shoulder. He examined the title page, scrutinized the script, felt with practiced fingers the fine grain of the parchment and turned the volume over to its torn and mutilated back.

For several moments not one of the three spoke. Then a long, slow sigh came from Sir Walter's lips.

"It is *the book*," breathed Maurice, "there can be no doubt of it! But what of the missing pages? Sure and it would be worth a king's ransom to find them!"

Hugh's heart was beating high with excitement and pride. He opened his mouth to tell them of his long guarded secret, of the pages he and Dickon had found in the underground treasure vault and how he had been working over them, hours upon hours, to fit them together and make of the book a more nearly perfect whole. But something restrained him and he said nothing, merely let the two look their fill and then reclaimed the volume and put it carefully back in its place.

"That is indeed a treasure," said Walter Mape as they turned away. "It is without doubt one of the most precious books in the world, even in its broken and imperfect state."

"It should be the property of the king," said Maurice. "No one but His Majesty should own such a priceless volume. There is no other place in all the world where one may read those stories of the Holy Grail; they would be lost forever if anything should happen to that book." He sighed. "I would I might borrow it and con the tales. Think you the Glaston folk would lend it to me?"

Hugh went cold at the thought. He had not realized how precious to him, personally, was the knowledge that *The Book of the Seynt Graal* was there safely in the Painted Aumbry in his Glaston. If it should be lent to anybody in the trail of the restless King Henry, nobody could guess what might happen to it.

"It may be Brother John will have it copied," said he hastily; "especially if—if more pages of it should ever be discovered."

"It should be in the king's possession now," insisted Maurice.

Dusk had almost slipped into night. As they left the shadowy cloisters Hugh thought for a moment that he had seen the tall form of Master Bleheris, but he must have been mistaken, for the walks and the terrace were empty. The abbot and the king and his party had all gone into the califactorium to warm themselves around the brazier, lighted for their comfort, though ordinarily the brothers made no such concessions to the chill damp of nights so late in spring. The bell for Compline rang clamorously. Hugh went in to the vast, dim, candle-lighted church with the brothers, and listened to the familiar service. He felt vaguely troubled; he wished he had not told those two men anything about the precious treasure in the aumbry. Tomorrow he must tell Brother John all about it. Perhaps he would be angry, but no matter, he must tell him without any more delay. He would also share his long kept secret about the recovered pages he had been working over. That had been kept from him much too long. Suppose something should happen to them!

He had scarcely paid any attention to the words and singing of the service of Compline. Now they broke in upon him, claiming his ear and mind. He

sighed and something in him relaxed. The old familiar intoned words, the deep rich voices of the
men quieted him, gave him the sense of peace they
had so often given him before.

"Into thy hands, O Lord, we commend our spirits;
Guard us while waking,
Watch over us while sleeping
That, awake, we may watch with Christ,
And asleep, we may rest in thy peace."

xiv. stolen treasure

THE NEXT DAY came the shrining. All the countryside for miles about gathered at the abbey church for the great event. After Prime and High Mass which the king and queen and all the court attended, a great procession was formed. Acolytes with crosses and novices holding candles and swinging censers came first, then all the officials of the monastic community, the obediendaries as they were called. Behind them in a cloud of fresh incense swung from another group of censer-bearers walked Abbot Robert, King Henry, and Queen Eleanor and six tall and stalwart monks bearing on their shoulders the huge hollowed oak wherein rested the bones of Arthur and Guenevere. Monks and lay brothers followed, marching two by two. Hugh was there, and

Dickon somewhat further behind with Brother Guthlac and other lay people belonging to the monastic family. All around the great Church of St. Mary the procession marched. The rich voices of the choir rang full and true, the metallic rattle of chains from the swinging censers sounded rhythmically, clouds of incense filled the air, and through it innumerable candle lights flickered and glinted like stars in a mist. The nave of the church was filled with lay folk, both high and low, and when the procession had passed three times around it, they joined in, following the last of the monastery people, out through the great arched central doors. The singing increased in volume as every voice took up the strains of the old familiar hymn, "Jerusalem the Golden." Then it thinned and straggled as the marchers wound around the churchyard, circled the little, old, deserted chapel of St. Joseph, and entered the cloisters, where it drew

259

together again around the garth. Then, at last, they returned to the church.

As many as could get inside the doors did so. The king and queen and a few other important personages stood near the chancel with the abbot and priests who would perform the ceremony. To the left, just where the north transept began, stood a large tomb of shining black marble, freshly built. After the sprinkling of holy water, much censing, and the intoning of suitable prayers, the great oak coffin was lowered into this, a slab of exquisitely veined stone was closed upon it, and the shrining drew to an end.

Hugh and Dickon had craned their necks and squirmed their way through the crowd until they could see and hear without difficulty.

In the middle of the service Hugh suddenly became conscious of Dickon's fingers digging him in the ribs.

"Do you know what?" said the boy in a whisper, after he had gotten his friend's attention. "There's something else that *ought* to be in that tomb—King Arthur's sword!"

"Excalibur!" exclaimed Hugh, so loud that several turned and frowningly bade the boys be quiet. "That's so!" he whispered in a lower tone. "I'd forgotten about the sword. It *ought* to have been here—you are right. But I don't suppose Bleheris would ever have consented to give it up."

"Well, he left the sword on the altar steps of the Old Church that last time we saw him there. Remember?"

Hugh nodded.

"I'm going to see if it's still there!" Dickon began at once to wriggle through the crowd toward one of the doors, but Hugh seized his sleeve and detained him.

"You can't get it now," he whispered decidedly. "And even if you did, who would believe it was King Arthur's sword without stopping to examine it?— and anyway it belongs to Bleheris—he—" But Dickon had worked himself free and was lost in the crowd.

Hugh turned back to the ceremony of the shrining, feeling somewhat uneasy.

When at last it was all over he moved with the crowd out of the church building and began looking around for Dickon. Suddenly he appeared at his elbow and Hugh was relieved to see that he was not carrying the huge iron-hilted sword. Appearing with it at that particular moment would have been as awkward as it would have been spectacular.

"Oh, so it wasn't there?" said he. "Doubtless Bleheris has taken it off again. Well, come on, let's go over to the guest house; maybe we can catch a glimpse of Eileen."

"Hugh," said Dickon, and his voice sounded so strange that the boy stopt dead and stared at him. "It *was* there, on the altar steps, and a lot more things, too; the crystal cross and my sapphire altar, and the very best and most precious of the old hermit's treasures, all there, laid out on the steps and floor. What on earth do you think is going on?"

"I can't imagine! Do you suppose Bleheris himself brought them there? Or somebody else?—And what for? I want to see them!"

Hugh started to turn back, but just at that moment they both spied the little Lady Eileen walking across the greensward toward them. She had her dog, Kenny, under her arm but her face looked so sad and woebegone as she drew closer that all thought save concern for her promptly left their minds.

They greeted her courteously, Dickon pulling off his cap and making a quick, ducking bow as if he were in a hurry to get it over with.

"Fair damsel," said Hugh with his accustomed ease, "is there aught amiss? We would fain help you if it be possible."

"By all the saints!" Dickon broke in emphatically. "If anyone hath done thee wrong or made thee sorrowful I'll—I'll—" He left his sentence unfinished, there being no adequate threat to offer in his present state of ignorance.

"It's about Kenny," said the girl miserably. "They say I have got to give him up. He chewed my Lady Imogene's slipper last night, and he is always getting underfoot, and he yapped at one of the page boys, too, and sometimes he runs away. But I love him— and I can't just leave him anywhere. He would starve or be killed by wild beasts." The tears were flowing fast now.

Dickon looked questioningly at Hugh, who nodded back.

"Could you now—would you leave him with us?" he said. "He could live at the grange with Brother Guthlac, and we, Hugh and I, would take care of him ourselves and—"

"And he wouldn't be the first homeless creature to

find refuge in Glaston!" Hugh added with a wry little smile, thinking of his own desolate state when he was brought to the abbey more than a year ago.

"That is most kind and gracious of you." The damsel dried her tears but still regarded them questioningly. "You—you would be very gentle and good to him? And the grange—would he be happy and comfortable there? I can't bear to part with him, but it would be good to know he—he was with friends who loved him!" A trembling little sigh which was half a sob made the boys more eager than ever to do her a service.

"After dinner we will take you to the grange and show you; it is a good place, and Brother Guthlac has a way with little beasts, big ones, too, for that matter, and whenever Kenny was not with us, he would be with him."

Dickon wondered as he talked, whether Guthlac would indeed allow them to keep a pet at the grange but—well, he would just *have* to!

At that moment the bell rang for the noon meal and after it, when court and monastery folk were all settling down for an hour or two of afternoon quiet, the two boys went again to the guest house, to wait until Eileen could slip away unnoticed from the ladies and tire women and join them.

Brother Guthlac smiled good-humoredly enough when the three appeared at the grange and made their request. Then they sought out a warm, comfortable corner in an unused stall, fixed a bed and let the little dog play about and sniff his new surroundings.

"It won't be like living at court!" declared Dickon.

Eileen made a face indicative of her extreme distaste. "I am glad of that!" said she, "and *he* will be glad; I know he will! Deary me, but I am weary of all the curtsyings and mouthings and mannerings, all the stiff clothes and stiff ways! Often and often I wish I were a simple village maid in a borel frock, and could sit at ease or play all the day long. It is not easy to be a lady!"

"Nor to be a knight," added Hugh sympathetically.

"But I would like to be a knight," said Dickon. "And if I were, would you be my lady?" He blushed to the roots of his hair as the words came tumbling out. He had not meant to say that at all. And now maybe she would be offended and not leave her dog with him.

She was not, however, for she smiled in the friendliest fashion and, taking the two yellow ribbons that bound her thick braids of brown hair, she gave one to Dickon and then handed the other to Hugh.

"You shall both be my knights," said she generously. "I give you each a token of my favor. If ever I am in danger or distress, I will send for one of you, if I can; and if ever you have need of a friend at court, send me my yellow ribbon that I may know, and then I will do for you whatsoever I can." She spoke graciously and gravely, and the boys gave heed to her words, pleased and touched by them.

Then she picked up Kenny, kissed him on his soft white ear and placed him in Dickon's arms.

"We shall be going early in the morning," said

she. "Take him now and get better acquainted so I can think of him being happy with you."

The little beast was friendly enough. He was a young dog and he licked Dickon's ear and romped and played with both boys in eager, impartial puppy fashion. It was agreed between the three that Dickon should stay at the grange and keep Kenny amused while Hugh escorted the Lady Eileen back to the guest house, a mark of really unselfish devotion on Dickon's part for he would have dearly loved the few extra moments of the young damsel's society.

"You are courtly born, are you not?" Eileen said to Hugh as they walked across the greensward together.

"Aye, that I am," said Hugh, but added nothing further.

"Then you will surely be a knight some day. Remember my favor—I am truly in earnest in giving it to thee."

"I will indeed remember," said Hugh, "whether I be a knight or no."

They said little more and, when they had reached the guest house gate, Hugh had barely time to bid the little lady a courteous farewell before she was whisked away by one of the queen's ladies who had evidently been looking for her.

Dickon spent the whole night in the grange barn in order to make sure that Kenny should not be lonely. He rolled himself up in a blanket on a pile of hay and slept so soundly that, even if the little beast had howled in despair and friendlessness, he never would have known it! But in the morning he found

his small charge contentedly hunting rats in a cob-
webby corner, apparently very willing to change the
luxuries of court life for a much more exciting if
simpler one in the monastic grange.

King Henry and his court were ready betimes, and
the abbot and chief monastery folk were already gathered around the guest house and the south gate to bid
them farewell and Godspeed. Hugh and Dickon
soon spied the Lady Eileen in the chattering crowd
of women who surrounded the queen. Dickon managed to get her ear and attention sufficiently to sig-
nal that Kenny was well and flourishing, but what
with all the stamping horses, lurching litters, and
servants rushing madly about, they could not approach her close enough to do more than wave to
her as she mounted her small, restless palfrey and
went clattering by.

At last all the visitors had got off and away, the
outer gate was shut, the porter went wearily back to
his post beside it, and the rest of the brothers prepared to take up their routine wherever they had left
it.

Hugh felt Brother John's hand upon his shoulder
as he turned rather listlessly toward the cloisters.

"Come, boy," said he, "there is much to be done.
Thou dost handle the script passing well by now
and I would set thee to copying a breviary. We have
need of many more."

He sounded as if there had been no break in the
monastic days, and Hugh felt the security of customary tasks slipping over him again, not unhappily.

When they came to the Painted Aumbry, Brother

John opened the top of it and took out fresh quill pens, lead rules, a medium-sized frame on which to stretch a sheet of parchment, and various other book-making implements, and handed them to Hugh who took them to a writing desk set against the wall a little further along. The hours of the morning passed, quietly, steadily, punctuated by the regular offices, then dinner.

Hugh was glad to stretch his cramped body and aching fingers as he rose from his desk and stept from the shade of the north cloister into the sunny garth. He hoped he would have the afternoon free and could go out into the orchards and marsh lands, for buds were bursting on bushes and trees, the willows by the Brue would be a golden yellow and the air was alive with the promise of growing things.

He also wanted to look in at the Old Church and see that odd collection of things Dickon had told him about. But no such good fortune. Brother John bade him return to his work after the noontide meal.

"So much precious time hath been lost," he grumbled. "What with all this pother about kings and queens, dead and alive! Books are far more important, at least beautiful ones are, and that is what we should be making!"

They went again to the north cloister while the rest of the monastic family betook itself to its hour of reading or rest. There was no relaxing in Brother John. After Hugh had settled himself to his copying again, the armarian, flourishing a dust cloth, applied himself to the Painted Aumbry. Evidently he was suffering from an attack of house cleaning. The two worked on, near each other but not speaking. Hugh became absorbed in his parchment. He liked to make the black letters clear and straight so that a written page was as lovely to the eye as to the mind.

Suddenly he was startled by a hoarse cry. He jumped, his pen making an ugly scrawl on the good fresh sheepskin, and turned to Brother John. The monk was standing motionless, his body bent slightly, his eyes fixed upon the lower part of the aumbry.

"What is it, Brother John?" cried Hugh, hastening to him. "What is the matter?"

The little monk straightened up and looked at the boy with white face and an expression of utter desolation.

"It's gone!" he said, scarcely above a whisper. "Our treasure! *The Book of the Seynt Graal!*"

Hugh caught his breath. For a moment the cloister walls seemed to reel about him. He thrust Brother John aside that he might look for himself and see the hidden, secret cupboard, unwilling to believe what his ears and eyes told him. It was empty. The broken book had vanished.

Speechless, he looked back at Brother John. His mind registered only one scene, one thought, Maurice, the king's minstrel, and the cynical face of the clever archdeacon, Walter Mape, peering over his shoulder as he, Hugh, displayed the treasure of Glaston; the look of unmistakable greed in their faces as they gazed at the soiled and worn old pages.

"The king should own that book," Maurice had said.

"There is none other in all the world," Walter Mape had added.

Could it be that those two had taken it, "borrowed" it, ostensibly for the king's library, really for themselves, that they might pore over it and learn the age-old stories and traditions that were the loveliest in the world, and which could not be found in any other place?

Still Hugh gazed mutely and despairingly into the face of Brother John. If they had taken it, those two, then it was his fault, *he* was responsible. He should have known enough, he who had seen so many examples of the unscrupulousness of courtiers and hangers-on around the king!

"Gone!" Brother John was repeating. "Gone! But who could have taken it? Not a brother in the whole of Glaston would have laid hands upon it; few know that it is here; only one or two know what it *is*. Hugh, how *could* it have gone, and where?"

Then Hugh poured forth the whole story, not only how he had shown the book to Maurice and Walter Mape, but why he had done so; how he had recognized the story of the loathely lady which the minstrel had told as the same tale that was incomplete in the broken book.

"And, you see, Brother John, I had found a lot of those missing pages that told other Grail stories, but not the very end of the adventure, so I asked Maurice where he had got it and—"

"You had found some missing pages! Where? What do you mean?" Brother John laid a shaking hand on the boy's arm. "By all the saints, boy, tell me quickly—you say you had found—?" He left his sentence unfinished in his excitement.

Then it all came out, of course. Hugh told of Dickon's underground treasure vault, of the chest with the loose pages in it, and how he had been working over them for months now, and kept them hidden behind a loose board inside the door of the Old Church.

"I wanted to wait until they were all done," he said, tears of distress coming into his eyes. "Then I—we—Dickon and I—were going to present them to you as our find, our work, a sort of gift to Glaston. And—and it would have meant so much to me, particularly, because—because, Glaston has been so good to me—in spite of my father—and everything." His voice trembled and for a moment he could not go on. Brother John continued to stare at him without a word.

"And now the book has been taken—and it is all my fault! What good will the loose pages be without the book they belong to?" the boy finished miserably.

At last Brother John roused himself. "The minstrel and Sir Walter Mape," said he, returning to the subject of the theft. "If they have taken our book they must return it, and that right speedily! The king shall make them give it up! Come, boy, we must see the abbot. Thou and I shall mount nags and ride after the king's train."

They started across the garth, Brother John almost running. Hugh caught at his sleeve as he hurried after him.

"Brother John," said he, "I pray you, Brother John; it is my fault that the book is gone. Let me ride alone and recover it. You are—" He was about to say too old, but thought in time to stop himself. "I can ride fast, I have ridden since I was a babe in arms, except when my lameness got worse, and you can see how much better that is! I can ride on a swift horse, and—Brother John—I will bring back our book myself, no matter what I have to do to get it!"

The monk stopped so short that Hugh actually bumped into him, and stared at the boy for a long moment as if he had never seen him before.

"Perhaps thou art right," said he at length. "Thou art young and thou knowest the ways of courts and kings. I will get thee a horse now, this moment, without waiting for my Lord Abbot's permission. Canst go at once?"

Hugh nodded, his heart pounding. They turned their steps toward the grange and the boy did some reckoning on his fingers. The king's party had been gone since shortly after dawn. From the look of the sun it must be around four o'clock now. They had eleven hours start of him, at least, but with ladies in the party they must perforce move slowly. Perhaps he could catch up with them before black night set in, if he made the best of every moment. But if night came on and caught him on the lonely country roads, would he have the courage to ride on, alone and without weapons of any kind? Would he be able to ask his way sufficiently, learn which direction the cavalcade had taken, and follow along with the least possible loss of time? He wished Dickon could ride with him, but that would delay him, for the boy was no horseman. Well, he must not think of difficulties, only ride, ride with all possible speed, overtake the king and his court and recover the book!

It did not take long to find a stable man and get him a horse. Hugh looked around the big barn eagerly, hoping to catch sight of Dickon. He would like to have told him where he was going and why, but the boy was nowhere to be seen. He took time to make sure of a comfortable saddle, then forced a hopeful smile for Brother John, who was looking as if the foundations of his life had collapsed beneath him.

"The loose leaves thou didst find—" called the monk after him as he mounted and rode out through the great door, "didst say they were in the Old Church?"

Hugh nodded. "Behind a loose board, to the left as you go in." Then he was off and away, cantering over the grounds to the high road, then turning to the west as the king's party had turned. He dug his heels into his horse's flanks, spoke to him, urged him, then leaned forward clinging with his knees as the good beast broke into a gallop.

It was smooth enough going at first, the road straight ahead with no forks nor puzzling turns, but at the very first town, Hugh must pause and ask, "Which way did the royal court go?" and thereafter, whenever he came to a branching road or a possibility of two directions, he must inquire, and thereby lose precious time. And somehow he felt that time was all important.

In spite of all his haste, twilight came upon him before he had any reason to believe he had lessened the distance between the king's party and himself by any appreciable amount. And with the dusk came a soft, persistent spring rain. Hugh did not mind it at first, except that it made the oncoming night swifter and darker, but it soon began to increase in volume. At the end of an hour he was wet to the skin and his horse was clopping and splashing through thick mud that hindered his progress. He slowed down to a walk, for his steed was already showing signs of fatigue, while he himself ached in his unaccustomed muscles, for it had been a long time since he had bestrode a horse. He began to wonder what he had best do, and as the cold rain trickled down his neck and his soggy clothes grew heavier upon his shoulders, he looked about uneasily, thinking perhaps he would have to seek shelter for the night and continue his pursuit in the morning. Until that moment he had not really thought out any plan of action; his one idea had been to get hold of the minstrel fellow, Maurice, and Master Walter Mape, and demand of them, in the name of Glastonbury, the torn *Book of the Seynt Graal*. It never occurred to him for a moment that it might not have been they who had taken it. The covetous look he had seen in their faces when they had been examining the book, and the feeling among many unscrupulous courtiers that they could appropriate anything they wished in the name of the king, made the whole thing seem inevitable to him. However, he would have to move warily in the matter. It would hardly do to burst in upon two full grown men, highly respected at that, and bluntly demand the return of the Glastonbury treasure. Hugh groaned aloud, unable to think of anything more definite than to get where the book was, quickly. He relinquished all thought of begging shelter somewhere for the night. The farther the court got ahead of him, the harder it would be to catch up with it. He urged on his horse again; the rain beat in his face, but he lowered his head against it and rode on.

Soon the road became an indistinct line in the surrounding blackness. He had left a fairly good-sized village behind him and was now in open country, what was probably pasture land and rolling hills, though he could not make out much of anything, with the rain pouring down upon him. He held his bridle loosely, leaving it to the horse to keep to the road which he himself could barely make out. No sound broke the stillness around him save the clopping of the horse's hoofs, the straining of the saddle leather, and the monotonous beating of the rain.

Suddenly he heard a long low whistle, his horse, startled, flung up his head, and shied. Another whistle answered, more near at hand. Then a man's voice shouted, and another; there came the sound of feet running in the mud, and out of the black dark on every side appeared men. One seized Hugh's bridle, forcing the frightened horse back almost on his haunches. The boy could make out, dimly, forms and faces, though how many, or what sort of men, he could not have told.

"Who is it rides so late upon the highway?" spoke the man at his bridle in a mocking voice.

Hugh did not answer.

"Why, 'tis but a boy!" said someone else from the darkness.

"Who let you out of the nursery?" the first voice spoke again.

"Speak up now, who are you, whence came you, where are you going?"

They must be footpads, robbers or criminal out- laws! Hugh was shaking with fear, but somehow man- aged to keep his voice calm and steady as he answered. "I be a boy out of Glaston on my way to the king's court. I have naught about me that is worth your taking."

"We will judge as to that!" said one of the voices.

" 'Tis a good horse, at the least," said another.

Hands reached up and pulled Hugh roughly off his saddle. Someone thrust a lantern in his face, which blinded him for a moment, and then enabled him to see his would-be despoilers a little more clearly. The leader, the man still holding his horse's bridle, was a tall fellow with a bold, impudent face and a cap with a curling feather in it. He regarded Hugh with a smile at once disdainful and a little curious, as the other men felt about his clothing for possible money or arms.

"And why do you ride to the king's court?" said he. "Henry the Second is no friend of mine; if thou dost love him—" He paused, leering unpleasantly.

"I do not love King Henry," Hugh answered coldly, "but he is my liege lord and I will tell him how his highways are beset with thieves who molest honest folk going upon their honest business! Sir, I bid you, in the name of the law, to let me go!"

The man laughed. "Boldly spoken, my poppy-cock! I like your manner well. But you have not yet informed me why you seek the king. I have a fancy to know."

Hugh turned away angrily. For some reason he was not afraid any more. It would be wise to conciliate these men, he knew, yet something about their bold lawlessness made him wish to resist them even where resistance was impossible. Refusing to answer, he stood sullenly silent.

"There is naught in his pocket save a yellow ribbon," said one of the men, flaunting the favor that the little Lady Eileen had given him, in the dim lantern light.

Hugh snatched it back and put it in his pocket again before any hand could stop him.

"Odd's blood! A lady's favor!" cried the man who was evidently leader. "The lad beginneth young! Let him keep the trinket and if there is naught more of worth to him set him again upon his mysterious way!"

There had been a guffaw of laughter at the ribbon which made Hugh flush indignantly in the dark.

"Give me my horse then," said he.

"Nay, not so fast, young blade; the horse looketh to have mettle. He bides with us. Get you along on shank's mare. Know you the saying? On your own two legs!"

Someone gave him a buffet on the back which nearly sent him sprawling. Then the lantern moved away into the darkness. The men's voices followed it and the tall fellow, still holding the bridle of Hugh's horse, led it down the road and away.

The rain still fell steadily, relentlessly. Hugh shivered with cold and the reaction to his fright. He could not see a yard before him; his lame foot ached and, when he sought to walk on it, a pain running through his thigh stabbed him like a knife. Feeling his way, groping, reaching for the bushes which bordered the road to guide him, he struggled on, not knowing for a surety whether he was retracing his steps or advancing.

It was slow going, desperately slow. Hugh kept peering into the blank dark on all sides, hoping against hope that he might see a light or some sign of human habitation. At last he could go no further, twice he had fallen, his weaker leg, aching intolerably, had given out under him, and the second time it seemed as if he simply could not stand up on it again. He crawled into the bushes that crowded the edge of the road. At least he would find some shelter from the cold rain underneath them. It was not pouring so hard now and, when he had pushed himself well into the thick underbrush, he found a relatively dry spot in which to lie down, but his wet clothes kept him shivering, and the ground was chill. He could not sleep, but at any rate he could rest his aching body until dawn. However, he must have slept, finally, in spite of all his discomfort, for he started broad awake suddenly and saw that the night had broken and the dim twilight of dawn lightened the sky above the road.

He found his muscles stiff almost beyond endurance, but at least the sunrise told him in which direction to go. Woods and bushes still bordered each side of the narrow road as he pushed on slowly and painfully; the day grew gradually lighter and before long a warm sun slanted encouragingly upon him from between the budded trees.

As he rounded a bend in the road he was startled to come suddenly upon a horse which looked surprisingly like his own mount that the robbers had taken from him. Yes! It was indeed, and there beside him, stepping out from the underbrush was the leader

of the band. Hugh stopt, uncertain whether to go
on or turn and try to run away. The man, noting his
hesitation, motioned to him.

"Come, boy, you have nothing to fear," he called.
Hugh advanced cautiously towards him. He was conscious of his limp which was much worse than usual
owing to the stiffness and fatigue in his muscles and
the chill of wet clothing. He struggled against it and
held his head high and proudly because of his uncomfortable self-consciousness.

"So you are going to see the king," said the man
when he had got quite close. "And though you love
him not, you are loyal to him?"

It seemed unnecessary to repeat the information he
had given the night before, so Hugh remained silent.

"I am not so disloyal to the king, myself, as you
might think, though, in sooth, I have much cause to
hate him, my outlawry being the result of his high-
handed, overswift judgment. But enough of that. It
hath come to my knowledge that one of the king's
sons is instigating a revolt against his father; would
be king in his stead without waiting for death to be-
stow the crown lawfully upon him. I like it not, and
I would warn His Majesty, yet I dare not show my
face at court. Wilt thou take a written message to
the king, boy?"

"Aye, that I will," said Hugh, "though in truth I
owe you nothing after last night's mistreatment! But
for the king—I would do that much."

The man drew from the pouch that was hanging
from his belt, a soiled scrap of parchment folded
into a small square.

"If thou couldst read," the man continued, "I would let thee see that the message is even as I tell thee."

"I can read," said Hugh, "but I need not. There is something in thy face that promises truth though thou art consorting with outlaws and footpads."

The man grinned in not unfriendly fashion. "Thou art a bold spoken youth," he said, giving the parchment into the boy's hands. " 'Twill be quite useless to send the king's men after us, for we shall be gone past recovery in the twinkling of an eye."

"That I would never do!" said Hugh stoutly. "I know too well what it means to a man to suffer the hue and cry."

The two looked at each other, friendliness growing between them.

"For the favor that I have asked thee," the man said, "here is thy horse again. Ride straight along this forest road for an hour or better, then you will come upon a highway wider and in more constant use than this. Turn north and, before the sun has reached the high noon mark, thou wilt come to a large manor castle. It is there that the king and his court have bided the night. If they have not been minded to go further thou wilt still find them there. Farewell, boy, we shall not meet again." He vanished into the underbrush as completely as if the earth had opened and swallowed him.

Hugh climbed into his saddle, thankful indeed to have his good horse between his knees again; thankful also that the outlaw had not returned it to him out of pity for his lameness. He drew a long breath and straightened his shoulders. "Come on, old man," he said aloud, pressing his heels into the horse's flanks. "Come on! The sun is shining warm now; I shall soon be dry. Pick up your hoofs and hurry to the rescue of our treasure!"

xv. henry the king

W HEN HUGH REACHED the manor castle where King Henry and his train were said to be lodging, he clattered over the drawbridge and outer parade ground with considerable confidence. He passed through the great gate with some peasant folk who were bringing in supplies, and then proceeded alone to the inner gate which admitted only noble guests and those who had direct business with them. The porter who answered his ringing of the heavy metal gong, looked troubled, as well he might, for the sovereign of England was no easy guest for any manor lord to entertain, and before his none too friendly scrutiny, Hugh felt his self-assurance slipping away from him.

"What wouldst thou of the king?" the man asked, barring the boy's entrance with his broad bulk.

"I have a message for him," said Hugh, "which may be of grave importance, and I have also business with Maurice, the king's minstrel, and Sir Walter Mape."

"They be occupied, I have no doubt, all of them, and I know my duty better than to trouble such high and noble folk for a boy such as you." His eyes traveled critically over Hugh's bedraggled, rain soaked clothes as he continued, "Give me the message for His Majesty; I will convey it to my betters and they to him."

But Hugh shook his head. That message from the outlaw might be his sole means of getting into the center of the courtly folk and finding what he had come for. He would not let that out of his hands if he could help it.

Suddenly he bethought him of the Lady Eileen's ribbon. He pulled it from the pouch under his tunic where he was carrying it.

"If you will take this," said he, holding it up, "to a young damsel who is the queen's ward, the Lady Eileen, she will vouch for me that I am nobly born and, what is more important, honest and loyal."

The porter took the ribbon, hesitated for a moment and then, evidently deciding that Hugh was not the disreputable character that he looked, let him pass through the gate, bidding him dismount and wait until he should return. Then, with the yellow streamer still in his hand, he trudged away into the castle.

Before long he was back again, the little Lady Eileen beside him.

"Hugh of Glaston!" she cried joyfully as soon as she had got near the boy. "Oh, but I am glad to see thee! And Dickon the oblate—is he with thee? But what is it brings thee here so soon? Is it Kenny? Oh, Hugh, do you bear ill news of my little dog?"

She scarcely paused long enough to get even the briefest answers to her questions, and then chattered on so fast that Hugh began to think he would never have a chance to explain himself.

"But come," she said at last, taking his hand, "let the porter have a care to thy horse and come with me into the hall; then we can *really* talk." And she led the way, leaving the bewildered porter to catch the horse's bridle rein and take him away to the stables.

When they were within the lofty castle hall, Eileen drew Hugh through an arras covered door onto a terrace where they were quite by themselves and could talk freely. "There," said she, seating herself on a stone bench, "now, sit down and tell me everything."

So Hugh poured out his story without a break, telling of the precious broken *Book of the Seynt Graal;* how he had shown it to Sir Walter Mape and the minstrel, Maurice; how they had both declared it should be the property of the king, and then how it had vanished with the departure of the court, so that one could not fail to believe those two had taken it, ostensibly to present it to the monarch. Such things had been done before. Brother John had once told him how a beautiful and priceless volume had been taken in a similar way, during the reign of a former king, from the neighboring Cathedral of Wells. In that case His Majesty had sternly insisted on the return of the book to the ecclesiastical library, but he need not have done so, for did not everything in the realm really belong to the king?

When Hugh paused, Eileen said loyally. "*Our* King Henry is just and honest, too. If the book is given to him and he knows where it came from, he will give it back, immediately, I know he will!"

Hugh sighed and looked doubtful. "If and when— but Eileen, they may not give it to him for ever so long; they want it for themselves, really, both the minstrel and Sir Walter. And the king moves around so fast it might so easily be lost. And, oh Eileen, we of Glaston need it *now!*"

And then he went on to tell why *The Book of the Seynt Graal* was so unique a treasure and how Dickon had found, and he had worked on, some of the missing pages, and how he was almost ready now to put them all together and present them to Brother John.

"Would you search their possessions?" queried the damsel in a troubled voice. "Faith! and that would not be easy!"

Hugh shook his head. "They be gentlemen and not common thieves; if I but charge them to their faces with the taking of our book, like as not they will laugh and say they have borrowed it. Then, if they will in no wise be persuaded to give it back, I will appeal to the king."

Eileen rose up. "Let us be about it immediately," said she.

They went into the hall again. Innumerable people were passing to and fro therein; knights, squires, pages, ladies, tire women, and servants. At the far end, a huge hooded fireplace jutted out into the room, and at one side of this sat a group, laughing and talking together, undisturbed by the stir and movement in the rest of the room. The leaping flames played on the faces of those who sat about it and made a spot of color and light in the dimly lit, high-ceilinged hall. Hugh and Eileen made their way into the outer edge of the circle. The king held the place of honor in a huge carved oak chair near the blaze. At his elbow stood Maurice, the minstrel, and farther off, talking to some gaily clad courtiers at the other side of the fireplace, sat Sir Walter Mape. It seemed hardly the moment to step forth and ask for the return of a stolen volume! Hugh decided to bide his time.

King Henry was speaking in his customary quick, authoritative voice. "It might well have been all an invention of the monks of Glaston," said he. At the name Hugh pricked up his ears and listened intently. "Our friend the archdeacon would have us believe it was naught else, but I am inclined to think otherwise. Walter—" he raised his voice and the talking in the small group on the opposite side of the huge fireplace ceased abruptly. "I say, Walter Mape, come hither and defend your cynical doubts in this matter of King Arthur's grave in Glastonbury. Tongues are wagging and the tale waxes or wanes with each telling."

"What tale, my lord?" questioned Sir Walter. He had risen and moved nearer the king.

"The lad and the vision," prompted King Henry somewhat irritably. "Thou shouldst know; thine own books have prophesied the finding of King Arthur's bones in Avalon, which, they say, is the marshy country round about the abbey, and a name frequently applied to the monastic property itself. But they say that which led the brothers to go digging and unearth the grave itself was a dream, a vision seen by a sick lad lost in the fog out on the marshes. Faith! We have all heard the story a dozen times by now! The monks were all agog with it. Why dost thou mistrust the truth of it?"

Sir Walter Mape shrugged his shoulders. "It may be true, Sire, yet it hath the sound of monkish invention."

"The grave was found, was it not? You cannot deny that," spoke up someone in the circle.

"Aye, that is sooth enough, but the vision; who can say *that* was true?" Sir Walter was evidently in the mood to argue.

"I would that I had summoned the lad himself and questioned him while I was in Glaston," declared the king. "I had much of importance to discuss with Abbot Robert, and the time was short."

Hugh had been edging his way toward the front of the group. He was breathing fast, his heart was in his mouth. Was there ever a more fortuitous time for him to declare his presence and make his request?

"So please Your Majesty," he cried, stepping forth and bowing before the king, "I am the boy who saw the vision of the burial of Arthur in Glaston, and it is all sooth and true, on my life and honor. If you desire to question me, I am here to answer."

A gasp of astonishment and then a moment of bewildered silence held the group in the circle. King Henry broke it with a quick, rather harsh laugh.

"By all the saints! This land must be enchanted! I have but to express a wish and the fellow I wish for literally springs up out of the earth at my feet!"

"May it be ever so when my liege lord graciously consents to honor my dwelling," said a tall man standing behind the king's chair. Evidently he was the host, the lord of the manor.

King Henry grunted, none too courteously, in reply, and kept his eyes still on Hugh.

"Who may you be, boy, and how comes it that a dreamer of dreams and a seer of visions follows after my very worldly court?"

"I am Hugh, son of Sir Hugh de Morville," declared the boy quietly.

There was a sudden, startled exclamation, then a hush. The king's face grew scarlet, the veins at his temples seemed to swell visibly, and the smile that had been on his lips grew strained and frozen. Hugh continued:

"I followed your train, Sire, because a book, which is old and broken but very precious in our eyes, hath disappeared from the Painted Aumbry at Glaston, and I bethought me there might be someone among your followers who had borrowed it."

The awkward silence in the group around Hugh was broken by an incredulous laugh which was almost a gasp. The expression on the king's face changed from painful remembrance to surprise, then relief and amusement. He suddenly clapped his hand upon his thigh and roared with laughter.

"Odd's my life!" he exclaimed, "the whole world is turning dizzy! Let me clutch one handle to this most remarkable business at a time! Whew!" He mopped his brow and the back of his neck, thereby turning into a humorous gesture his humiliating embarrassment. "Now, boy, begin at the beginning, and explain slowly. You are Hugh de Morville's son, how is it you are here at all while he is gone on pilgrimage for his murder of the Archbishop à Becket, to the Holy Land?"

Hugh winced at the raw reference to the ghastly deed. "My father left me at Glaston when he fled the country," he answered briefly.

"To become a novice and then a monk?"

"As to that I know not yet."

The king gazed at him silently for a few moments.

"Thy sisters are in France," he said at length, dropping into the familiar pronoun. "They be married, I am told, and happy enough. I wonder that thy father did not take thee there also."

"We love England," declared Hugh stoutly. "I think my father would have some of his blood still on English soil. And I—I am glad. I have been very happy in Glaston."

"Dreaming dreams?" The king's voice was soft and held no shade of scorn in it.

"Aye, dreaming dreams," assented the boy, "and seeking that which is lost, and rebuilding a book that had been broken—and is now lost also."

"Your Majesty," spoke a voice behind Hugh, and Walter Mape stood forth. "The lad is over bold but I think I know whereof he speaks. May I have your gracious permission to ask him a further question, and perchance lay his doubts to rest on a certain score?"

The king nodded.

"Is it *The Book of the Seynt Graal,* the volume hidden in the Painted Aumbry, to which you refer, boy?"

"Aye, Sir Walter, that it is. It hath not been seen since—"

"Since Maurice and I gazed upon it covetously and held it in our itching fingers! And, naturally enough, you thought we had borrowed the same to enrich our own or the king's library! Well, lad, thou hast guessed wrong. We laid no impious hands upon your Glaston treasure. Did we, now, Maurice? Speak up, man; our characters and honor are in question!"

"By the bones of Saint Bridget, I swear we never touched the volume, boy, though I will confess I would have deemed it no sin to transfer it to the king's chamber!"

Hugh looked from one to the other of the two men who were now standing on either side of him. Walter Mape had spoken in a light, bantering tone, the minstrel was forceful and emphatic. But the faces of both were open, honest, concerned. Somehow he could not doubt the truth of either. His heart sank, but there was nothing further to be said. With a little bow to the king, he was about to step back into the circle when the monarch motioned him to remain where he was.

"Art satisfied, lad?" said he with a teasing grin at Maurice and the archdeacon, "for if thou art not, I will have the possessions of these two brought forth and searched—Odd's blood, I will! They have played me many a prank in their day, the both of them, and I would not trust them, at least as far as books and tales are concerned!" His quick, roguish laugh belied his words, and everybody felt at ease again and in a good humor, the unhappy, fearful mood created in them by the mention of À Becket having been already forgotten.

Hugh smiled also. "Sire," said he, "I need no more than the honest word of a gentleman. We must look elsewhere for our stolen treasure."

"But first, boy, tell me of thy vision of King Arthur. I had thought the gods had dropt thee into my presence for no other reason."

So Hugh told the story of his wanderings in the marshes of Avalon, of his strange other-world experience, and of how Dickon and Bleheris, the mad hermit, had found him and borne him to Beckery, and how, later, the monks had dug between the two pyramids in the graveyard outside the Old Church and discovered the king's grave just where the vision had foretold. But of the Holy Grail and the age-old tradition that it had been lost or buried somewhere in Glaston, he said nothing. That was too deep a matter, too sacred and, for him, too precious, to bring forth in this little company of idle courtiers, so worldly-wise and incredulous. Instinctively he knew they would not have understood. But perhaps he was mistaken, for a hush lay upon them as he ceased speaking, and in the king's face was a look of wistfulness as well as interest.

"I would I had a son like thee, my boy," he said impulsively.

The remark thrust a knife, as it were, into Hugh's

heart and memory. He had forgotten the message from the tall outlaw, bringing ill news to this father of a rebelling son. He wished he might withhold the folded bit of parchment, but that, of course, he could not do.

"Sire," said he hesitantly. "I had almost forgot; as I passed through a wooded road on my way hither a stranger bade me give Your Majesty this written message."

He knelt as he handed the king the note and then stept back among the courtiers, watching the sovereign's face with concern and real sympathy as he opened and read the missive. The round face flushed darkly, the color sweeping up in waves from his thick neck. He leaped to his feet, his stocky body alive with energy and determination.

"By God's eyes!" he cried, using his own peculiar oath, "the ingrate, the inhuman creature that would take up arms against the father that begat him and that loves him! Oh, my son! My son!"

The little company about the fireplace broke up instantly. Those sitting rose to their feet. Faces paled and grew troubled. "What is it? What hath happened?" one after another whispered to his neighbor. King Henry brushed them aside, calling for his personal servants and closest friends.

"My son, Henry, has taken up arms against me!" they heard him state in a voice cold with fury. "We must get back to London at once, without a moment's delay!"

In the confusion that followed Hugh was quite

forgotten. He managed to get himself out from underfoot of the courtiers and servitors who immediately began rushing about. Everyone was far too busy to notice or delay him if he wished to depart, and he did so wish. There was no further need for him to stay, save to find the little Lady Eileen again and bid her farewell. She, however, seemed to have been swept away with the hurrying, whispering women folk who had rushed off to prepare the queen and themselves for departure. He made his way toward the outer court to find his horse but, as he was crossing it toward the stables, a light footstep sounded behind him. He turned and saw her running after him.

"Eileen," said he. "My Lady Eileen! I had feared I could not tell thee my thanks for thy help and—"

"There is naught to thank me for," interrupted the girl breathlessly. "But I wanted to see thee again and tell thee I am sorry about the book—that it was not here to be recovered. Oh, Hugh, what *can* have happened to it? Who would have taken it? What wilt thou do about it now?"

At the sound of his very own thoughts being put into words by the sympathetic girl beside him, all the discouragement and despair Hugh had not yet allowed himself to face seemed suddenly to rise up and overwhelm him. Tears started to his eyes and his lips trembled so that he dared not trust himself to speak.

"Hugh, thou art weary beyond bearing!" Eileen laid a hand gently on his sleeve. "And I doubt not

thou art hungry also. Hast eaten at all since leaving
Glaston?"

The boy shook his head, forcing a little smile.
He was hungry, faint for lack of food. That must
be why he seemed to be behaving like such a baby.
Things had happened so fast and he had been so
desperately eager to overtake the king and his court
before they moved beyond his reach, and scattered,
perhaps. He had not even thought of food until
this moment and, now that the girl mentioned it,
he realized how completely empty and hollow he
felt.

And Eileen, womanlike, did not need to be told
anything further.

"Come with me," she commanded, seizing Hugh's
hand and moving down the court in the direction of
the cook houses.

In no time at all she had got hold of a friendly
servitor, who found a seat for Hugh in a corner of
one of the great kitchens and supplied him with a
bowl of rice soup and a generous slice of pigeon pie,
thick, juicy, and succulent. The boy fell to with a
good appetite and soon found both courage and conversation coming back to him.

The little lady hovered over him, replacing his
empty soup bowl and his dish of pie with other del-
icacies, serving him with her own hands, and keeping up a running stream of talk that was friendly
and comfortable, but needed little more than nods
or brief comments in reply.

When at last the boy stood up, replenished to the

full, he felt that he was a new man entirely. Eileen smiled up at him.

"There now," said she, "that is better! I wonder thou wert able to stand on thy two legs at all with nothing inside thee since yesterday noon!" She dug into the silken pouch hanging at her girdle and produced the yellow hair ribbon. "My favor is still thine. May it help thee again and to better purpose!"

"Oh, Eileen, thou hast been mortal good to me!" said Hugh, accepting it. "I will never forget thee!"

"I think thou wilt find the book," she continued with hopeful assurance. "Nay, I am certain of it! Thou canst not fail! Farewell and God go with thee!"

Hugh knelt and kissed her hand in true knightly fashion, and then watched her as she walked with easy grace to a door of the cook house that led into the manor hall. Just before she disappeared in the doorway she looked back and waved to him, smiling her wide friendly smile. Somehow Hugh felt immensely cheered and turned with a far lighter step back into the courtyard to find his horse.

After a bit of searching in the manor stables he spied the beast, untethered him and mounted. Everybody about was too busy getting ready for the sudden, but already announced, departure of the king to bother or question him. He rode across the courtyard and out over the drawbridge, then turned in the direction of Glaston. As his horse fell into a steady trot and the muddy road stretched out evenly before him, his heart grew heavy again. He realized with renewed and devastating force that the treasure of Glaston, the priceless, precious *Book of the Seynt Graal,* had vanished completely. He had not even the vaguest idea as to what could have happened to it, or who could have taken it.

xvi. the great fire

IN SPITE OF his downheartedness Hugh urged on his horse whenever he showed a tendency to slacken his speed. A strange feeling of haste was upon him, though he knew not why, and he was glad when at long last he galloped into the little village which straggled upon the outskirts of the abbey grounds. It looked quite deserted, as it had upon that other occasion which now returned vividly to his mind, the time when he had come upon Jacques de Raoul fleeing from the hue and cry that was raised hotly after everyone connected with his father's household. He wondered what had happened to Jacques. It was good to know that his sisters were safe in France and his father in the Holy Land. Hugh thought of the king and was surprised to find

how completely his feeling of resentment and hatred had vanished. Those short glimpses of the monarch when his remorse had been so apparent, and then his sorrow and hurt pride at the rumored rebellion of his son, had somehow shown the boy very convincingly that the king was an erring human being who suffered for his mistakes and wrongs as intensely as ordinary folk. Evidently he worried about his children, felt disappointment and regret for them and, perhaps, just because he was king, he knew greater loneliness than other people and found little sympathy and less honest friendly affection to lean on. Hugh not only forgave him in his heart for all the tragedy and pain in his own life and family that the king's impulsive words had been at least partly responsible for, but he thought of him with a pity that was almost akin to affection.

Strange that the little town through which he was

riding should be so completely deserted. Hugh roused himself from his wandering thoughts as he spied an old peasant sitting in the sun before his cottage door. He was the only human being about and, as the boy rode closer, he recognized him as the ancient gaffer who had hobbled along beside him that day he had found Jacques and helped him on his way to sanctuary on the Galilee Porch of the abbey. He drew rein and greeted the old fellow with a friendly smile.

"How comes it that there be no folk about the village, saving yourself, good neighbor?" he said.

"Gone to the fire," answered the old man briefly. "I could na go; legs be stiff and unsteady these days."

"Fire!" exclaimed Hugh. "Where?"

"Abbey grounds. Hours and hours now they be a-burning."

The boy waited for no further word but dug his heels into his horse's side, urging, shouting, beating him, tired though he was, into a gallop again. Before long he could see smoke rising in great clouds, then flames, like angry red tongues shooting through them. Half the monastic buildings must be ablaze! He raced on; his horse seemed to catch the sense of disaster and redoubled his speed. They reached the south gate which was crowded with peasant folk. Unable to force his way through on horseback, Hugh slid off and, leaving the beast to take care of himself, rushed into the grounds.

A scene of desolation and confusion met his eyes. Already the dorter, chapter house and several other buildings, all of wood, were a mass of smoldering ruins. A great wave of smoke, heat, and cinders blew toward him from the Church of St. Mary which was a blazing furnace. He skirted it, running around to the west. There he found the brothers gathered in a body on the lee side of the suffocating flames and smoke, watching it burn. Hugh joined them, but no one seemed aware of him. They all stood or knelt with tragic, white faces turned toward the fire. Some were praying, others weeping; the faces of many were black with grime and cinders, their habits torn and scorched. Some still held buckets half filled with water, useless utterly in the magnitude of the blaze, some clenched helpless hands, wringing them in despair. St. Joseph's Chapel was burning, too, though the flames there had not yet got such a start. Hugh watched in agonized helplessness with the others.

Suddenly someone clutched at his sleeve. Turning, he saw Dickon, his eyes wild, his face chalk white, his whole frame trembling.

"Brother John!" he said, raising his voice almost to a shriek to be heard above the roaring and crackling of the flames. "Brother John! He is in the Old Church! I saw him go in a few moments ago and he hasn't come out! He can't *get* out! See, the wooden walls are blazing all around it now, and the door has fallen in!"

A hoarse cry from one of the brothers standing near enough to hear; exclamations, shouts from others; half articulated, half sobbing groans and sentences that died on the lips. Hugh rushed nearer the blazing building, Dickon following him.

"He must be trapped inside there," he cried through clenched teeth. "Dickon, quick! Get people with picks to go to the cleft near the old north gate and *dig!* Make the entrance bigger—you know—the entrance to our passageway, so they can get to us that way or we can get out! I'm going to try to go through the flames here, through the door, and show Brother John the underground way out."

Dickon gasped but had no time to reply. Already Hugh was halfway across the ground that separated them from the door of St. Joseph's Chapel. He paused only for a moment to watch breathlessly as his friend reached the doorway which was belching forth heavy smoke and flame, lept through it and was gone. Others beside Dickon had seen him go, but it all happened so quickly they had no time to realize what the boy was about until he had vanished into the burning building. Then a shout rose up, a shout that ended in a groan of anguish. The roof and the inner walls of the chapel were of lead. When the heat grew great enough, they would fall, molten and searing, destroying utterly anything they fell upon.

Hugh had only one thought, Brother John. If he were indeed inside that fiery furnace he must be got out. Perhaps he was already overcome with smoke and, for that reason, had not at least tried to come out again through the door. Perhaps he had tried and been beaten back by the heat and flames which were growing worse every moment. In that case only the trap door and the underground passage would save him, and of these the boy was certain, he knew nothing.

Once inside the building, he instinctively threw himself upon the stone floor where the air was less dense and choking with smoke. His eyes were blind with tears from the stinging soot, the heat from the burning walls was almost intolerable, but he crept along toward the sanctuary, stopping every few moments to wipe his streaming eyes and peer about. No sign of Brother John. Perhaps he had already found and lifted the stone above the passageway. He must himself get to that, and quickly, for there was no going back now, the way he had come.

The low wall that separated the nave from the chancel offered some protection from the heat of the flames behind him and, when Hugh had crept through the arch of it, he found he could stand upright, though breathing was still difficult. The cloud of smoke was thinner also; he could see the sanctuary steps and rail. And behold! There, kneeling upright before the altar were *two* figures, one slight, tonsured, in the black Benedictine robe—Brother John. The other towered, even in his kneeling posture—Bleheris the hermit, with shaggy beard and matted long white hair, dressed in his customary gray-white mantle, girdled with a rope. They knelt, the two of them, as tranquil and still as if they were in some quiet lovely spot with naught in all the world to threaten danger or disturbance. All about them, heaped high on the chancel steps and at the foot of the altar itself, was a strange assortment of articles. Hugh gasped in astonishment and then remembered what Dickon had told him and realized what they were; the treasures from the black chest in the hermit's hut, all the antique things the old man had found and cherished, loved so passionately and called his own. Glimpsed through the smoke was the shine of gold and silver and bronze. The old-fashioned chain armor of King Arthur's day lay heaped there, with Excalibur in a place apart, as if singularly precious. The pectoral staff with its jeweled crook was there, the chalice and patten and the odd castle-like reliquary. And directly in front of the old man, kneeling in such rapt absorption, lay a broken book. Hugh started forward with an instinctive motion to catch it up, for he knew at once what it was—*The Book of the Seynt Graal!* And all around it were piles of loose parchment pages, the very ones that he had labored over so long and lovingly. Perhaps the ones Brother John had deciphered were there also. He must seize them, all of them, and carry them out, safe. But at that moment heat and flame suddenly wrapt the boy about, making him realize anew the peril of his position. Though the smoke had been less dense, the fire less menacing at this end of the church, they were rapidly encroaching upon him. There was not a moment to be lost, yet still the two men knelt motionless before the altar, their heads raised, their eyes fixed, completely oblivious of everything around them.

Hugh lifted his eyes to see what it was the gaze of the two rested upon so intently. The ancient wooden altar with its stone altar top stood before them unadorned, as always. A cloud of smoke hung low over it, obscuring its surface and then, unaccountably, the heavy, opaque smoke thinned and grew lucent like a mist. Flame shot through it, shone within it and round about it, and yet not flame so much as light. Light rested on the surface of the altar, diffused at first, then contracting into a central spot of intense white radiance. It seemed now to stand upon the altar, now to float above it. Then it took form and substance in the semblance of a Cup, a Chalice covered with a shining white cloth. Brighter and brighter grew the light streaming from it until Hugh's eyes could no longer bear to look upon it, and he covered them with his sleeve. When he looked again the intense white radiance and that which contained it were gone. Only red, angry, leaping flames darted from the wall behind the altar and dense black smoke billowed and settled above it.

At that moment a rumble and then a crash sounded behind him; the ground shook and the blinding black smoke became thick with soot and flying dust. The ancient lead roof of the Old Church had sagged and fallen in over the nave. Only the part directly over the chancel still held.

"Quick!" shouted Hugh, coming to his senses as out of a dream. "Brother John! Master Bleheris! The trap door over the passageway!" He fought his way through the blanket of smoke, coughing and choking, toward the sanctuary steps.

Another crash and roar; charred and burning wood and hot pieces of lead fell all about him. One of the walls had given way. Blindly, forced to his knees more than once, with one arm over his eyes and face to protect them, he struggled forward amidst the searing flames and falling debris.

Brother John lay crumpled on the sanctuary steps. Hugh could just make out the form of the hermit lying prone just beyond him. For a moment smoke and flames veered away and he could see more clearly. Across the body of the old man lay a heavy beam. Hugh ran to him and struggled to lift it, straining with all his might till the sweat poured from him, but he could not. For a long, trembling moment he bent, sobbing, over Master Bleheris with his hand upon his heart. No flutter of life; the old man was dead. But there was a look on the white face that the boy would remember as long as he lived. It held no sign of pain or terror, no expression of confusion and discontent and longing such as had so often rested upon it in life. Even in that moment of great danger Hugh forgot his fears, noting only that large quiet face, how radiantly glad it was.

But Brother John! There was not a second to be lost! Hugh turned from the dead to the living. Brother John still breathed, though he was unconscious. With a whispered prayer for strength, the boy leaned over him and, half lifting, half dragging, managed to carry the inert form down the steps and around behind the altar. With a mighty wrench, straining every nerve and muscle, he pulled up the marked stone which concealed the passageway. A draft of musty smelling air rushed up, bringing momentary relief to his stinging throat and smarting eyeballs. A strange, almost supernatural power seemed to surge through him as he bent again over Brother John, grasped him under the arms and dragged him down the rough stone stairs into the black darkness of the cave below. Feeling his way step by step he found the broken wall of

the well and gently laid the still unconscious monk
on the rough earth floor beside it. Then he tore off
a piece of the hem of his tunic and, soaking it in the
well water, bathed Brother John's face. Slowly the
warmth of life came back into the cold hands, Hugh
felt the eyelids flutter and heard a long trembling
sigh.

"Art thou all right, Brother John?" said he, his
own voice unsteady.

"Aye," said the other shortly.

Hugh knelt back on his heels. He was still breathing hard from his enormous exertion, and now that
the greatest of his terrors was over, as if in reaction,
he began to tremble violently, his teeth chattering.
Above them the sound of crackling flames and falling timbers was muted; the air, though smoky, seemed
clear by comparison, and felt cool and damp on his
hot skin. For several moments they remained motionless and silent, Brother John lying on the ground
breathing more regularly now, but not yet venturing
to stir. Hugh crouched beside him, the trembling of
his body growing less. A quiet of infinite relief, an
inexplicable sense of security and peace gradually came
over him. He forgot the danger they were still in, the
difficulties they must yet meet in getting out of the
pitch black cave, his old friend, Bleheris, dead, and
the enormous tragedy of Glaston burning so ruin-
ously over his head. His mind held only one thought,
one image, that shining Chalice that he had seen
standing upon the plain square altar of the Old
Church. Brother John's mind must have been filled

with the same thought, for his voice came at length out of the darkness, filled with awe and wonder and exaltation and no fear at all.

"*Sanctum Gradalis!*" he said, "the Holy Grail! O God in heaven receive my thanks, for I have beheld a miracle! And thou, too, boy, thou didst see it, didst thou not? Strange—passing strange! Truly the ways of God are not to be comprehended by mortal minds! The mad hermit of Beckery, the lad without name or family, and old Brother John who had no wish in all the world save to fashion beauty in books, and look with the inner eye on things that are lovely. To think that we three have been vouchsafed that glorious vision! The Lord be praised! The Lord be praised!"

"Vision!" Hugh caught up the word. "Vision? It was *really* there, Brother John, was it not? Bleheris must have found it at last and placed it there upon the altar with all those treasures of his that lay upon the steps below it."

"Nay," said Brother John, "he did not find it, and it hath been borne in upon my mind that the Holy Grail is never found by seeking. The sight of it, the vision, is *given* by God to whom He will. Why He gives it and when, no man can tell; that is a deep and sacred mystery."

"But Bleheris *did* seek the Holy Grail," continued Hugh after a few moments' silence. "You said no one ever found the Grail by seeking; *he* must have found it!"

"Nay, he did not find it! All his seeking was in vain; it was shown to him, as to us. Mark my words, lad, not to *seekers* but to *givers* do the visions and the gifts of God come. Bleheris gave himself and all he had, before his eyes were clear enough to see the thing he longed for."

"But *I* didn't give anything," said Hugh, wondering.

"Lad! Lad!" Brother John's voice was warm with affection. "Hast thou not even now offered thy life for poor old Brother John? And thou hadst naught else to offer! It is I who am fain to wonder why the vision was vouchsafed to *me*."

They fell silent again except for the coughing that wracked them with increasing frequency as the smoke in the close air of the cave grew thicker. Another thundering crash shook the earth above them and a faint glow issued from the stairs behind the well. Evidently the fire above was raging more fiercely than ever. Hugh peered uneasily about him wondering whether the roof of the cave above their heads might fall through. He imagined that the heat of the place was increasing. Sweat broke out on his forehead. The light of the flames beyond the passageway and stairs pierced the blackness about him sufficiently for him to discern dimly the form of the monk lying at his feet, and to make out the walls of the cave.

"Brother John," said he, standing up, "if I could get you to the other side of the cave, I think I could find the stone slab over the secret passageway and then we could go through it into the treasure vault. It would be safer there, and Dickon *must* come soon.

I can't see why it takes so long for them to make that cleft in the moor wider and get through to us!"

"There is nothing to fear, lad," said the brother tranquilly. "But go thou, alone, if thou wilt. The others will come anon, and if they come not—faith! I am more content to die now than I am ever like to be again!"

"Of course I am not going without thee!" cried Hugh indignantly. "See now, if I support thee, very gently—" He put his arms under the monk's shoulders and slowly and with great tenderness got him to his feet.

A groan escaped Brother John in spite of his efforts to make no sound. "It is my leg, boy; I fear me 'tis broken, here at the thigh. But no matter, it will mend in time. I will lean upon thee, but not too heavily."

Very slowly they made their way across the cave. The slight lightening of the dark caused by the flames above disappeared, leaving them groping in a deeper blackness than ever. But somehow Hugh managed to feel his way to the right slab of stone and pull it open. With the monk leaning now against the wall and now upon him again, they managed to get through the passage to the bolted doors of the aumbry which stood across the entrance to the treasure vault. It seemed as if the bolts would never draw and Hugh struggled with them until the sweat poured down his face, but at last they slid back and the two almost fell through the opening into the room beyond. The air was distinctly clearer there and they could wait in safety until rescue came from the other direction.

Nor had they long to wait. Soon they heard voices and steps coming toward them, and a faint light issued from the arched doorway across the room, growing brighter as the rescuers drew close. At last they were upon them; Dickon first, with a lantern, then two of the brothers, their faces full of wonder as they gazed around at the chests and aumbry in the treasure chamber.

There was no time then for explanations. Tenderly and carefully, in spite of the immense difficulty, they carried Brother John between them, while Hugh and Dickon followed, down the twisting underground way to the cleft in the moor. This had been dug out so that it was broader and they all passed through at last into the open air. Then came the long way back to the abbey grounds.

Hugh groaned within himself as he drew near and beheld the devastation. The churches were gone, both St. Mary's and the little old Chapel of St. Joseph. A few charred and blackened walls still stood, though most had fallen, and the interiors of both lay open and roofless, a smoldering mass of ruin. Refectory and dormitory buildings were in a similar condition; the green garth was trampled and black, the cloister walks were charred and broken; guest house and almonry still flamed internally like belching furnaces. Only the new bell tower and the chapel that Abbot Henry had left unfinished and Abbot Robert had planned to complete, stood untouched and whole.

Some vagrant shifting of the wind had spared them, and a portion of the kitchen building. Toward the former the two brothers, carrying Brother John, and Hugh and Dickon following after, now turned their steps.

Inside this building the old and infirm monks had already gathered and the infirmarian moved restlessly among them, filled with anxiety for the ailing ones, too disheartened and despairing himself to give much comfort and encouragement to any. When Brother John was brought in, he gave his attention at once to the injured leg. Yes, it was broken but, miraculously enough, the bones seemed to be in place. With skilled and accustomed hands he bound the leg upon a stiff board and placed the brother on a makeshift bed in a corner, where he would be as much out of the way as possible. Brother John's face was white and drawn with pain but he smiled up at Dickon and Hugh as they bent anxiously over him.

"Praise God, my children," said he in a whisper. "Let us praise Him and thank Him with all our hearts! I have never known such joy, such gladness, in all my life!"

Then he shut his eyes with a little sigh of contentment as if he would sleep.

"Joy!" said Dickon bitterly; "Joy! he can talk of joy when our Glaston—" the boy's lips trembled so that he could not finish.

Hugh said nothing, but put an arm awkwardly about Dickon's shoulders and the two moved through the growing crowd of monks out into the desolate grounds again. They had walked thus together for a number of yards when Dickon suddenly thrust Hugh from him, staring at him in round-eyed astonishment.

"Run!" he exclaimed unaccountably. "Hugh, run over yonder and back again!"

Hugh stared back. "Are you crazy?" said he. "What do you want me to run for?"

"Never mind, do it, please! Run out into the grounds. I want to see you!"

Completely at a loss, but willing to humor his friend, Hugh dashed off across the trampled green and returned. He found Dickon laughing and crying at the same time. "Whatever is the matter?" he cried, shaking Dickon's shoulders, irritated as well as puzzled.

"You walk—you run—straight! Hugh, you aren't limping any more! Not the least bit! I could feel the difference when you were leaning on me! You are healed!"

Hugh started in astonishment, then looked down at his erstwhile dragging foot as if he did not believe it was truly his. In all the excitement and exertion of the fire and his rescuing Brother John, he had not given himself a single thought. Yet something must have happened to him; a miracle! He had been lame almost all his life—at least as far back as he could remember—and now he stood and walked firm and steady, on two legs so like each other in strength and wholeness that, by the feel of them alone, he could not have told which had been the ailing one! When had it happened? The vision in the flame-swept Chapel of St. Joseph flashed before his mind's eye. *That* had been it! Healing had come in the presence of the Holy Grail! Wonder flooded the boy's mind. He did not understand; it was all too big for him. Perhaps all one could do about it was what Brother John had done, praise God and be glad. He turned to Dickon who was still staring at him, speechless with amazement.

"Hugh, you have seen something," he cried, finding his voice at last. "You've been somewhere or done something that has made you different! What is it? What happened? Tell me! Tell me!"

Hugh found it hard to begin. Somehow, dearly as he loved this friend, this sworn brother of his, he knew he could never make it clear to him. Something had indeed happened that had changed him, made a new and different person of him in more ways than just in curing his lameness. But no one could really understand that experience who had not lived through it. Yet he could not turn from Dickon's eager, questioning face and not *try* at least to tell him.

"I—I don't know how to explain about it," he began hesitantly. "In the Old Church, in the smoke and flames, I saw it for a minute—and I think just seeing it must have worked a miracle and cured my lameness."

"Saw what?" interrupted Dickon.

"The Holy Grail."

"The Cup itself?" cried the other in an awed voice. "By all the saints! What was it made of? What did it look like? How did it get there? Couldn't you have brought it out with you?"

Hugh shook his head. "I don't even know for sure whether it was real or not. Oh, I *saw* it all right, as surely as I am seeing you now, as surely as I saw all those treasures of Master Bleheris's at the foot of the altar. But the Holy Grail was not the same as those things—it was *different*, I don't think anyone could ever hold that in his mortal hands."

"No one could ever hold anything again that was in that blazing furnace, that is certain!" Dickon's voice grew suddenly bitter. "Seems as if the fire has taken all that we have, and that everything, every single treasure of Glaston is gone now—forever."

The enormity of the loss came over Hugh more appallingly than it had before. "Aye," said he, his voice also growing tense with emotion. "And the book, Dickon, our precious broken *Book of the Seynt Graal,* that is gone, too. Bleheris had taken that in there with him, and all our pages."

"But *why?*" interrupted Dickon again, "just to be burned up? I never knew he was that crazy!"

"He couldn't have known they would be burned," Hugh defended him. "I think I understand a little the way he was thinking. He loved those things, and he had the feeling he wanted to *give* something he loved; offer a sort of sacrifice—the way he did Excalibur, don't you remember?"

Dickon grunted. "Whatever he thought or was trying to do, it is fixed now so nobody in all the world knows about the Holy Grail, or how it came to our Glaston, or any of those wonderful things that happened long ago."

"I do," said Hugh quietly. "Everything that was in

that book and in the loose, recovered pages, too, are in my mind now. And the story was almost complete. And the tales, too, that Bleheris told now and then about it, the fire hasn't destroyed those either. They are all here." The boy touched his forehead meaningfully.

"A lot of good that will do anybody," Dickon turned his back on the desolate waste of smoking ruins that had been Glastonbury, unable to endure the sight any longer. But in a moment he resolutely faced them again. "Guess I'll see if Brother Symon needs any help," said he. "One has got to keep going, somehow."

Hugh cast a wistful look toward the cloister walks. They were a mass of smoldering debris; the Painted Aumbry must be among the ashes, and the books he had brought from his old home. They were gone too. The guest house over by the south gate where he and his father had come that stormy March night, a year and more ago, stood stark and empty, its roof fallen in, its walls blackened with smoke, its interior a heap of wreckage. Glaston, thought Hugh, a great lump rising in his throat, his Glaston that had opened its friendly arms to him in his hour of greatest need, was now a thing of naught, a dead place of meaningless ashes. He had not realized how dear Glaston had become to him in the short time he had dwelt within its walls.

Disconsolately and silently he and Dickon made their way between the charred skeleton buildings to the one remaining chapel with its incompleted bell tower. The place was crowded with monks, a somber, desolated company who stood or moved about, saying nothing, doing nothing, held in an apathy of despair. Dickon elbowed his way through the crowd until he found Brother Symon, while Hugh sought out the corner where Brother John's makeshift bed had been laid. Unconsciously the two lads derived a measure of security from the presence of the men under whom they were in the habit of working.

After a while there came a stir among the brothers and all eyes turned to the doorway through which Abbot Robert had just entered. His face was pale and there were dark shadows under his eyes, but the eyes themselves were full of life and fire. His lips had a determined look and he moved with assurance and confidence. Silence fell upon the crowded room as he mounted the chancel steps at the far end of it, and lifted his hands in blessing.

"My children," said he, "let not your hearts be troubled. Our Glaston is not gone or destroyed, even though scarce one stone be left standing upon another. For the real Glaston is not made of stone and wood and mortar, which fire can destroy, but lives, indestructible and forever, in the minds and hearts of men. Over and over again in the long history of our abbey, its outward frame and structure have been laid low, broken, burned to ashes, by accident as in fire and flood, by evil intent at the hand of enemies. And in the future it will happen again and yet again; the walls of our Glaston will be thrown down, its noble buildings will become as now, heaps of rubble. Yet out of its ashes Glaston has always risen anew, it will always rise anew. On these charred and smoking ruins will be built a yet more lovely Glaston, more beautiful perhaps than we have ever dreamed. To build and build and never be cast down though every outward evidence of our labor perish; to give and give no matter what the cost, to serve with all our hearts, no matter how little or how great the service we can render—it is *that* which makes the life blood of our Glaston, it is that spirit that will ensure for our Glaston an eternal life."

A little sigh ran through the listening group of monks, as when a breath of wind moves among fog and mist, dispelling it and letting the sunlight through. Faces that had been dark and haggard took on an expression of light and of new life. Heads lifted, hands moved involuntarily, brother touching the sleeve of brother in reassurance and affection. Heads nodded, and then, after a little pause, voices began again.

"There be some of the gold leaf rescued from the cloister aumbry."

"Praise be the saints! The cook house hath scarce been touched! We shall have enough to eat."

"It is marvel truly, that of all our people only poor old Bleheris, the hermit, hath met his death, and none has sustained aught but minor injuries, save our good armarian."

"And Brother John will mend apace! You shall see!" It was Brother John himself who spoke thus cheerfully from his straw bed in the corner. His eyes were shining, his face radiant.

Hugh bent over him to straighten the covering and ease his position somewhat.

"Lad! Lad!" whispered Brother John in his ear.

"Didst thou hear—'to build and build, to give and give'—that is the soul of our Glaston! And to the builders and the givers will come the vision—when God so wills it!"

xvii. the choice

DAYS PASSED. The exaltation produced in the monks by the abbot's short talk began to wear off. They were crowded and uncomfortable in the half-finished chapel and bell tower, and a spell of cold wet weather added to their difficulties. The half-demolished kitchen made feeding the eighty or so who had lived in the conventual halls possible, but a real problem, and an epidemic of colds reduced spirits to a very low ebb. Dispositions were edgy, work lagged, and idleness gave ample opportunity for self pity and complaining. Abbot Robert was tireless in his efforts to set the routine of the Benedictine life going again. The daily offices were said in the crowded little chapel; there were no books to read but the novice master increased the time all the brothers were

to spend in conning the music of the services, albeit without accompaniment. Labor in the fields could go on as usual, and Brother Symon went quietly about his work among the poor and sick again. The village folk did what they could to help out, though that was little enough, for the peasants were, at all times, desperately poor and overworked. The near-by manors sent food, clothing, and bedding, which did more than anything else to relieve physical discomfort. But daily life continued to be a pretty dreary business and eagerness to make the best of things began to slip into apathy again.

Then came a day when a messenger clattered down the road to the south gate and demanded audience with the abbot and, when he had gone, the news spread like wild fire from one end of the abbey grounds to the other.

The messenger had brought word from King Henry

and Queen Eleanor that they themselves would finance the rebuilding of Glastonbury and that at once. Architects had already been summoned from France, stone would be bargained for shortly; the new Glaston would be all of stone with no wooden buildings to catch fire again; no expense would be spared, and the king himself would come presently to confer with Abbot Robert about actual plans.

The spirits of the community rose as if by magic. King Henry's name was blessed on every tongue, and everybody stopt talking about himself and his own griefs and discomforts, and began to discuss the future plans of the abbey with the greatest animation.

"*Now* what do you think of King Henry?" Dickon demanded of Hugh triumphantly, after he had helped to spread the good news of those generous promises.

"The king?" answered Hugh. "Oh, I got over hating him long ago—before I saw the—" he hesitated, wondering how much Dickon had really understood about his strange vision of the Sacred Cup. "Before I had that experience in the Old Church. I guess if I had still held hate in my heart I could not have seen the Holy Grail at all. So the king is going to help us rebuild? Oh, I am glad, *glad!* Then he must love our Glaston, too. It will be wonderful to watch it growing up again, won't it? And maybe we can take part in the work ourselves."

They were interrupted by the porter who still kept his watch by the main gate though his quarters above it and the almonry buildings just inside it were empty skeletons of their once solid selves. He came hurrying now across the grounds to where the boys stood.

"Two strangers are come to the abbey gate," said he, "a knight in the habit of a Templar and a younger man with him. They asked for Hugh. Ah me, 'tis a sad thing that we have no guest house in which to lodge them!"

The boys turned quickly in the direction of the main gate. While they were yet some distance off they spied the strangers, still mounted on their horses, just inside it. The taller of the two had a long white surcoat about him with a red cross on the left shoulder and the distinctive red hat over a white under-cap with lappets over the ears, that the Knight-Templars always wore. The man beside him was evidently an esquire or attendant.

Dickon suddenly gave a cry of surprise and delight. "Hugh, it is Jacques de Raoul! Do you see? It is Jacques himself, and some other!"

But Hugh made no answer. Already he had outstripped his companion and was racing on.

The knight dismounted as he saw the boys approaching and Jacques, for it was indeed he, did likewise and then took the bridles of both horses into his own hands. The other seemed not to know what he did, but stood staring in stupefaction at the slight boy figure outrunning his companion toward him.

"Jacques!" he whispered. "Do you see what I see? Am I dreaming or is that truly my son?"

"Aye, Master, that is indeed thy lad." The man's voice was husky with emotion and he paused a moment. " 'Tis thine own Hugh, no longer a cripple, but sturdy and whole and free!"

By this time the boys were upon them. If he had

stopt to think; if he had been his old shy, self-conscious, unhappy self, Hugh would have held back, repressed his joy and eagerness and waited for his father to call him, but he thought of nothing at all, nothing in the world, save that his father was there.

"Father!" he cried. "Father!" and rushed into the knight's arms.

Jacques turned away with a lump in his throat. It was not fitting that he should look upon his master, warrior, and man of iron that he was, with tears coursing down his sun blackened cheeks. Dickon had turned away too, his face working with an odd mixture of a grinning welcome and emotion.

"Well, young Dickon," said Jacques heartily, "so we meet again. The world is not so large nor time so immeasurable, after all. I had thought our parting was a matter of eternity, that day you accompanied me upon the road to port and exile; that I would never know peace and security again, nor a durable roof over my head, and that *you* would never know aught else. Now I find your haven roofless and I—I ride under the open sky, 'tis true, but in the safety of pardon from His Majesty, the King, and also from his Holiness, the Pope."

"So that is it?" Dickon looked at him wonderingly, then glanced at the knight and Hugh who were talking in low tones, their arms still about each other. "And he, Sir Hugh de Morville, is he pardoned too?"

"Aye, that he is," replied Jacques. "I found my master in France and went with him to Rome, and then I followed him also to Jerusalem."

"Did you have many adventures?" asked Dickon eagerly. "Did you fight the Moslems and rescue the oppressed? I would give *anything* to go on such a pilgrimage and see strange sights and do great deeds—!"

"Lad, you forget, this pilgrimage was in the nature of a penance, and it was no lighthearted nor easy adventure."

"But, anyway, it must have been wonderful fun!"

They were interrupted by Hugh's calling for Dickon. "This is my friend and my sworn brother," said he, drawing his father's hand toward the boy.

Dickon bowed awkwardly and fidgeted with the round cap which he was holding.

Sir Hugh put his hand on the lad's shoulder. "The friend of my son is my friend also," said he.

"Father, you have not said why you have donned the Templar's robe, or why you are here at all. I was so full of gladness to see you that I thought of naught else save that it was indeed you yourself standing inside the gate."

"I have indeed taken the vows as well as the garments of the 'Poor Fellow-Soldiers of Jesus Christ,'" said Sir Hugh, turning again to his son. "It is our sacred right and duty to protect pilgrims and guide them safe to the Sepulchre of Our Lord, and to keep the Temple precincts—and indeed, all Jerusalem—safe for those who would worship there. We live a life of austerity and devoted service to that cause, and I am minded to return soon and live and die in combat for the Holy Land. But Hugh, lad, I could not stay there without seeing thee once again. I thought I had put thee from me completely, with all my old life, my home in England, my service to court and king. But I could not. Boy, I have longed for thy face as a man thirsteth in the desert for springs of water. I would see thee once again, I told myself, just the once, and then leave thee with the good monks, knowing as I doubt me thou didst not know before, that thy father loved thee."

No one spoke for a moment and, when the knight's voice broke the silence, it was on a more cheerful note. "And now, boy, thou art whole and well! Thou hast not told me yet—but thou shalt how the healing came upon thee. No matter now! Thou art no longer a weakling but hale and strong, and nigh fourteen years of age, if I mistake not! High time to be a squire and anon a knight, spurred and accolated! Hugh, thou shalt ride with me on the morrow, as my squire-at-arms. We shall travel, a-horse and by boat, over the long, long way back to Palestine, and when thou art man grown, perchance thou too wilt be both knight and Templar."

A little ghost of a sigh drew Hugh's attention from his father's face to Dickon's. The boy had been drinking in every word and now his expression was filled with passionate longing, and yet there was no trace of envy in it. Dickon would rejoice wholly and fully in his friend's good fortune, but he could not keep back that little, little sigh for himself.

Hugh's eyes dropt. "Father," said he, "we must see to thy comfort, and that of Jacques, though 'tis little enough we have to offer. My Lord Abbot will, perchance, ride with thee to a neighboring manor to spend the night. Here, as thou seest, we have scarce place enough to stretch out side by side on the floor of yon one small building left by the flames. Many of the brothers sleep in the shelter of the ruined walls or out under the sky these last few starry nights."

He moved restlessly, as if to lead the two men to the abbot, but Sir Hugh stayed him for a moment. "We too shall lie out under the sky this night, my boy, or against some fire-blackened wall. Thy father is no longer the ease-loving courtier that he used to be. A Templar, lad, lives under as strict and simple a rule as the Benedictine. But lead the way to some place where our horses may be tethered and, if they will permit us, we will eat frugally with the brothers."

At this moment the porter, who had been watching from a tactful distance, approached again, took the horses into his care and bade Hugh lead the guests to the bell-tower Chapel where Vespers were about to be said.

After Vespers came the customary time for quiet talk and relaxation among the brothers. Hugh took his father to Abbot Robert and then to Brother John, where he lay in his corner uncomfortably strapped to the rough board splint. Both men spoke of Hugh with such high regard and with so much genuine affection that the boy reddened with pleasure. But he, himself, said very little. He seemed almost dejected, strangely enough, at the very moment when he had every cause for joy and anticipation.

That night Hugh slept but little. His mind seethed with memories, plans, questions. Before dawn he arose from his resting place hard by Brother John on the floor of the chapel, and made his way silently between the forms of the sleeping monks, out into the open. The trampled greensward, the broken and blackened walls of the ruined conventual buildings looked fantastic rather than ugly in the half light of sunrise. Hugh looked over the vast grounds, his heart heavy within him. Glaston had given him quiet, security, peace, and loveliness at the very time in his life when he most needed them. He would always be grateful for this year and more among the brothers. Out of the ruins Glaston would be rising up again, more nobly beautiful than before. He would like to see it grow, to have some little part in the rebuilding of it. He moved thoughtfully in the direction of the grange and the apple orchards and plucked a little green nubbin of an apple from one of the low branches, noting how heavily loaded they were already with the beginnings of fruit. It would be a good apple year; Brother Guthlac would have everybody picking when autumn came, and then storing the apples in big barrels at the grange for the cellarer to call upon whenever he needed a fresh supply.

Beyond the orchards lay fields and then the marshes began. Hugh could see Weary-All and Chalice Hill and the great conical summit of Tor rising beyond them. Chalice Spring lay in a little valley pocket beyond his view. He pictured in his mind the ancient well with the odd shelf in it where he and Dickon had stood together, wondering, after they had climbed up from the underground passage. How long and uselessly they had sought for the Holy Grail! But it had been fun—and a mighty good thing they had plumbed the mystery of those passages from

beginning to end! If they had not, Brother John—
Hugh shuddered and resolutely put all recollection
of the fire out of his mind. He wanted to go to
Beckery, had an unaccountable longing to visit Bleheris's island again before he left Glastonbury, in all
probability forever.

It took some time for him to cover the distance,
but at last he stood at the sagging door of the little
old hut. Everything was just as Master Bleheris had
left it, just as Hugh remembered it, when he had
lain in the corner of it during that long feverish illness. Only the black chest was empty now, its cover
thrown back displaying its cavernous interior. He sat
down on the rough block of stone that had been the
hermit's favorite resting place. Good old Master Bleheris! Hugh's eyes smarted with tears and he tried to
swallow down the lump in his throat as he thought
of him. Bleheris had seen his heart's desire and died
beholding it, and the joy in his face would be what
Hugh would remember about him longest, that and
his love for the old stories and traditions about the
Holy Grail. He must have been a wonderful minstrel in his youth. And now all those noble tales
would be lost forever. With the broken *Book of the
Seynt Graal* burned, and Master Bleheris dead, no
one would ever know, no future age would ever hear
those stories, the loveliest in all the world. Unless
someone should write them down, unless some one
who knew them now, to whom they were as clear
and fresh as if they had happened but yesterday.

Hugh rested his head on his hand and gazed out
over the marshes back toward Weary-All, but his

eyes were not looking for St. Joseph's thorn or resting on the blue line of sea beyond Tor Hill. A sudden thought had gripped him, a plan that was absorbing all his attention. At length he rose up and walked back to Glaston with a sure and decided step.

When breakfast had been eaten and the monks had gathered on the abbot's terrace, there being no longer any chapter house in which to hold their morning meeting, Hugh sought out the Templar.

"Father," said he, touching his sleeve gently. "Father, I have a boon to ask thee, something I desire with all my heart."

"It is thine before thou dost ask it, child," said Sir Hugh heartily. "What dost thou desire with all thy heart?"

But Hugh found it difficult to go on and stammered hesitantly.

"I have no doubt but that thou wilt be wroth and disappointed with me, but—Father—I do not want to go with thee now—to the Holy Land—not yet. I have somewhat to accomplish before I leave our Glaston, something to do that none but I *can* do."

"Not go with me, my son?" cried the knight in astonishment. "But what can be better to thee than to become a knight and fight nobly in a noble cause?"

"It is hard for me to tell thee," continued Hugh, "but I somehow feel—nay, I know that knighthood can wait—that it *must* wait, until I have accomplished that task to which I feel myself bounden."

"What task, boy?"

"The writing of a book that will last long after

any deeds of knighthood that I might do will have been forgotten; the recording of tales that belong to our Glaston and must not be lost, and which none but I now know. Father, I must stay here and tell those tales again in a form that is durable! It is my gift to Glaston, the one thing I *can* give and must give toward her rebuilding."

Sir Hugh stood silently looking down at the boy. His face wore a puzzled frown but showed no anger or resentment.

"And Father," continued Hugh, taking courage from the man's quiet attention, "the boon I ask is this: take Dickon with thee as thy squire-at-arms instead of me. Let him learn knighthood and follow thee. He will be faithful and devoted, a brave and stalwart knight. And when Glaston is built anew, more gloriously than before, and when the tales of the Holy Grail are told again, then Father, oh, then, if thou and he should come riding back—!"

Hugh's eyes were shining. His father caught his two shoulders in his hands and smiled down at him.

"Hush, lad, I know not rightly what thou art talking about! But if thou art minded to be a builder and a giver in this poor broken world, I would not stay thee—nay, I shall be proud of thee! As for Dickon, I like the boy much, and if thou wilt not squire thine old father, faith! then thy friend shall do it for thee! Run quickly and fetch the lad, for we must be upon our way."

The abbot must be consulted about releasing Dickon from the vows taken for him by his father, but there was little fear that he would not consent, especially as Sir Hugh was a Templar under an order very similar to the Benedictine, and was going back to serve the Holy Sepulchre and all pilgrims going thereto. While his father sought the abbot, Hugh raced off to find his friend. He came upon him, as usual, helping Brother Symon with his poor.

"Dickon!" he cried. "Dickon!" He was so excited himself that he could scarcely get the words out. "You are going with my father and Jacques to the Holy Land! You are going to be a squire and then a knight, just as you have dreamed of all your life! Dickon, hurry and come to my father; he is even now talking to Abbot Robert about you, asking to have you as his squire!"

Dickon stood perfectly still for a moment, his round blue eyes getting bigger and rounder, his mouth half open. Then he poked Hugh gently, with a trembling finger. "Say that again, Hugh, all of it! I don't think I heard you right."

When Hugh had repeated the essential part of his message, Dickon let out a whoop that might have been heard from Tor to the Mendip Hills, and then stood on his head. Having thus relieved himself of his first emotion, he fell upon Hugh and began pummelling him, and rolling on the ground with him. Then he sat back and hugged his knees, breathless and grinning ecstatically.

"*Me* going, along with you! To be squire-at-arms and then knight! *Knights!* Hugh, we'll be brothers-in-arms as well as sworn brothers! I can't believe it! I just can't believe it's true!"

Hugh sobered. "Not brothers-in-arms, Dickon—

at least not yet—but brothers, always and always—
Dickon—I'm not going. Father is taking you instead.
I'm staying here at Glaston."

All the joy and enthusiasm died out of Dickon's
face so that he looked stricken. "You—are—not—
going?" said he slowly. "But Hugh, *why?* Couldn't
we both go? Wouldn't your father take us both? I
wouldn't ask to be squire—if I could just follow along
—be a servant and mind the horses."

Hugh shook his head, smiling affectionately at
his friend, but speaking with finality. "No, Dickon, I
think now it was fated to be this way—that—maybe
that was why I was shown the vision of the Sacred
Hallow. Bleheris is gone, the broken book is gone,
no one will ever search again in Glaston or anywhere for a Holy Grail that can be held in one's two
hands. But the stories, the tradition—all the meaning and the marvel of the Holy Grail—*that* mustn't
be lost and it *will* be, if I don't write it down. Nobody knows about it or could tell it from beginning
to end now but me. I've got to stay here and make a
book of it, the most beautiful book in the world. I've
got to do it—and I want to do it for our Glaston."

Things happened fast after that. Dickon recovered his excitement and enthusiasm to a certain ex-
tent, grieved though he was at the thought that he
must leave Hugh behind him. He said good-by to
Brother Symon with a catch in his voice, and ran
with Hugh to the grange to see Brother Guthlac.

"It's a queer thing," he said huskily. "I thought I'd
be so happy about going away from Glaston, especially to seek adventure in a strange land, and now,

when I say good-by to all these good folk, seems as if I could just bawl like a baby because I *am* going."

"You won't feel that way long," encouraged Hugh, "and you'll be riding back some day, you mustn't forget that, with your shield and spurs and all sorts of knightly honors upon you."

Dickon's face cleared and he smiled happily again. "True enough; and everything I do, all the battles and the honors that I win, will be for Glaston!"

After the grange, they went into the bell-tower chapel to say good-by to Brother John. He had already learned that Dickon was going instead of Hugh and his face wore a comical mixture of relief and delight that his favorite would remain with him, and concern for the boy who was going out from the sheltering walls that had been his home ever since babyhood. The friendly advice that he poured forth upon Dickon's head was interrupted, however, by a summons to hasten to the south gate.

Father Robert was standing with Sir Hugh and Jacques near the half-ruined entrance to the monastic grounds. The horses of the two men were pawing the earth near them and another horse, one that belonged to the abbey, had been saddled and bridled ready for Dickon to mount. The boy had nothing of his own to take with him except the clothes on his back, and Hugh had told him his father would doubtless have him fitted out in proper livery for a squire when they had got to a neighboring city. There was nothing more now except the saying of the final farewells.

"My son," said the abbot gravely, laying a hand

on Dickon's shoulders. "I am giving thee into the charge of Sir Hugh de Morville, to be his squire-at-arms and to be his man. Be dutiful, obedient, faithful. Serve God as truly and as lovingly out in the world as thou wouldst serve Him here in the shelter of our abbey. If, when thou art grown to manhood, thou dost wish to return and take the Benedictine vows thy father purposed for thee, well and good; if thou dost not feel thyself called of God to enter our brotherhood, then I absolve thee of the vow thy parents made for thee. Thou art free to choose, but let it be God's way thou dost choose, not thine own way, wheresoever thou art and what-soever thou doest. Farewell, my son, and God Him-self bless thee and go with thee." He made the sign of the cross over the boy, who knelt before him.

Then the seriousness of the moment broke. Jacques stept forward with his master's horse, bidding Dickon hold the other two. Sir Hugh put his arms about his son unashamedly and kissed him. The two looked at each other for a long silent moment of mutual un-derstanding.

"Good-by, lad—until thy task is done," said the knight.

"Good-by, my father."

And then—"Farewell, Jacques—and Dickon—oh, Dickon, good-by! good-by!" Hugh called to first one then the other.

They were all mounted at last and moving toward the gate, Sir Hugh first, then Jacques, then Dickon. The long shadows of late afternoon were falling and a shaft of sunlight shone through the trees directly

on Dickon as he turned for a last wave of farewell. With a sudden chuckling laugh, he seized his round borel cap and made a lunge with it at the streak of sun. Then he caught it again as it was about to fall, almost tumbling off his horse as he did so.

"No use!" cried Hugh, laughing. "You just can't hang your hat on a sunbeam! You're no saint yet!"

"You wait!" Dickon shouted back. "Someday—" but the last of his sentence was drowned in the clatter of the horses' hoofs as they passed under the stone gate and out onto the highroad beyond.

Hugh turned back into the cluttered and blackened abbey grounds. Father Robert still stood beside him. The two looked at one another for a moment in quiet friendliness.

"Tomorrow," said the abbot, "we shall begin to build. It will be good to see Glaston rise again out of her ashes."

When he had got back to Brother John he found the little monk happily fingering a sheet of fine new parchment.

"Hugh, lad," said he, "there be a few clean, newly stretched skins in yon remnant of a kitchen, and some minium—the clearest red—and ink and gold leaf, a little, and the novices have found some rules and pens and other aumbry material in the ashes of the cloisters, still unharmed, miraculously unharmed. Thou canst begin at once."

"Aye," said Hugh, "tomorrow I can set the title page."

"And we shall soon have more materials; we can borrow from Wells Cathedral—we can go right on with the work."

"Capitals in gold leaf, with a good red ground," continued Hugh dreamily. "How about it, Brother John? And scroll work all down the page; S for *Sanctum* and G for *Gradalis,* big and floreated, and for a subtitle, written in good clear black in the pointed Gothic lettering—

" 'The Book of the Holy Grail' "

note

A WORD TO those who like to ask of a story, especially one with an historical background, "Is it true?" Many of the incidents in this tale of Hugh and Dickon in Glastonbury really did happen, a good many more might actually have taken place, if we are to believe persistent tradition, and the details of the setting are as authentic as a good deal of research can verify.

The Glastonbury of the twelfth century stood much closer to the sea than the present abbey ruins would indicate, for that was before the extensive drainage and reclaiming of land of a later age took place. A little old wooden church overlaid upon an alloy of lead is believed to have stood until the Great Fire upon the exact spot where Joseph of Arimathaea built his original beehive-shaped oratory, with the twelve cells around it. This disastrous conflagration which laid waste almost all the monastic structures, took place in the year 1184. (We have pushed the date forward a little, to fit in with the story of Hugh as a young lad, and to keep it still within the period of good, kindly Robert of Jumiège who was abbot of Glastonbury at the time of our story.)

Under this little basilica-shaped Chapel of St. Joseph, ancient records tell of a chamber hewn out of the limestone foundations, with a well in it, and extensive underground passages radiating from it. One of these led, at one time, to the sea, and included a secret treasure vault not far from the old north gate, built and used during the time of Danish incursions and subsequently forgotten.

Perhaps the imperfectly recovered recollection of some such underground passages and hiding places lies at the bottom of the constantly recurring suggestion that the actual Cup, the material and substantial Holy Grail, still lies buried in Glastonbury. In many of the old stories Joseph is supposed to have brought the Holy Grail with him "to Avalon in the Isle of Britain," and the confusion between an actual and material vessel and the symbol of a spiritual reality is far from being limited to the experience and understanding of the two boys, Dickon and Hugh!

As for the Grail stories, the vast and complicated question of where and how they arose can, of course, scarcely be touched upon here. But this much, at least, may lend interest to our story:—The tradition of a lost book appears again and again, no matter which lane one travels down in search of Grail source material. Some say it was written in Latin, some in Provençal, some that a hermit, inspired by an angel, wrote it, others that it came out of Wales as part of some hidden and secret minstrel or ecclesiastical lore. And, of course, many trace the whole Christianized version of the stories to monkish sources in which the name of Glastonbury frequently figures. The late twelfth century is said, also, to be the period in which the Grail stories began to take form. So it is not at all beyond the bounds of possibility that a lad in Glastonbury, like Hugh, should have collected and written them from some unknown source, about the time of the Great Fire.

All that we have recorded of Sir Hugh de Morville is historical, as is also the account of the finding of King Arthur's grave, and the description of St. David's sapphire altar which was lost for long years and then found "hidden underground." The ravages of the Great Fire and its promised rebuilding by King Henry II are authentic, and the visit of Walter Mape and Maurice the minstrel in the king's train at Glastonbury is, at least, probable.

To the tireless and loving labor of such monks as Brother John we owe far more gratitude than has ever been given. Patiently copying by hand, in clear black script, books that would otherwise have been lost to us, they kept alive not only the substance of men's thoughts, but also the art of binding and illuminating which made of those books treasures of beauty beyond price. There were countless Brother Johns in the Middle Ages, and a few saintly souls like Brother Symon. Life was by no means dull and stuffy in the vast monastic communities of those days, and a boy might easily find in them friendships and happy tasks and high adventure, as Hugh did, in his year of searching for

THE HIDDEN TREASURE OF GLASTON

about the author

ELEANORE M. JEWETT was born in New York City in 1890. She found it to be a somewhat lonely city for an only child, but the fact that one side of her family had been there since it was a small Dutch village made her feel like she "practically owned the place." Her solitude caused her to create imaginary friends with whom, at around the age of nine, she even formed a literary club. Since young Eleanore was the only one who actually could put pen to paper the club died a natural and early death, but she dates her ambition to write for children from this time.

When Mrs. Jewett was doing a Master's degree in comparative literature at Columbia University she became deeply interested in the medieval period, a fascination begun many years earlier after hearing a story about King Arthur. *The Hidden Treasure of Glaston* and *Big John's Secret,* a story of the fifth Crusade which takes place in 1218, were direct and satisfying results of this interest. *The Hidden Treasure* received a Newbery Honor in 1947.

The truth and nobility which she infused into her historical novels was also something valued in her daily life. In the dedication to *Big John's Secret* the author writes: "This book is dedicated to my husband, Charles Harvey Jewett, a physician who has shown me that a doctor's life, consecrated to his work, is nobler than that of any knight in shining armor."

After their marriage, the Jewetts moved from New York City to a town in upstate New York where they lived with their two daughters. Eleanore Jewett died in 1967, leaving a small but solid contribution to the field of children's literature.

LIVING HISTORY LIBRARY

The Living History Library is a collection of works for children published by Bethlehem Books, comprising quality reprints of historical fiction and non-fiction, including biography. These books are chosen for their craftsmanship and for the intelligent insight they provide into the present, in light of events and personalities of the past.

TITLES IN THIS SERIES

Archimedes and the Door of Science, by Jeanne Bendick

Augustine Came to Kent, by Barbara Willard

Beorn the Proud, by Madeleine Polland

The Hidden Treasure of Glaston, by Eleanore M. Jewett

Hittite Warrior, by Joanne Williamson

If All the Swords in England, by Barbara Willard

Madeleine Takes Command, by Ethel C. Brill

The Reb and the Redcoats, by Constance Savery

Red Hugh, Prince of Donegal, by Robert T. Reilly

Son of Charlemagne, by Barbara Willard

The Winged Watchman, by Hilda van Stockum